To the memory of Sue Accord, friend and fellow gamer,
beloved and greatly missed. Shine on, Luna.

A YEAR AGO—

A year ago, I was a different person, just one of the Hunters at the Monastery on the Mountain. A Hunter who kept our area free of monsters, under the tutelage and direction of my Masters. A Hunter who'd lived in a place so different from Apex and the other big cities it might just as well have been on another planet.

A year ago, I'd never given a thought to Apex, except once in a great while when I'd watched some important news vid, or someone decided to play something that had been sent out to us turnips by the mail-car that came once a week on the supply train. I'd never thought I would leave the Monastery, and never wanted to.

A year ago, the Elite had been an untouchable legend to me, mysterious heroes I wasn't entirely sure were real.

A year ago, I had never faced a Folk Mage on my own.

My Masters always told me that a lot can change in a year. Well, now I was in Apex, I was one of the Elite, and it didn't look as if I was ever going to go home again. I didn't even recognize the person I saw in the mirror anymore.

A mere two months ago I hadn't been sure Apex was going to survive. I'd been even less sure that *I* was going to. Because two months ago, the Othersiders had hit us at the Prime Barrier around Apex with everything they had, and they very nearly ran over the top of us. It would have been the Diseray all over again, at least as far as the capital city had been concerned.

We'd won in the end, but the two Battles of the Barrier had nearly flattened the Elite. I still could scarcely believe we'd not only survived it but had driven them back.

Of course it would have been too much to ask that the Battles of the Barrier had finished the Othersiders. Far from it. We got a month of respite, and then they were at our throats again. Except now the Othersiders were concentrating on targets away from Apex: smaller cities, towns, even villages, but by chopper, all within a couple hours of Apex at most.

So far as the Cits of Apex were concerned, everything was back to normal. The Hunters and the Psimons had driven the monsters away, and there had never been the slightest danger that their safe and ordered lives were about to come crashing down around them.

If I thought about it at all, it would make me crazy. On the Mountain, we all lived our lives with a healthy sense of paranoia and self-preservation. Here . . . the Cits were oblivious.

Be that as it may, the army and the Elite were still getting hammered. Callouts every day and every night, never less than two in twenty-four hours, sometimes six, even eight on the horrible days. The Elite were split into a day and a night shift, twelve hours on, twelve off—except any of us could get called out even when we were asleep, if things were bad enough. No one had died—yet. But now I remembered fondly the days when I was "just" a Hunter of Apex and got a day off if I had two strenuous Hunts in a row. And the days when I'd been a Hunter on the Mountain—when we had all the resources of each other *and* the Masters at the Monastery— seemed a far-off dream.

Today the callout was a town fifteen minutes by chopper from the Prime Barrier, not even a fortified one. At this point, I didn't even remember the names of the towns we were defending any- more. This was a grain-farming center, that much I knew. They'd had walls and heavy defenses at one point, but they must have figured they were safe, that the Elite could handle anything that got close to them, because those walls and defenses had been taken down years ago.

Anyone who'd been raised on the Mountain and in the com- munities we protected could have told them that removing defenses was a bad move. But there it was again; they were close enough to Apex that some of the complacency had bled over.

The army had gotten there before us; they were based on the west side of Apex, a lot closer to this spot than we were. I was in the last chopper the Elite sent out, riding solo. I'd been the last one *in* from the previous fight, and I'd literally jumped from a chopper running low on fuel to one waiting for me at HQ.

"*Joy,*" Kent said over my comm channel, as the new chopper

slowed to let me drop off. *"Some of the Othersiders have penetrated the town."*

I swore to myself; Kent continued. *"We're to the west. Most of the Othersiders are facing off with the army. There's supposed to be three Folk Mages here."*

Of course. Since the Battles, we'd never seen Othersiders without at least one Folk Mage with them.

The chopper hovered, and I bailed, hitting the ground and rolling, then to my feet again. "I'm on the ground, east side of town, Kent," I replied.

"Hammer and Steel were in the chopper before you. I sent them into town. You follow and hook up with them."

"Roger," I replied. I did the quick and dirty summons, bringing the Hounds over by opening the Way purely on magic energy, will, and the Mandalas on the backs of my hands. I'd been doing this so much lately that I didn't even notice the Mandalas burning as I brought the Hounds over. I ran in on foot, with Hounds in front of me acting as scouts, Hounds behind me guarding our backs, and Bya and Myrrdhin right beside me. My original seven were in their *Alebrije* forms, appearing as weird animals with crazy patterns and colors, the better to be seen at a distance. Hold and Strike, ahead of me, were a pair of wolves, if wolves were made of shadow. They had been Karly's before she was murdered. Myrrdhin and Gwalchmai, both dark-silver gargoyles with silver eyes, had been Ace's before he betrayed us all by trying to murder me. I could speak telepathically with all of them except Hold and Strike, but the others would tell them what they needed to know.

We passed the wrecked grain silos, following the paved main road into town. Probably held several thousand people. About half the buildings were "old-style," built defensively, solid blocks of 'crete with very narrow windows, if they had any windows at all. Unfortunately, the other half of the buildings were wooden and brick structures, and while I am sure they were pleasant to live in, they were . . . flammable. And dead easy to break into. I just hoped that the Cits here had had the sense to make for the old-style buildings when the attack came.

Because a lot of those other buildings were burning.

In moments, I was deep into the town, and by now the air was thick enough to cut. I could tell by the noise that the army was pounding away at the Othersiders outside the town limits. I was wearing my gas mask and goggles as protection against the smoke, or I wouldn't have been able to see or breathe. And I was keyed up and alert, with a nice edge of fear. *The Hunter that isn't afraid is soon to be a dead Hunter,* as my Masters said. The trick was making your fear into something you could use, rather than letting it use you.

The Hounds and I went in deeper and passed more buildings on fire—most likely the work of some sort of incendiary Othersiders like Ketzels. I kept Dusana with me and sent the others ranging along to either side, including Bya and Myrrdhin. As pack alphas and pack seconds, they would keep the others coordinated.

There was no sign of Cits, but there *were* drifts of that gray ash the *Nagas*—four-armed Othersiders that were snake on the bottom and something vaguely human on top—turned into when they were killed, with discarded swords in or near the ash. Hammer and Steel must have caught up with the Othersiders inside the town limits. Fortunately it looked as if the *Nagas* hadn't gotten as far as breaking into houses to go after the people sheltered there. And clearly the guys hadn't had as much trouble with the snake-men as I'd had when I'd first encountered them.

I stopped Dusana for a moment and tried contacting Kent. "Looks like the guys hit *Nagas* and cleared them out. They're somewhere ahead of me."

"Roger, carry on," he replied. Static flooded the channel as a plume of magical energy erupted to the northeast, visible as a dense tower of sparkling glitter over the roofs of the buildings nearest me. *"I know it looks bad, but I need your eyes and talents and, most of all, your pack right where you are. These bastards could be using their Folk Mages as a distraction from something else in town, and if they are, I want you there to deal with it."* He cursed, then continued. *"Two of the Folk Mages are here—fancies, not ferals. The third disappeared just before we got here. Keep your head on a swivel looking for him. They're using bale-fire."* I shuddered. Bale-fire was kind of like napalm and just as hard to put out. Just as he said that, I heard a distant shriek over his freq and more plumes of magic appeared over the rooftops. I hoped the team could get a handle on the situation.

The smoke was thicker, billowing down the street in dense gray clouds mingled with streaks of black. I tried not to think about people who were going to come out of hiding to find everything they owned had burned up. Hopefully *they* weren't burned up. "Yes, sir," I replied. "Out."

We rounded the last corner and came out at one edge of an open space with a watchtower in the middle. It was *really* hard to see, but I thought I spotted two moving figures on the other side of the watchtower. I urged the Pack toward them. A sudden gust cleared the smoke between us; it was Hammer and Steel. Hammer was farther away from us, shooting at something on a rooftop with a shotgun loaded with slugs instead of shot. Steel was closer, and his Hounds were packed up with Hammer's. I started to shout at him.

And that was when a flash of blue and copper suddenly appeared next to him.

Fear blazed up inside me. It was the third Folk Mage. This one didn't have a staff; he just thrust out both his hands, and Steel *flew* across the road, hit the wall of a building, and slid down it. The Folk Mage raised one hand with a fireball in it. It flamed a hideous green. Bale-fire.

"Bya!" I screamed; I couldn't pull up a spell fast enough to save him. Bya *bamphed* away from me, appearing beside Steel, and threw up his Shield, just as the Folk Mage hurled the fireball. It splattered against the Shield. The Folk Mage turned to face me. I expected him to be furious. It was a lot more unnerving to see that his face was absolutely expressionless.

I Shielded; my Hounds were already moving, rushing him. I saw a brief moment of surprise in his eyes, then he was gone. Not through a Portal; he *bamphed*. I had no idea the Folk could *bamph*. My Hounds plunged through the empty air where he had been.

I ran to Bya and Steel. Steel was just coming around; he raised his head and rubbed the back of it. I helped him sit up, and a moment later his brother was beside us. *You are the best Hound ever,* I thought at Bya. He lolled out his tongue and grinned smugly at me.

"Give me your flashlight," Hammer said. I got it off my belt and slapped it into his outstretched hand. He half supported Steel with one hand while he flicked the flashlight at his brother's eyes, then grunted in satisfaction. "I knew that hard head of yours would come in handy someday," he said. "Breathe deep." Steel did so. "Any stabbing pains?"

His brother shook his head slowly, then coughed. "Just got the wind knocked out of me," he said. "Where in *hell* did that come from?"

"The third Folk Mage *bamphed* in next to you," I said. "He knocked you across the square."

"Damn smoke. I didn't see anything," Hammer muttered.

"It was awful fast and your back was to him," I replied. "I wouldn't have seen him if I hadn't been looking right at you."

Hammer reached out and patted Bya. "If it hadn't been for this guy..."

Bya grinned even bigger. Which, in *Alebrije* form, was kind of unnerving. He has a *lot* of teeth. *Tell him he's welcome,* Bya said into my head. *And he owes me a Goblin at the least.*

I repeated Bya's message faithfully. Steel managed a laugh and slowly got to his feet, just in time for all three of our Perscoms to light up with a message from the armorer.

"Team HSJ, come in."

"Roger, Kent," Hammer said, speaking for all of us.

"*We're getting our asses kicked out here. We're already down one army Mage. If you two think you've got the worst of it taken care of, leave Joy to clean out the small fry in town and you two rendezvous with me.*"

They both looked at me. I nodded, and Hammer replied, "Roger that. On our way."

Hammer hauled his brother to his feet; their Hounds packed up around them, and they lit out at a trot, disappearing into the smoke. I looked at my Hounds. "All right. Same groups as before, same tactics. Let's go."

We split up. I kept expecting more big surprises, but everything else we encountered was relatively small. Clots of Redcaps with their wicked two-foot-long knives, a single Ogre (which looked like a shrunken version of the two-eyed giant called a Magog and carried a big wooden club for a weapon). I finally found out what it was Hammer had been shooting at: Harpies. I *really* wished that Knight and his winged Hounds were with us; I couldn't even see the Harpies, much less shoot at them.

I listened to them calling and screeching at each other up on the rooftops, veiled in smoke, and cursed. "I wish I was any good at casting illusions," I said to Dusana. "I could make the image of something small and helpless out in the street and—"

You don't need an illusion, Dusana interrupted.

Bya snorted. *Of course you don't,* he concurred. *Give me a moment.*

I'd seen him change from *Alebrije* form to greyhound before, but as he shimmered and glowed for a moment, I didn't know what to expect. When the glow faded, I was astonished to see a human toddler in Bya's place.

Is this convincing enough? he said anxiously. *I've never had the chance to practice this form.*

I got over my surprise and looked him up and down critically. "It wouldn't convince another human, but I think you'll fool the Harpies," I told him. The shape he had taken was a little crude; the face was blobby, the hair too coarse for a small child, and the limbs were too stubby. But the Harpies weren't going to notice any of that. My astonishment was more that he could actually shape-shift into human form at all. It was one more thing my Hounds could do that I had never heard of anyone else's doing.

As long as those stupid birdbrains are fooled, he replied with a snort. Then he waddled out into the middle of the street, plopped down in the dust, and started to cry.

Needless to say, he got the Harpies' attention immediately.

I might not have been able to see them through the smoke, but I could certainly hear them. Not only were they noisy fliers, but they kept screaming at each other. Dusana and I pressed ourselves back into the shadow of a doorway and waited as Bya sobbed convincingly. His imitation of a child crying was really excellent. My heart was pounding, more with excitement than anything else. This took me right back to my days on the Mountain when I used to shoot down Harpies all the time.

The Harpies couldn't resist Bya's performance, and it wasn't long before they swooped down into the street to nab him. There were three of them, practically colliding with one another in their eagerness to snatch up the tasty morsel.

That was when he turned the tables on them.

Quick as a shot, Bya morphed into *Alebrije* form, snatching the legs of two of them with tentacle-like arms and chomping down on the tail of the third. They screeched and flapped, beating him over the head with their wings. He probably couldn't have held them for very long, but he didn't have to; I got three shots off within a minute and nailed all of them. Unlike Minotaurs, they had no resistance to bullets. Dusana jumped into the street quickly enough to suck the manna off the last of them.

About that time, the other three sets of Hounds came back to us. *We have not sniffed in every doorway and under every bush,* Myrrdhin said for all of them, *but we are certain there are no more enemies here to Hunt, unless someone opens a Portal.*

Bya regarded his second-in-command thoughtfully. *If they do that, they will do so in the middle of town,* he said. *I think that is what that Mage intended to do, and he was not expecting us to be there.*

I licked my lips, aware of how dry they were. "That would account for why he didn't just kill Steel on the spot," I said. I got my canteen out of my pack, pulled off my gas mask, and took a long drink. "He was expecting the place to be clear of us, and he reacted without thinking." I quickly put the mask back on; just the whiff of smoke I got while I was drinking was enough to make me cough.

Then we should go back to the middle of town and hide, Bya said, nodding. *Just in case.*

We made our way back to that watchtower and found doorways and overhangs to give ourselves some concealment. I crouched down behind a 'crete barrier intended to keep something from running straight at the door behind me and breaking it down. We did things like that all the time back home. Of course, it wouldn't stop a Gog, but then, there wasn't a lot that would.

I was about to feel guilty about being able to sit there and rest, when Gwalchmai alerted and a wave of *Nagas* poured through the streets straight toward us. It got . . . very busy.

By the time we were done with them, I was soaking wet with sweat, and the only thing keeping me standing was the wall at my back.

"Kent to Joy."

"Joy, copy," I replied. "We're clear here for the moment."

"Good. If you can still stand, and the town is still clear, we need you out here."

"Roger that," I said, finding another reserve of energy and pushing myself off the wall. Too bad the Hounds couldn't feed me physical strength along with the magic they fed me.

Then again, I should be counting my blessings that we'd discovered the Hounds *could* feed their Hunters magic. Without that boost, we'd have gone under months ago, at the second Barrier fight.

We made our way to the side of town where the fight was still raging. Twisty, maze-like streets such as these were another defense; only *Nagas* could "charge" through the sharp bends every twenty feet or so. But the narrow streets had trapped the smoke, which was coming from somewhere behind us now. I wondered if something had set the grain elevators on fire. If the Othersiders had settled on a war of attrition with us, taking out some of our food supplies would be a logical thing to do.

Between the streets and the smoke, I couldn't tell that we'd come to the edge of town until we were just past it. Suddenly a gust of wind blew the smoke away and I found myself looking at the back of another Folk Mage.

There weren't *three* Folk Mages, there were *four*! And not just *any* Folk Mage—this one was floating about three feet in the air, encased in his Shield bubble, a Shield so damn good and tight that it was keeping the smoke out while still letting him breathe. This was one of their big guns, someone with as much power as any three ordinary Folk Mages put together.

But this wasn't "my" Folk Mage, the one that had taken an inexplicable interest in me, although his outfit was just as elaborate as the one in lavender wore. His blond hair was shorter than the lavender one's hair—it barely came below his shoulder blades, and it was fastened into several tails by gold bands. From the back it looked to me as if he was wearing a combination of fanciful armor and ankle-length robes of various shades of gold. The armor was engraved with elaborate designs and inlaid with gemstones. The robes were heavily embroidered with gold bullion and gemstone beads.

My nerves rang with fear, like guitar strings, and my Hounds suddenly clustered themselves around me, adding their Shields to mine. Then he turned.

Like "my" Mage, he was so handsome he was somehow . . . *too* attractive. In the uncanny valley where inhuman perfection lives.

But his gold eyes lit up with an expression I did not like at all, and his smile mirrored what was in his eyes.

"Well, well, well," he said in a voice like icy velvet, if such a thing were possible. "The famous shepherd. Save your sheep, shepherd—if you can."

And before I could react to that, he conjured a Portal, stepped through it, and was gone.

Great, was all I could think, as I reeled from the shock of being recognized. *I'm famous among the Folk. This can't possibly end well.*

2

IT APPEARED I HAD disturbed the mind behind the battlefield strategy, because when I looked out over the battlefield from my vantage at the edge of town, it was obvious things fell apart at the moment he vanished. Portals popped up all over the place. The Othersiders who could retreat were doing so, leaving the rest behind to be slaughtered. By the time I joined up with the rest of the team, their Hounds were harrying the last reluctant *Nagas* through the final open Portal.

The Hunters were all moving slowly, unlike their Hounds, who were romping about like puppies. I envied the Hounds. I suspect all of us did.

I wasn't moving very fast myself; once I got over the jolt of adrenaline caused by coming face-to-face with *another* top-rank Folk Mage, I felt as limp as an old, wrung-out dishrag. But

I counted heads and came up with the same number we'd arrived with. *Any landing you can walk away from, I guess. Or any battle.*

The team was slowly gathering around Kent, while two of the army Mages led several squads of soldiers into the town to make sure the Hounds and I hadn't missed anything, give the Cits the all clear, and evacuate the injured. "... they're going to demand walls," Kent was saying to Archer, as I got within earshot.

Archer rolled his eyes. "They pulled down their walls six years ago," he pointed out. "It's their own damn fault that they don't have any now!"

Kent just shrugged and looked around for something to sit on, as his four Hounds plopped themselves casually down around him, looking sleek and satisfied. "Any objections to waiting for transport while the army gets themselves out of here?" he asked in general.

"They have wounded, we don't," Hammer pointed out, as one of his massive Hounds positioned itself so he could use it as a backrest. Dusana did the same for me, and I took the invitation to plant my butt on the dirt, while my eleven made a pile around me. I pulled off my gas mask and got another drink of water. It tasted like smoky ambrosia.

"I nearly ran into a really fancy Folk Mage at the edge of town," I said. "A fourth one. I think he was playing general. I startled him, and I guess he didn't want to take the chance I wasn't alone, because he Portaled out of there, and that was when the fight fell apart." I wasn't sure if I should mention what he'd said just yet.

Kent demanded a description, and I obliged as well as I could, while they all listened. When I finished, there was silence, except for the distant *whumpwhumpwhump* of choppers approaching.

"He looked kind of like the one that stopped the train when I was on the way here," I said. "Only gold instead of lavender."

Archer and Kent exchanged a look. "You think?" Archer asked.

"Beginning to look like it," Kent replied.

"You guys going to enlighten us, or pretend we're all Psimons?" Steel demanded irritably, then coughed as the wind blew smoke over all of us.

Both Archer and Kent grimaced. "Not here," Kent said, with a quick look around. "Back at HQ. Joy's people back home are right; thinking or talking about *them* can get their attention, and we don't want him coming back."

I sagged my head against Dusana's back, buried my hand in Bya's coat, and closed my eyes. I didn't want to think about anything; I just wanted to concentrate on getting every tiny little bit of rest I could get while we waited for the choppers, because odds were we'd get a callout while we were still in the air. We'd already had one callout this morning that half the Elite team, including me, had gone on—the other half had been on night shift and were still sleeping after last night's callout.

The regular Hunters were working harder than they were used to, too. No longer going out on solo patrols, they were pairing up to patrol places like the storm sewers and the edges of the Barrier, and even parts of Spillover that *we* used to handle. I was pretty sure that going out to do fan service or having fun at clubs at night wasn't happening for them anymore. Or at least, nowhere near as much.

The one good thing was that all this activity seemed to be concentrated around Apex. Kent had put out a call to other cities for Hunter volunteers to come to Apex, so we had some new—but *experienced*—blood, and we needed them. I hadn't actually met any of them yet, but the roster was larger by just over a dozen.

Truth to tell, I was tempted to ask for help from the Monastery, and feeling a bit guilty about hiding the Monastery from everyone here. But the Monastery Hunters were spread out over just as much territory as the Elite defended. I didn't know if they'd be able to spare anyone. And even if they could, until I could figure out how we could explain the "sudden" appearance of one or more seasoned Hunters from an area that wasn't supposed to have any at all, I didn't want to do that just yet.

"Hunters, your rides are incoming," came the word from HQ over the general Hunter comm channel.

"Roger, HQ, and thanks," Kent said wearily. We all remained where we were, sprawled on the ground among our Hounds, unwilling to get up until we actually had to. When the choppers landed, we hauled ourselves and one another to our feet and opened the Way for our Hounds to go back, then shuffled off to our rides like a bunch of sleepwalkers. And once we were in and strapped down, we all fastened chin straps too, hoping to get just a few more minutes of rest.

We made it through the rest of our shift undisturbed, and I woke up the next morning with the memory of Archer and Kent being enigmatic about those fancy Folk Mages in the front of my mind. I threw on the clothing I'd set out last night without even paying much attention, and when I was decent, I headed for the mess. I was the fourth out of the eight of us to arrive. Kent and Archer were already there, just starting on their bowls of eggs-and-stuff. The kitchen always gave us eggs and something, first thing, to remind us it was morning.

"What were you two talking about yesterday?" I demanded. "When *you* said 'You think?' and *you* said 'Beginning to look like it.'"

Everyone turned to Kent and Archer. "You did say you'd explain back at HQ," Steel pointed out.

Archer and Kent exchanged another one of those looks. Archer shrugged. "You're the senior Elite," he pointed out, and went back to eating.

"It's a theory," Kent said carefully. "There's no proof for it, of course. Most people who know the Folk exist say that they are anarchists. That they have no leaders as such, just loose alliances, and they have little or no interest in acting like human warlords would by establishing themselves inside set territories. Certainly during the Diseray they acted that way—if two Folk came upon humans at the same time, it was even odds they'd fight each other rather than joining forces. But the longer it's been since the Diseray, the less that's been happening. We definitely saw differently at the Barrier Battle—that wasn't a disorganized mob; that was an army. Until now, though, we've never actually *seen* one single Folk Mage directing everything. But what you saw, Joy, is proof. They have real leaders. Real generals."

This wasn't exactly news to me, although I acted as if it was. The Masters had known there was something like this going on with the Folk for as long as I had been a Hunter, at least.

"He sure seemed to me as if he was acting like some sort of general," I agreed, glad to finally have done with keeping my knowledge a secret. "We know the Folk have psionics. He could have been giving them orders that way. In fact, if he was concentrating on doing just that, it accounts for how I managed to get so close to him before he noticed me."

"Well..." Hammer said heavily. "That's just terrific."

"It doesn't change much," Archer pointed out. "Except that..." He rubbed his ear. "Those of us with extra Hounds, or flying Hounds, might want to think about deploying one to look for a Folk Mage acting like a general. We chase him back to where he came from, we can end these fights a lot quicker."

"Huh. That's true." Hammer brightened a little. "You're not as dumb as they say you are."

At just that moment, the alarms blared and we got a four-man team callout. Kent assigned me, Hammer, Steel, and Archer, and we sprinted for the chopper pad. Word was this was Minotaurs and Ogres, which meant we'd be in for some heavy fighting.

By the time we got back, Kent, Scarlet, Mei, and Flashfire were gone on another callout. We had about enough time to grab ammo and other supplies when we got back, and then we went out again, bolting down energy squares in the chopper. This time, it was "just" a really big Drakken....

We dragged in at sunset. The Drakken had not gone down without a huge fight; the wretched thing was easily the size of the ones Ace had called his "new Hounds." The rest were already back, and they looked just about as hauled-over-the-rocks as we did. "Anybody spot a general?" Kent asked as we joined them in the mess. We shook our heads, and he sighed.

I happened to glance up at the vid-screen, which was showing a Hunter channel. It was Tober and Dazzle taking out a pair of Ogres. I immediately recognized where they were.

"Huh," I said aloud. "That's PsiCorps HQ. So why isn't there at least one Psimon pitching in to help?"

"Oh, they aren't helping Hunters anymore," Mei replied, with a sardonic lift of her lip. "Abigail Drift did *not* like the public reaction to the noble sacrifice of her Psimons at the first Barrier Battle."

This was news to me. But anything that displeased Drift sounded interesting. "Public reaction?" I prompted.

Flashfire snickered. "More like lack of public reaction. Oh, and I heard that someone anonymously left a big wreath on the front steps of the PsiCorps HQ, with a ribbon across it that read 'It's a good start.'"

Well, my reaction to that was mixed. I really loathed Abigail Drift. She was the reason I broke up with Josh, who was Uncle's Psi-aide. To say she manipulated and used her Psimons in every way possible was an understatement. She'd had no compunction whatsoever about putting them into a situation she *knew* was going to kill some of them, and I'll bet she never let them have the faintest inkling of the risks they were about to take, either. I'd have happily used her as bait for a Drakken, and I wouldn't have been too quick about coming once the Drakken got hold of her.

But if she hadn't sent the Psimons to the Barrier, we'd probably all be dead now and the city would have been overrun. Okay . . . she did do that. But those poor Psimons hadn't deserved what had happened to them, dropping dead with exhaustion or whatever it was that had killed them. And she'd sent them there *knowing* that was going to happen to them. *Yeah, PsiCorps isn't the problem. It's Drift. And I'd still use her for Drakken-bait.*

From the look on Kent's face, he felt the same. Flashfire glanced at him and flushed. "I'd throw Drift under a train in a heartbeat," Kent said slowly. "And PsiCorps used to be . . . better than this. I'd like to think that some of the Psimons are still people who won't take a stroll through your skull just because Drift wants to know what you're thinking. Maybe even most of them. And . . . I'd hate to find out that the ones that died at the Barrier were the ones she couldn't turn into her personal errand boys." Flashfire nodded a little, and that was that.

And that was when we got a very small miracle. All our Perscoms *and* the alarm in the mess gave what I now knew was the "dangerous weather" signal, and our heads all snapped around to look at the vid-screens—which were showing a glorious, *glorious* storm coming in—a nice big red-and-purple one. It wasn't moving so fast as to be driven by Thunderbirds, but it *was* blowing up nicely, and would probably give us at least twelve to twenty hours of respite. Maybe a bit more, if it picked up energy and moisture as it got closer to us. The collective sound that came out of all of us was more groan than sigh, but it *was* relief.

"Stand down, Elite, we're getting a break," Kent said. "Who wants to join me for a drink?"

"Not me," Archer said, as Mei, Scarlet, and Flashfire shook

their heads. "Sleep. I'm so short of it right now I'll probably pass out on the way to my room."

Hammer, Steel, and Mark all raised their hands. I tried not to look hopeful, but Kent pointed a finger at me. "Unless you're ready to pass out, you too, kid. You're Elite; you're an honorary adult."

"In that case," Scarlet said, "I change my mind. Joy and I can walk each other back to our rooms." Scarlet's suite was across the hall from mine. That made it real convenient if one or the other of us had sprains or strains we needed wrapped, or bandages changed. Bonding over wrenched ankles might seem weird to a Cit, but that's life as a Hunter.

Now, I'm not one to self-medicate, but I couldn't help remembering how relaxed that very tasty sweet stuff had made me the last time I'd had a drink in the Elite bar. Right now, the knots in my muscles had knots in them. My Masters would probably have suggested meditation instead of medication, but I knew if I tried to meditate I'd fall asleep and wake up just as knotted as before. A drink now . . . a hot steam bath in the morning . . . I might be human again sometime in the next twenty-four hours. I cheerfully trotted along with the herd to the second-floor bar, reserved for members of the Elite.

The lights came on as we entered. The bar looked almost exactly the way good bars looked in old pre-Diseray vids: lots of wood, padded two-person booths along the walls, some overstuffed leather chairs with little tables beside them, a real wooden bar with tall chairs lined up in front of it, and a vast array of bottles on shelves behind it. On the walls were framed photos of Elite who had been killed. I had the feeling that this room tended to see a lot of use when things were "normal," since none of the Elite seemed inclined to go clubbing. Not so much lately, of course.

We all took those tall chairs, and Kent went behind the bar to play bartender.

Kent poured; whiskey for himself and Mark Knight, that creamy tan stuff for me, something clear for Scarlet, and something clear from another bottle for the brothers. This was a much bigger selection of hard liquor than we had on the Mountain. There, we had one type, good old-fashioned moonshine, which came in two forms—clear and raw, or aged in wood barrels. We also had beer and berry-wine, which kids were allowed to have in moderation, but I didn't much like beer, and more than one glass of wine made my head ache.

I sipped at the tasty stuff and felt my muscles beginning to unknot. Oh, the relief! Even more of a relief knowing I could actually allow myself to sleep properly rather than always being on the edge of sleep, waiting for a callout alarm to go off in the middle of the night. Even through the massive walls of HQ, I could hear the thunder getting nearer.

I was still cautiously sipping my first drink, the others already on their second rounds, when the storm hit. The building shook and the lights flickered for just a moment, a momentary blip as a lightning strike somewhere close interrupted the power.

Kent raised his glass. We all did the same.

"My Jessie is going to be glad to get a break," Mark observed. He and I traded a knowing look. Sure, Mark had been a Hunter back home, but back home there hadn't been cam feeds of his battles where his new wife could see them. For Jessie, it would be a break from watching and worrying about him, not just from working.

"We all are, that's a fact," Kent said. He turned his attention on me before I had a chance to take another sip. "Now that we don't have dozens of ears around us, what did that Folk Mage say to you?"

Oh, blargh. He must have called up all the cam footage before he went to bed. But I answered, of course, repeating the Mage's words verbatim.

Kent mulled that over. "What do you think he meant?"

Fortunately nothing I planned to say involved lying about "my" Folk Mage. "First thing, he obviously recognized me, probably from when we beat Ace and his tame feral, so I guess that's another clue that they've gotten really, really organized. The business of 'shepherds' and 'sheep,' though, that's pretty clear. *We* call ourselves Hunters, but to them, we probably look like sheep dogs protecting a herd. From their point of view we don't actually hunt anything—if we did, we'd be out going after them on their own territory."

"Wherever that is," Steel muttered.

But Kent nodded with satisfaction. Scarlet ran her finger around the rim of her glass. "We need a better name for these new ones," she said. "What about Folk Lords?"

I made a face, but nodded in agreement. "He surely acted all high and mighty."

"Folk Lords it is," Kent said, after thinking about it a moment.

We sat there, listening to the continuous thunder, the bar top vibrating faintly under our arms. "I've sent for more help from some of the other big cities. We're getting another wave of reinforcements. No Elite, but very experienced Hunters."

Mark Knight grimaced a little. "We need 'em, and I hope you're right about them being prepared, Kent. We're being worn down to the point where we're going to start making fatal mistakes just out of exhaustion."

Now... I'd been thinking about something. *What the heck*, I decided. "Armorer Kent," I said, "what if we took volunteers as apprentices from the rest of the Hunters? You know, an Elite as the master and the volunteer as the apprentice?" That, of course, was how the Masters worked up at the Monastery: each Master had one or more apprentices under him or her. When they sent you out to Hunt on your own, you knew you were no longer an apprentice.

He gave me such a strange look that for a moment I was afraid I had said something horribly wrong. Finally, he swallowed the last of his whiskey in a gulp and said, "That's not a half-bad idea. We should have just enough people coming in from outside to replace the volunteers, if we get a full fifteen to agree to this apprentice thing."

"I'd have said nobody was going to volunteer and lose their standing in the ratings," Mark replied. "But after the Barrier Battles... I don't think anyone gives a rat's ass about their ratings anymore."

"I'll drink to that," said Scarlet, and held out her glass. We all got refills. Even me. Kent reached under the bar and brought out roasted nuts. I went back to sipping, but by the end of my second

I was definitely starting to feel more than just relaxed. Then Kent looked over at me and said, "I think you're right. I think we should get volunteers to be . . . apprentices, although I don't like that name. And since it was your idea, I think you should be the one doing the recruiting."

I nodded. "I can do that, sir." Part of me was sitting back and shaking my head at my audacity. But that part of me was a lot smaller than it had been the last time Kent told me to step up and take charge of something. Heck, I was Hunter Joy, the one with eleven Hounds who was *still* famous enough to get a lot of vid coverage without being ranked or having my own channel anymore. I should learn to use that, or it would go to waste.

"Good," Kent replied.

I'd have to talk to both the night shift and the day shift . . . and the best time to do that would probably be now, during this storm, while everyone was in HQ. "Permission to issue an all-Hunter Perscom message, sir?" I said. "I want to talk to everyone in the morning."

"Permission granted," he replied with a grin, and then walked me through the process, which involved getting hold of the comm operators. Five minutes later all our Perscoms went off with the text message.

Scarlet finished her drink and contemplated the empty glass. "Another?" asked Kent, picking up her bottle. But she shook her head.

"No, I think I will walk back to my room while I can still do so without bouncing off the hallway walls," she said, getting off her chair. "You coming, Joy?"

"That's the plan," I told her, and got off my chair as well. "We can leave the guys to serious drinking now." So we left, and managed to get back to our respective rooms and beds, only staggering a very, very little.

3

I WOKE UP THE next morning much earlier than I needed to. I started thinking about what I was going to say to the others while I was getting dressed, and kept reconsidering how to word my speech all through breakfast. I guess I must have had a "deep thinking" face on, because while the couple of other people that came in while I was eating nodded at me, they didn't sit down and try to talk to me. At about eight thirty I sauntered over to the hangar and sort of set myself up at one end, waiting. People started trickling in a little before nine, and the place was full right on the dot. I cleared my throat, and the speakers picked that up, which made everyone that wasn't already looking at me turn and give me their full attention.

"Hunters, those of you who I haven't met yet, I'm Elite Hunter

Joyeaux," I said, trying to keep my tone casual. I noticed the rest of the Elite filing in and sort of arranging themselves at the back of the group. "We've all been hammered lately, and it doesn't look like it's going to get any better anytime soon. As you know, Elite Armorer Kent has gotten some help from outside the city, and thank you for volunteering, Hunters"—I nodded at a couple of faces I didn't recognize up in the front—"and he's going to ask for a second wave, because I suggested something some of you might be interested in. Obviously this is no time to be holding Elite Trials, but would any of you consider signing up as sort of Elite junior partners?"

I paused and waited for a question. "Would this be permanent?" asked Dazzle.

"Only if you wanted it to be—then you'd have to go through the Trials once this current situation is over. And we wouldn't put any of you out there solo," I assured her. "You wouldn't have to give up your channel or anything like that. You'd just be partnered up with an Elite with complementary powers, so the Elite will be able to spread themselves out a little more."

"Sounds like a fine plan to me," said Tober, in his deep, gravelly voice. "Sign me up."

"Same," said Raynd, before anyone else could say anything.

"Ditto." That was Bithen. Cielle just held up her hand, followed by Dazzle. Shortly we had fifteen, enough for each of the Elite to get a new partner. I wasn't too surprised by Trev and Regi and Sara—but I was absolutely floored by Tober, Bithen, Raynd, and Cielle. They'd all been part of Ace's crowd, and while they had not been unpleasant to me now that Ace was locked up, I hadn't expected any of them to fall in with something I suggested so quickly, much less be the first to volunteer.

Kent cleared his throat and the speakers picked it up, which told me he was taking over the meeting. "All right, Hunters, go back to relaxing until the storm is over, except for you volunteers. You come with me to my office and we'll get you matched up with a complementary Elite."

As I passed Cielle, heading back to my rooms, she stopped me. "If you're wondering, and I bet you are," she said, with a wry little twist to her mouth, "ever since Ace . . . well, it feels like we have something to prove. Like, we're nothing at all like him, you know? I mean, he used to be snarky funny, and he knew all the greatest places to club, and being seen with him kicked up our ratings a treat. But what—" She shook her head. "Nothing about him, even after his brother got killed, rang any alarms. You know? None of us saw *that* coming." She made a sour face. "So, like, we haven't talked about it much, but I'm pretty sure the others all want to prove we're *Hunters*. I know I do."

"Hey, he did a good job of fooling Kent, you know," I pointed out. "You were manipulated; not your fault. But I see your point. And you guys *are* top-ranked Hunters. If I was going to get a choice, instead of waiting for volunteers, I'd have picked you guys. We're glad to have you on board."

The twist left her lips, and she actually smiled a little. "You're not half bad, Joyeaux Charmand."

"I have my moments," I replied, and went on my way to my room to check the weather.

It looked as though the storm was going to stick around longer than we'd thought, maybe even lingering until tomorrow morning. I thought about watching a vid or reading a book... but at the moment, there was nothing as appealing as actually *using* my fancy shower-steam-bath-hot-soaking-tub thing. In fact, I decided I was going to finally try out every darn function it had until my sore muscles stopped being sore.

I was feeling a whole lot better when I left the bathroom, wrapped in a big, warm, soft robe. The vid-screen had the "message" light blinking in the corner, so as I flung myself down on the bed I ordered it to play.

It was Kent. "I'm pairing you with Cielle," he said. "She's got some impressive tricks that work at a longer range than yours do. I think you can teach each other a lot. Plus, her Hounds fly, which will come in useful. Kent out."

Well, now I was *really* glad we'd made peace with each other.

The only toad in the cider was that I *still* hadn't made up with Josh. And I didn't dare. I was pretty sure Abigail Drift was trying to figure out ways of combing through my brain, and I couldn't trust any Psimon, much less one that had started to get romantic with me. So far as I was concerned, there were still some lingering doubts as to whether or not Josh had really felt anything about me. I mean, he had never actually *lied* to me, but... well, of all the people in Apex, Uncle and I are the two who can least afford having a stray thought slip, if that thought betrays the secrets of the Mountain and the Monastery.

When it came down to it... the longer we were apart, the more I realized I didn't know that much about him. Back home, my best friend, Kei, could have told you not only what every single one of her boyfriend's favorite colors was but what his favorite song had been back when he was knee-high, and any other detail you wanted to know. I knew...a little about Josh. That his mother had brought him up, rather than a crèche, because she'd been a Psimon too. But I didn't even know why she hadn't been together with his father, or what his father had been. In fact, what I actually did know, compared to what I didn't, was like a gallon of water compared to the swimming pool. I'd just let what I wanted dictate what I did and how I reacted. So maybe I was lucky that circumstances had broken us up.

That was what I kept telling myself, anyway.

If he and I had still been together, we'd probably have been playing a vid-game; I didn't have the heart to go on solo with the one we'd been duo-ing, so I probably would never find out what the endgame was.

And before Mark Knight had gotten married, we'd probably have hung out in the lounge, or gone swimming, or spent some time in the garden trading news from home. That wasn't going to happen—he and I both knew better than to do anything that would exclude Jessie. Like most Christer girls, she'd been raised to think that if a guy spent time alone with someone who wasn't his wife or girlfriend, he was probably cheating on his wife or girlfriend. And even if we invited her along, our shared experience as Hunters would make her feel excluded anyway.

Besides, this would probably be the most "awake" time they'd had together since the attacks ramped up, and it wasn't exactly fair of me to rob her of any of that.

Instead, I did a subject search through the library and found some fiction books about magic at the turn of the twentieth century—a good thing to read anyway, because I might get some more ideas for what I could do. I picked one at random, set an alarm to remind me of supper, and started on it. I got so deep into it that I yipped when the alarm went off.

I bookmarked my place and made a note of the author's name. Some publication details came up, and I noted with some surprise that she'd been alive and put this book out just before the Diseray, at a point when some people in charge had decided they "didn't believe" in climate change, or "didn't believe" it was happening because of burning fossil fuels, and had just started in wholesale on digging, drilling, and fracking, and burning, burning, burning. Eventually that had led to a massive release of frozen methane in the tundras of the world, then complete and catastrophic climate meltdown, and that had led to starvation wars, and *that* had led to someone nuking the Middle East. And that had brought on the Breakthrough when the Othersiders came over, if my Masters were right. Of course, the earthquakes, droughts, killer storms, and volcanic eruptions hadn't helped.

That just made me wonder: Had the author seen and understood what was happening? Had she felt helpless and afraid because there was absolutely nothing someone like her could do to stop it? Were these books about Victorian magic her way of trying to escape from that feeling of helplessness? I have a good imagination; I could feel myself right back there, seeing everything coming apart. It kind of made me sick to think about. My life might be in danger almost every waking hour, but at least I wasn't helpless. I could do a lot about steering the course of things.

I picked a quiet spot in the mess and mulled over things as I ate. Now that I wasn't distracted by the book, my thoughts kept veering back to reality and the Folk Lords who recognized me, *talked* to me—Lavender, and now Gold. How had I ended up being well known among the Folk?

Idiot, I chided myself. *There's no mystery about it; Lavender knows you from when he tried to attack the train. And as for Gold, a Folk Mage witnessed you taking down Ace and those two Drakken he was controlling.* Someone who had taken out two of the biggest Drakken I had ever seen? Yeah, that probably raised some long, pointy eyebrows. I hadn't done it alone, far from it, but that Folk Mage who'd left Ace to our tender mercies hadn't known that.

"Save your sheep, shepherd . . . if you can." That was an interesting statement, and very close to a traditional challenge, without actually issuing one.

Or was there more to it than that?

Just how many Cits had been lost in that raid? Was there something more going on than just the kinds of attacks we were used to?

Before I could get any further with that thought, Cielle appeared at my table with a tray full of food. "Breakfast pizza," she said. "They were making some for the night shift. I don't suppose you want some, do you?"

"If you're looking for a way to get me to ask you to sit down," I replied, with a wave of my hand at the seat across from me, "you found it. Sit down, oh wandering stranger, and tell me of this strange thing you call 'breakfast pizza.'"

She plopped down in the seat I'd indicated, put the tray on the table, and shoved it a little toward me. "Breakfast pizza, oh mighty wizardess, is not unlike regular pizza, except the spell required for its making uses yellow cheese instead of white, plus onions, bacon, and eggs." I think we both found it easier to talk like this, sort of "acting" as we sorted through our feelings toward each other.

"Sounds yummy." She gestured at the plate nearest me, and I took a piece. "Um. It *is* yummy. Thanks!"

She smiled tentatively at me, and both of us did our best to turn the tray full of "breakfast pizza" into a memory. Since she had approached *me*, I figured this was as good a time as any to interrogate my new... partner, I guess. "Feel like talking about Hunting with the Elite?" I asked.

She nodded. "That's kinda why I was bribing you with food." I have to admit, I was liking this side of Cielle a *lot* better than what little I had seen of her before.

"Okay, then let's start with the basics. How many Hounds do you have? Kent told me they fly."

"The usual," she said. "Four. Like coyotes with bat wings. They're tough, tougher than Harpies. They talk to me."

"That's a plus. That's you, Scarlet, Defender, and Mark with the only flying Hounds in all of Apex." I studied her a few moments. Cielle's pink-dyed hair was cut asymmetrically; her Hunting colors were dark rose, pale pink, and white, and the overall impression that gave was one of someone soft... which absolutely could not be the case. But it was so ultrafeminine, and so completely unlike me. "How on earth do you stay clean?" I finally asked.

She gave a startled laugh. "I used to Hunt the city," she reminded me. "I never went down in the storm sewers, I never went out in Spillover. I never got dirty until the Barrier." She chewed on her perfect lower lip for a moment—have I mentioned how gorgeous she was? It had been intimidating when she was with Ace, and it was still kind of intimidating. "Have you got any ideas?" she asked. "About how to fix my Hunting gear so it's better for out there?"

Well, the last thing I expected was to give fashion advice to *Cielle*. "Uh...make the main color of your Hunting gear in the darkest color, let them gray it out a lot, and just use the other two for trim? Have them make the trim waterproof?"

But her eyes lit up, and she smiled and reached for her Perscom. I finished my share of breakfast while she ordered up new outfits, then she turned her attention back to me. "So, what is it you *do*, exactly?" I asked. "Your magic, I mean." I had seen her at the range, and I already knew she was a darned good shot with just about any gun. But I hadn't seen anything she could do magically.

"Well, it wasn't horribly useful until you figured out the Hounds could feed us magic," she admitted. "I can—I can make something like a fat laser-blast, only before the Hounds could feed me I was only good for one shot and then I had to rest at least a half an hour to recharge."

I blinked because that sounded...well, like something out of an old pre-Diseray vid. "Distance?" I asked.

"If I can see it, I can hit it," she said confidently. "I've hit things half a mile away if they were big enough to see at that distance. Only it's magic energy, of course, not like a real laser, so if the thing I'm aiming at has a good Shield or something like that, it just splashes off."

"I can still see a use for it, if I can grind a hole in the Shield," I mused. She nodded.

"When you showed us how to do that, that's what Ace and I did." She made a face again. "I hate to keep bringing him up, but—"

"But you got partnered a lot, and anyway, I'm pretty sure when he went rogue he wasn't actually sane anymore." I let that drop but didn't give her any details. No one was supposed to know that Ace had been playing footsie with the Othersiders shortly after his brother died. Heck, *I* wasn't supposed to know that, but Uncle had slipped me in to watch Drift interrogate Ace, probing his mind psychically while she did so, and I had heard all the important parts.

Cielle nodded thoughtfully. "He never was right after his brother died. We . . . kind of stopped spending time together, actually. I was trying to be sympathetic, but he got really distant, and finally I just gave up. I figured he was handling things his way, and eventually we'd go back to normal. Except he didn't." She traced a pattern on the table with her finger. "I guess that sounds pretty shallow."

I didn't say anything because, really, what could I say? *Yeah, it does?* Or *I guess you didn't have much of a relationship?* I'm not the most tactful person in the world, but that would be pretty awful even for me.

"We didn't have much of a relationship," she said out of the blue, echoing my thoughts so closely I was startled. "I guess we were sort of using each other for ratings, you know?"

Actually, I *did* know, but I was not such a terrible person as to say so out loud. "It is what it is," I said with a shrug. "Look, I'm not in any position to get judgmental. My boyfriend was a Psimon who was probably just trying to get into my head to find out if I could be used against my uncle. From everything I saw, Ace was more focused on staying number one in the rankings than anything else. Kind of hard to compete with that level of ambition."

A look of relief flashed over her face. "Yeah, that," she said, and changed the subject to ask very detailed and pointed questions about what it was like out beyond the Barriers.

She smiled and shrugged when I asked her about her background. "My father and mother are both APD. The last thing I wanted to do was go into APD myself—it's all work and no fun— but I got lucky and popped Powers, so here I am."

Well, that explained quite a bit.

"And this *isn't* all work and no fun?" I pointed out. "When was the last time you went clubbing? Or did fan service? Or had a full night of sleep?"

"It's still more fun than I'd have in the APD," she retorted. "And *way* better outfits. I still have my fans, and I'm in the top twenty. Besides, Hunting is tons less boring than walking or driving around on regular patrol, the same patrol every day, doing the same things on the same schedule. That would drive me insane with boredom."

Suddenly, she stopped, put her hand over her mouth, and flushed. "Oh my god," she said, looking stricken. "I mean, people are really in horrible danger and these monsters are destroying entire towns or trying to, and I'm...talking about trending...." She went even redder. "Somebody should drown me."

Until she'd said that herself, I was thinking the same thing. Now, not so much. "Hey, it's the way you're used to thinking," I pointed out. "Back when I first got here, people got whole days off just because of one tough Hunt! I bet it's hard to get out of the habit of thinking about trending and fan service first."

"Yes, but *you* don't think that way!" she replied with a grimace.

"And I'm a turnip who was raised in a place where we start training our kids to use firearms at about age six. And where we regularly have people killed, all the time." I shrugged. "We can't help what gets installed when we're little."

"You're being a lot nicer about this than you should be," Cielle said after a moment.

I shrugged. "You didn't stop being nice just because you said something you caught yourself on the next second. I stick my foot in my mouth often enough, too, you know." I changed the subject, then, to the APD, partly because I really did want to know more about what they did, but mostly to get her mind off her fumbles. In that moment, I decided I really did like Cielle—for herself, as well as what she could do. She was nothing at all like Kei, but somehow, she reminded me of Kei. By the time breakfast was finished we were trading jokes.

We moved from the mess to her rooms (and oh my god, the pink overload), and I called up all the private Elite vids I had access to and reviewed the Hunts since the attacks had resumed. She listened, and she watched, and she just absorbed it all with focus and concentration. After the first hour or so, she began volunteering things. Like when her Hounds would have come in handy, and when that magic blast of hers would have taken out this or that monster.

"Oh, *Nagas*—" she said, when I decided to bring up the vid from the last Hunt. "They've got no chance against me. Once the

Hounds feed me, I can cut a whole couple of rows of them in half with one sweep."

"Nice," I commented with approval. "You are definitely my new best friend."

She laughed at that.

At some point we were both starting to yawn, and I called things to a halt before it got too late. "Early morning," I pointed out. "We always meet in the armory and suit up. From there, either Kent or Dispatch sends us out, and we're usually on the move before the dew is burned off the fields—unless, of course, the night shift is still in the middle of something, and in that case we move as soon as we can get ourselves out the door."

"Has that happened yet?" she asked. For the first time, she sounded apprehensive.

"No," I admitted. "But keep it in mind, and keep energy squares in your kit in case that ends up being breakfast in a chopper."

"Ugh," she said, making a face. "Well, I volunteered . . . but ugh. I'll see you in the morning, then."

"Absolutely." She let me out, and I headed back to my room, mentally chuckling. Drakken, Harpies, *Nagas,* Ogres—none of these things fazed her. But making a breakfast out of energy squares in a chopper did.

I WOKE UP IN a good mood, an hour ahead of my alarm and well rested, thanks to the storm. I felt more like myself than I had in weeks.

Cielle and I had hit it off, and it was beginning to look as if I was going to have a female friend relatively near my own age for the first time since I got here. I *missed* that. Of all the people I'd met since I got here, it was Mark and Karly that I'd connected with the best. Now Mark was keeping his distance for the sake of his wife, and Karly, well . . . Karly was gone.

But Cielle—yeah, I could see that. I got the same feeling from her as I did from Kei back home. There'd probably be some rough patches, but there was real potential there for a *friend*.

I grabbed my breakfast and ate in a hurry. Cielle came in just as I was leaving and we waved to each other. I was thinking about getting in some practice on the range with a couple of the weapons I hadn't been able to use in the last few weeks.

I had just turned the corner to the corridor that the armory was on, when I *literally* ran into Josh.

I jumped back about five feet, managed not to squeak, and stared at him, my heart racing.

There were dark circles under his eyes, and his blond hair was disheveled. He stared at me, the same way he'd stared at me the last time we'd encountered each other, his blue eyes full of emotion. But there was something new in his expression this time. I thought it was desperation. "What . . . are you doing here?" I managed finally, surreptitiously triggering the Psi-shield on my Perscom. I was calming down, fast. I'd faced two giant Drakken not that long ago; one human wasn't going to keep my heart racing for very long, even if it *was* Josh.

He looked around, then grabbed my elbow. I let him. There wasn't anything he could do to me, not right here, not even if he'd been sent by Drift personally to kidnap me. I could put him into a wall if I wanted to, and I was pretty sure that Psimons didn't get martial arts training. "Can we go somewhere else?" he asked nervously. "Please? I'd rather not talk about this in an open corridor."

I stared pointedly at the hand on my elbow. He removed it, flushing. "In here," I said, going a few more feet along the corridor and opening the door. "Ammo storage. Nobody is going to come in here until the ammo in the armory runs out."

This was one of several small, fireproof, blast-proof rooms along this corridor fitted with heavy metal shelves filled with case after case of ammunition. Heaven help anyone who was in here if there was ever an earthquake. I had wondered why the Hunter HQ was so big when I first arrived; once I became Elite, I learned the reason: HQ was supplied for a prolonged siege. We had enough stores of just about everything to hold out with the current complement of Hunters and staff for at least a year. We also had independent emergency power, and in a pinch, the swimming pool could easily serve as our water source after distilling the water.

There was zero chance we'd be overheard here. No sound would get past the heavy door.

When the door was closed, he turned back to me. He still didn't look any better. If anything, he looked even more wretched, as if he had been sleeping badly, and maybe not eating. "Joy, I need your help," he said, pleading. "There's no one else I can trust."

Which was, of course, *exactly* what he would say if Abigail Drift was setting me up for something. I folded my arms across my chest, controlled my breathing, and tried not to think how much I owed him (and how much I liked him). "And I should trust you, why, exactly? Your boss—"

"My boss is the problem, and I don't mean your uncle," he replied, interrupting me. He took a deep breath. Glancing down, I saw his hands were shaking. "I'm in trouble. I think. I mean, I don't know for certain but—"

"In trouble with Drift?" It was my turn to interrupt, since he was babbling to the point where I was willing to accept that this might not be a setup.

He nodded. "I've got a friend in PsiCorps Admin, and my friend says that Drift has been trying to get me transferred, but your uncle keeps fighting it. Now with things getting worse and worse, attacks coming on all those towns just outside the Barriers, and people outside the Barriers going missing, my friend says she's probably going to appeal to the premier and tell him I'm needed elsewhere."

People going missing?

Hold that thought for later. Concentrate on Josh's problem now.

"She's going to tell him you're needed for the project that overclocks Psimons and kills them." I set my jaw. "I can see that. Your punishment for not getting dirt on me she could use, I guess?"

"I guess." Josh wasn't on the verge of hyperventilating anymore, but he still looked miserable. And now I could identify the other emotion—he was *scared*. I didn't blame him. I didn't know how many Psimons Drift had killed with her overclocking experiments, but the number wasn't insignificant. "It's supposedly not exactly the same thing, and she's supposedly getting better results, but that's a lot of supposition. My friend thinks she's not going to approach this as 'I want Josh,' but instead she's going to go to Premier Rayne and present him with her data, and Rayne will give her pretty much anything she wants. I'm not the only Psi-aide she wants, but . . . Drift holds grudges. And I didn't perform to her specs."

That was the first admission I'd gotten from him that he knew Drift intended him to pick my brain. And it was a funny thing, but rather than making me madder at him, it made me feel more sympathetic. There had been any number of times that he could have said that my Psi-shield was giving him a headache and asked me to turn it off, and I might have. And that would have given him another chance to snoop on my thoughts. But he hadn't.

"I'm not sure what I can do," I said slowly. Then an idea occurred to me. "You know what, though, why don't you drop some hints that I might be thawing? That might buy you some time. If Drift holds grudges that badly, she's got a bigger bone to pick with me than with you."

All the tension drained out of him. He grabbed one of my hands, held it in both of his, and babbled his thanks. I let him. This looked *genuine*. Genuine fear, and genuine relief. I didn't think he was a good enough actor to fake it.

And dammit anyway, I wanted it to be real. I wanted him to have really liked me, and maybe even done his best to keep me out of the political tangles at the top levels of Apex.

"You'd better make some tracks back to work," I told him, opening the door and shoving him out. "You don't want to arouse suspicions by turning up late. I'll start accepting your texts again— just make them look tentative. And don't send too many. Just one at first. Like we're making up."

"I will. I can do that," he said fervently. And then he sprinted for the door, probably to call a pod in order to get to work before Uncle got there.

And me? I headed to the armory to check in with Cielle. I had a lot to think about, and I wasn't going to do that *now*.

When we bailed out of the chopper, Cielle and I weren't entirely sure what we were going to get into; our information was only to talk to the mayor, and something about a building. But the mayor of the village had seen the chopper incoming and ran out to meet us as we jumped out—at a proper chopper pad, no less, marked by a big *H* painted on the grass.

I summoned my Hounds before I said anything; without my Hounds, to strangers who don't recognize me, I'm just a girl in Hunter gear. With a pack of eleven, I'm *Holy crap, it's Hunter Joy!* As expected, the trick worked again; when the Way opened and all my Hounds poured through, the man's face went from *Crap, they sent me just two girls?* to *OH!*

Cielle followed my lead and brought her handsome fellows over as well; she had neglected to say that while her Hounds did indeed look like coyotes with bat wings, they were also a delicate shade of slate blue. Which, of course, literally paled in comparison to my *Alebrijes.* "Elite Joyeaux and Hunter Cielle," I said to the mayor, when all the Hounds were across and I could close the Way. "We didn't get any details on your situation, just that it required Elite."

"We keep all our farming and transportation machinery for the whole village in there," he said, pointing at a concrete dome in the middle distance. "After the storm we went to open it up and get what we needed, and Ogres rushed us. We got the door shut and locked and called for help."

I didn't bother to ask how many, because counting the Ogres would not have been a high priority for them at that point in time. I just assumed: a lot.

We had lucked out. Ogres, even a whole tribe of them, are not that bad, and certainly nothing we couldn't handle. Obviously the Ogres had been moving on the village when the storm broke, so they rushed in, found the door to what looked like a concrete hill could be opened, and holed up. After almost two days in there without food, they'd be angry and hungry. Under other circumstances, the right answer would have been to lob a few grenades in and slam the door again, but these folks couldn't do that. Not without wrecking every piece of large mechanical equipment they had.

"Let's look the situation over," I said, and our guide nodded. "If I were you, I'd get people in the village to take cover while we handle this. I'm pretty sure nothing is going to get past us, but there's no point in taking chances."

The mayor seemed very relieved at that; he nodded and headed into the village, while the two of us and our Hounds headed for the building.

This wasn't going to be pure cake, but it was something I could have handled alone, which meant it was a really excellent way for Cielle and I to shake out our partnership.

We paused outside the building; the door, probably steel, was a great big thing that moved on a track, certainly big enough for a good-size harvester to fit through. There wasn't a lock on it per se, but there was a bolt holding it firmly shut. Something was beating on the door from the inside.

"Well," Cielle said, eyeing the door without any sign of alarm. "We need to make some kills to power up the Hounds so they can power *us* up."

"Agreed," I said. "My Shields are pretty good. How about I wall off that opening, we open the physical door, and I let through one or two Ogres at a time?"

"Mine aren't good enough to pen up anything that can hit that hard, so if you want to do that, the Hounds and I should be able to take them," Cielle replied, looking happy that I had come up with a plan. This could be her real weakness; that she either didn't know how to concoct a plan of attack, or she didn't *think* she could. In either case, that could be easily cured with practice.

But meanwhile, I'd take over the planning for this incident, unless she spontaneously came up with some good ideas.

I looked around. There didn't seem to be anything she could get on top of, so I positioned her with Chenresig and Shinje next to her for extra protection. I put my Shield up, covering the entire opening of the building, then slammed the bolt back in its socket. A single push sent it quickly sliding along its track, and I jumped back as an Ogre crashed into my Shield and bounced off.

The Ogre was about eight or nine feet tall, with an oversize head covered in long shaggy hair, heavily bearded, dressed in a fur tunic, and carrying a great big honking club. His hair was kind of greenish, as if it was growing mold or something. And oh dear gods, he *stank*. Not as bad as a Gog or Magog, but . . . feh.

He was back on his feet in an instant, and another one—a female—rushed past him, hitting the Shield and bouncing off. She was shorter and kind of squat, with white hair and incongruously dressed in a long leather dress with a leather apron. Ogres are ridiculously strong and a lot quicker than they look; quick enough to have killed my Hounds if my pack hadn't been so clever and careful. They can swing those clubs far faster than they ought to be able to, and their aim is so precise it might as well be laser-guided.

The first one rushed the Shield again, and this time I allowed him through. He was charging so hard that he ran right past me. I let him have it. I was using my assault rifle with steel-jacketed bullets, and at a short distance like this, I almost didn't have to aim.

They don't do well with steel bullets or buckshot. Two in each knee, two in each elbow slowed him down; he dropped the club and turned with a howl to face me, and that was when Cielle got him.

She was right; whatever she wanted to call her magic, it looked like a laser beam about an inch in diameter, and it went through his skull like a laser beam, too. Since he was turning as she nailed him, he spun as he collapsed. Cielle's Hounds swooped down out of the sky to get his manna; mine held back, knowing I didn't need extra magic energy at this moment.

I let the female through. There was stirring and howls inside the building—must have been at least five or six more in there. Way more than the village could have handled on its own, especially with just conventional weapons. The female got the same treatment, and then things went quiet. Ogres weren't as stupid as Gogs and Magogs; they had figured out that running out to kill us only got them dead.

I'd have felt sorry for them, except that they eat humans, just like Gogs and Magogs do, and they prefer to eat children when they can get their hands on some. It's really hard to have anything like sympathy for something that thinks the best possible start to the day is with a baby sandwich.

Cielle said aloud what I was thinking. "We need a new tactic. Something to drive them out."

As she said that I saw her face light up. At the same time an idea popped into my head. "Skunk spray!" I said as she said, "That stink stuff you used on Ace!"

So . . . she actually could come up with plans. Made me wonder if being paired up with Ace had impeded her. I could easily see him just taking over, making all the decisions, not even listening to her, and she'd just taken the path of least resistance.

But it was pretty clear she was sharp and could think for herself.

We nodded at each other and dug into our gear.

Standard load-out these days included our gas masks, and both of us put them on. The Hounds, of course, had their own means of dealing with stink or toxic fumes. I dropped the Shield for a moment, cracked and shook up a chem-light, and tossed it into the dome. It took me three tries before I could get one I could see from where I was standing, but once I did, I put the Shield back up. The light would be my target.

I'd been cautious when I'd unloaded the stink on Ace at the Trials, since I was inside the same Shield as he was. I didn't need to worry about that today; I cranked the potency up as high as I could.

The howls of outrage, followed by coughing and gagging, started almost immediately. The Ogres rushed the door in a mob, and I had a hard time just letting one of them through at a time.

I fumbled the Shield once and let two through. "Look out!" I yelled. Cielle got one, missed the second by trying a hasty second shot, and the Hounds had to intervene to save my ass before she got it with a third shot.

We stopped then, breathing heavily, and looked at each other. I could see she was angry. But I could also see she was keeping her mouth slammed shut on her anger.

"My fault," I said first, before she could speak.

That surprised her for a minute—and I could guess why. I could never imagine Ace apologizing for anything.

She took two or three measured breaths, then the anger faded and she shrugged. "The second one squeezed through. I'll be prepared for more than one at a time from now on."

And that was it; we went back to work. After the first three went down, Cielle was powered up by her Hounds, and she was able to snap off laserlike shot after shot with ease. Between her magic and my rifle, we made short work of them.

By the time we finished them off, all our Hounds were sated, and it was pretty clear that we made an excellent team. I dismissed the skunk-spell—it would be too cruel to subject those poor villagers to *that*—and called in for pickup while Cielle texted the mayor to let him know his building was clear. Ogres, thank goodness, were one of the Othersider types that would go to goo and sink into the earth pretty quickly after they were dead, so there wasn't going to be anything to clean up.

Our chopper arrived at about the time the villagers came to get their vehicles out, and I was happy to see that Cielle ran for it and jumped right in rather than standing around and doing fan service. I wouldn't have *blamed* her if she had, and I would have waited for her to sign autographs and all that. But the fact that she understood without my needing to remind her that we were on the clock just pushed her further up in my books. I hoped everyone else's partners were working out just as well.

And sure enough, we hadn't been in the air more than ten minutes when we were diverted to handle a flock of Wyverns trying to make a communal nest. Despite the storm, it didn't look as if we were going to get much of a respite.

"Oh god," Cielle moaned, putting her head back against the headrest in the chopper. "I think I'm going to eat everything in the mess, then fall on my face."

I had already fastened my chin strap and was as limp as possible. "Well, night shift just went on duty, so we're done for the day. Think you can handle the pace?"

She cracked open the eye nearest me. "If you can, I can."

I grinned. That was what I wanted to hear. I would have replied, but Kent came on the Elite general freq.

"All incoming teams report to the armory. There will be something to eat and drink to tide you over until you can get real food."

We both groaned at that. Then we put our heads back and tried to get as much of a rest as we could on the ride.

We had to wait while another chopper cleared the pad; there was one in the air behind us as well. It looked like the Elite had been spread all the heck out today, putting out lots of (relatively) little fires. We were both too tired to sprint for the building, but we did manage a weary trot and found about half of the day shift already in the armory ahead of us. True to Kent's promise, there was a lot of ice-cold water and a tastier version of the energy squares waiting for us. When we were all sprawled on seats, munching and drinking, he looked around and smiled.

"Since I don't see any angry faces, can I assume this experiment is working?"

We all chimed in, Elite *and* Hunters, with varying degrees of enthusiasm. Cielle and I were about the fourth to speak. "Kent, I won't say this went like clockwork," I said. "But that's just a matter of not Hunting together before. I can't speak for actual statistics here, but it felt like we handled twice the Othersiders with half the effort it would take me alone."

I looked over at Cielle, who seemed a little cowed by so many Elite in the room; she took a long drink of water and gamely spoke up. "I don't know about the 'half the effort' part, but I can keep up, and I'll get better with practice. I'm still in."

About the only people who were a little cool on this were Knight and Scarlet, and after a little discussion it seemed to be more of a problem of Powers not meshing with their new partners than anything else. So there was some swapping around for tomorrow—neither Cielle nor I wanted to un-partner, of course—and Kent called an end to the meeting. He caught us before we left the room.

"So. You two getting along well, I take it?" He raised an eyebrow.

Cielle giggled, and for the first time she sounded like the Cielle that had hung all over Ace. I gave her a real close look and saw she was blushing slightly. Her posture had gone all girly; she'd ducked her head coyly to one side, and balanced most of her weight on one leg with the other foot just touching the floor with her toe. I realized I'd seen girls pose like that back home, when they were talking to boys they liked. She had a *crush* on Kent! Was that why she had volunteered? If so, it wasn't stopping her from giving 100 percent and more. I just grinned and nodded. "It was just like I said, sir. Twice the result, half the effort, so far as I could tell."

He consulted his Perscom. "Statistics would seem to bear out your feelings, Joy. Cielle, your channel is going crazy over the new footage. You've skipped up three ranks since this morning."

Her face lit up. "I *have*?" she squealed, then got her composure back. "I honestly wasn't thinking about that—" But she looked as if Kent's words had given her back all the energy she'd expended.

"Go eat half the mess, and get some rest," Kent said, in a "brotherly" tone that told me he had noticed Cielle crushing on him, all right. "Tomorrow you have to do it all again."

When I got to my room, though, I threw myself down on the bed with my hands tucked under my head; I needed to think.

I'd promised to help Josh without getting a chance to think things through, and that might have been a stupid move on my part. I knew for a fact that there was a power struggle going on between Abigail Drift and Uncle. I also knew for a fact that she'd use me to get to him. This might be a setup on her part; Uncle was in charge of all Hunters not in the army, and there had already been one traitor—Ace—among the Hunters. So if Drift was using Josh, getting him to talk me into helping him escape—was there some law against Psimons running away from PsiCorps? I was willing to bet there was; after all, there *was* a law that everyone with psionics had to be identified and trained by PsiCorps. Psimons were valuable assets to Apex. Josh running like this . . . would that be like a soldier deserting? And helping Josh would make me a traitor to Apex. Setting me up as another traitor would not just get rid of me, it would cast suspicion on Uncle. Nobody was blaming him for Ace at the moment, but if it looked as if I had turned my coat, well, that was a second Hunter gone bad on his watch. Plus, I was his niece, and he'd never escape getting tainted by my sins. It would be child's play for Drift to get Uncle booted at that point and put someone of her choosing in his place.

On the other hand, if Josh actually was in trouble, I *owed* it to him to help. If he vanished into that PsiCorps program that boosted Psimon powers at the expense of their lives . . . I would never forgive myself. I couldn't let that happen, I just couldn't.

All right, then. There was only one thing to be done at the moment, and that was to take this whole problem to Uncle. I was reaching for the remote to wake up my vid-screen and make a call to him when the screen lit up.

It was Kent. I sat up, both from surprise and because I didn't want him to see me sprawled like a drunk on my bed. "Joy, the prefect is on the way over for a meeting and suggested you sit in on it." His face and voice were utterly neutral. "He should be here in five minutes. Can you come to my office?"

"Right away, sir," I said, really glad now I hadn't changed straight into sleep gear. My muscles protested, but I managed to lever myself off the bed.

Just as I reached Kent's office, I saw Uncle coming from the opposite direction. Kent opened his door. "Excellent timing," he said. "Come with me, both of you."

I raised an eyebrow at Uncle, who shrugged. So he had no more idea what Kent had in mind than I did.

But I quickly got the idea when Kent led us to the indoor garden and koi pond at the center of HQ. There were no electronic devices in here other than our own Perscoms, so there was nothing that could be surreptitiously turned on to eavesdrop. And the noise of the waterfall that kept the pond aerated would cover the sounds of our voices outside this room. Kent locked the door behind us. We all got fish food, sat on the raised edge of the pond, and started tossing bits to the slow-moving koi.

"Psi-shields," Kent said, and I obediently turned on the one built into my Perscom. Uncle didn't move, and neither did Kent, so they must have already had theirs on. I didn't keep mine on all the time; it gave me an odd feeling, like a faint ringing in my skull, and it made it really hard to talk to my Hounds.

"So, Charmand, you indicated you had something to talk about involving your Psi-aide and Joy—that means Drift, then?" Kent said. My eyes widened just a little bit, and I nearly dropped all the fish-food pellets on the ground.

"Yes," Uncle said, and then recited a version of what Josh had told me, nearly word for word. Except that Josh had begged *him* for help.

"Josh ambushed me this morning before we went on shift, and said nearly the same thing to me!" I blurted.

Uncle nodded. "He told me he'd gone to you for help. If I am any judge of human beings at all, he's terrified, and he is genuinely afraid that Drift is going to dragoon him into this project of hers regardless of his unwillingness."

"You both know this sounds very much like a trap, don't you?" Kent finally said, frowning and throwing the last of his food to the fish, who surged for it, roiling the water. "If I were Abigail Drift, this is *exactly* what I would do in order to get you both out of the way. Drift isn't stupid; she knows if she discredits you and leaves Joy alone, Joy will move heaven and earth to clear your name and put you back in power. And getting rid of Joy alone doesn't accomplish her goal of getting rid of you. She has to get you both."

The lights were coming on all over the garden as night fell: soft, dim red lights that created a kind of cozy twilight. I listened to Kent and Uncle wrestle with the problem, then finally spoke up.

"I guess Josh didn't tell you, but I suggested we … get back together. That might stall Drift, if she thinks he can get inside my head and give her whatever the heck it is that she wants," I said. "It's not the world's best idea, but it might buy us some time."

"It's also not the world's worst idea," Uncle replied thoughtfully. "It's not as if you're going to be able to meet up in person for anything, with the Elite on twelve-hour shifts. But if Drift is still thinking in terms of the old normal, when the Hunters and even the Elite had plenty of downtime, she might not realize that for a while. She might just wait for you two to start going out on dates again, and it won't occur to her for a while that dating isn't going to be possible."

"It's about as good a way of stalling as I can think of," Kent agreed.

"So I'll go ahead and contact him on public channels and make up with him," I said decisively. And then I added, "He's never lied to me. I broke up with him in the first place because I thought PsiCorps was using him to get at me in order to get at you, Uncle. I know there's no good reason to trust him, and all I have going for me is my gut, but . . . my gut says he's never lied to me."

"I've trusted flimsier things," Kent mused. "And I have to say, if this is a trap Drift is trying to set up, it's not a very good one. It does depend entirely on all of us not talking to each other, which at least in the case of you and Joy is a rather stupid assumption."

"Don't get cocky—" Uncle and I said at the same time. We looked at each other and smiled sheepishly.

"Let's treat her as if she's a mastermind, because she probably is. If we overestimate her, we've lost nothing. If we underestimate her . . ." Uncle shook his head, and I swallowed. I could still vividly recall how Drift had looked at me, as if I were something on her plate she didn't want, except to feed to the dog.

"All right, then, we have a short-term plan, and we keep everyone in the loop on what's going on," Kent decreed. I nodded. Then I remembered something.

"Do either of you know if there are people missing from the towns the Othersiders are hitting?" I asked. I knew better than to ask about places like Spillover. No one ever bothered to keep track of the poor castoffs who lived there.

Kent raised an eyebrow. "How would I be able to tell people 'missing' from people 'eaten'?" he asked, reasonably. "Why are you asking?"

"I just wondered if there were people being carried off rather than killed on the spot," I replied. "Still thinking about what that

Folk Lord said. And . . . Josh said something about people going missing out there."

He nodded, then shrugged. "Nothing has been said to the Hunters about people being kidnapped. Right now, let's concentrate on what's in front of us. How are you going to convey information to the prefect?"

"I can code things by referencing books we both know," I said. "Uncle and I do that already."

"Smarter than using an actual code," Uncle agreed. "All right, let's go back to your office, Kent, and I can go over those reports on Joy's bright idea. Joy, you get some much-needed rest."

"Thanks, I will," I said, seeing no need to be formal right at that moment. I got up, gave them both an awkward little salute, and headed out.

I sighed as I got to my room. It would be nice to be friends with Josh again.

Too bad "friends" was going to be all I had time for.

HOT WIND SCORCHED MY face. Dusana ran so fast the ground beneath us was a blur. I was *really* glad he didn't have anything like a mane, or I'd have been beaten to death by it by now. Bya was just ahead of us, leading us through a twisty mess of magic tangle-traps only the Hounds could see—another one of Cielle's special magic spells and one I hadn't been able to master yet. Normally they were meant for much smaller Othersiders than a Drakken, and none of these traps were going to actually stop the Drakken we were currently leading, but we had figured they *should* start to slow him down as he accumulated them. Kind of like someone stepping in lots of the sticky flypaper we put out in high summer. By our reckoning when we'd made this plan, he'd be moving at half speed by the time we got to where Cielle would have a clear shot at him.

That was the theory, anyway. In practice, well, it wasn't working. The Drakken had blundered into dozens of the traps by now, and he wasn't one bit slower.

I heard the thing's tongue-jaw shoot out with a juicy *flup*, and my gut clenched as I instinctively ducked. Then I looked back over my shoulder. Suddenly the hot air around me seemed icy. "Cielle, this thing is as fast as ever, and we're going to be in range *quick*," I said over our freq. I hoped I didn't sound as panicked as I was starting to feel. "You need to get off your shot before I have to give up and *bamph* away from him, because if I do that, he might come for you!"

Cielle didn't reply, but I didn't expect her to. She needed to concentrate, since the target was moving faster than anything she had ever hit before. And much, much bigger than she had ever hit before. In fact, she had wanted me to call in a couple more Elite—we'd had our first argument over it. She'd had to cave because I pointed out there just weren't any Elite to spare. *You can do this, Cielle,* I thought at her fiercely. *You can do this.*

We came over the ridge that was blocking her view, practically flying. A split second later, so did the Drakken. Dusana and I turned to get him set up for the shot. He followed us like he was on a string, and in seconds we were running parallel to where Cielle was. I held my breath.

The bright white beam of light and power flashed toward us—but it was lower than it was supposed to be. She was going to miss the head! I wrenched myself around on Dusana's back, a dazzle-spell readied to blind the Drakken so we could get away . . .

. . . just in time to hear the thing give out a piercing shriek that turned my insides to mush and see its front quarters collapse. It hit the ground, momentum still carrying it forward, limbs jumbling and flailing over its body, while Dusana wisely dodged to the right to get out of the path of the meat avalanche.

Stuff was flying everywhere; we got pelted by debris as we put on more speed. We pulled up to a halt as the Drakken finally stopped somersaulting over itself, and we waited, tense and ready to run again in a split second if it showed any signs of recovery.

The thing's head reared up again, but I've killed enough animals, normal and Othersider, to know it was dying. It shrieked once more, nose pointing at the sky; then the head and neck fell limply to the ground with a huge *thud* and a cloud of dust.

Cielle's four Hounds came streaking in overhead to soak up the manna, and a moment later, the rest of my pack raced through the long wheat to join them. I got off Dusana so he could get his share, then started trudging the quarter mile or so toward Cielle, who was up in a tree with an unrestricted view of this side of the ridge.

This was a farm that grew strictly wheat or wheat-like grains, but as with everything else since the Diseray, it was scarcely the monoculture such fields of grain used to be. There were at least six different varieties of wheat and similar grains sown in these fields, all carefully chosen so they would all ripen together—that way if a disease or pest got one variety, there'd still be something to harvest. I only recognized one; the rest were all new to me, which made sense, since these fields were several thousand feet lower than the fields of home.

Cielle's tree was just one of a tree line that divided one field from another. When I got there, Cielle was sitting on the ground with her back to the trunk. "You did it!" I called. "I knew you could! Great work!"

"I didn't think I could get the head-shot, he was going so fast," she said, looking up at me wearily. "So I made the beam as big as I could and went for the body."

"You carved a big enough hole in him to drop him. Good call," I said, and dropped down into the grass across from her. "That was picture-perfect. We can call this one a win." I keyed in the HQ freq. "Team JC."

"*Team JC, go.*" Oh good. If they answered that fast, it meant no one was up to their asses in alligators, and we would get a little bit of respite.

"Drakken down. Ready for recall."

"*Team JC, roger. Got a chopper not far from you with room for one. Elite Joy, can one of you hold until the second chopper's free?*"

Quick calculation told me that meant Hammer, Steel, Dazzle, and Tober were inbound; with Hammer and Steel in a six-man chopper, there really was only room for five. "Copy that, HQ, yes, I can hold, and Cielle could use about five thousand calories right now."

Cielle mouthed *Thank you* at me. I grinned.

"*Copy that, Team JC. Chopper will be there for Hunter Cielle in less than five.*"

"I'll put up smoke." I went out into the field and set up a flare in the dirt. Cielle stood up just long enough to open the Way; her Hounds came flitting back, looking sated, and dove through the Portal without stopping to land. That was some very pretty flying.

As soon as they were safely Otherside, she dismissed it. Mine, greedy pigs, were probably vacuuming up every last bit of manna from the Drakken carcass—which would probably stay there until it was reduced to bones and scraps of skin by scavengers.

By the time red smoke had risen about a thousand feet into the air, I heard the distant *whumpwhumpwhump* of the chopper. Cielle did too; she got to her feet and we both stood at the edge of the tree line to wait. The chopper popped up over the ridge and down again, no more than ten feet off the ground, the wheat fanning out under the downforce from its blades.

The pilot was good; he dropped his skids right in between the rows to save the wheat, holding the chopper steady as a rock. Cielle ran out, staying low; when she got to the door, three pairs of hands grabbed for the shoulder straps of her backpack and hauled her in. The pilot rose straight up, swiveled the bird in place, then took off. I caught Steel waving to me from the door.

"*HQ to Elite Joy,*" my radio said.

"Go, HQ," I replied.

"*Your ride will be there in about thirty minutes. We'll call you at five so you can put out another marker. Meanwhile, relax and enjoy the view.*"

"Roger, HQ." I went and put my back to Cielle's tree and slid down it. The radio op had probably meant "enjoy the view" ironically, but I *did* enjoy the view. It was a lot cooler under the trees than out in the field. A light wind cut across half-grown green wheat, the closest thing I've ever seen with my own eyes to waves on a big body of water. And I liked all the sky, I seriously did. The only time I would see this much sky back home was if I was looking out a window at the Monastery, which is up above the snow line on the Mountain. Once below the snow line, the mountains around us cut off so much of the sky that sunrise was as much as an hour later than it was at the top of the Mountain, and sunset as much as an hour earlier.

For once nothing was chasing me, I wasn't chasing something, and I wasn't completely exhausted. The water in my bottle was even still cool. I sipped and put it back in my pack.

"It is a bucolic scene, is it not, shepherd?"

My blood turned to ice, and I jumped to my feet. Lavender was no more than six feet away from me, gazing out at the field of wheat.

He looked . . . exactly like he had the first time I set eyes on him, when he had stopped a train and tried to bargain with me for some of the people on it. Beautiful, of course—even the feral Folk were beautiful. But too beautiful, too perfect. Taller than a human, with a thin, seemingly delicate body and face, eyebrows like antennae, and pointed ears about as long as my forearm.

He wore—well, I couldn't tell if it was the *same* costume as before, but it was at least very similar, in the same colors. His long silvery-lavender hair, perfectly groomed and smooth as ice, was done in some sort of elaborate style with strings of sparkly beads behind his right ear. He had a silver headband stretched across his forehead, with a lavender stone in it that matched his lavender eyes. His costume was less warlike than Gold's had been—it was all made of some soft, shiny silvery-lavender stuff, with floaty sleeves and lots of layers, and every visible bit of it was covered in silver embroidery and more sparkly beads.

But this time, instead of floating a couple of feet above me, his feet were firmly on the ground. And he had no Shield.

He glanced at me sideways, eyes glinting, mouth curving up ever so slightly. I felt the sudden agitation of my Hounds, and knew that they were racing across the field to get to me.

"You are in no danger from me, shepherd," he said, as if he was reading my—

Of course he was! Hastily I triggered my Psi-shield.

That faint smile got just a fraction larger.

My Hounds came tearing across the last few feet, then stopped dead. And stared at him. They packed up around and behind me but made no aggressive moves.

"Peace, faithful ones," Lavender said. "I told your shepherd I am no threat. And indeed, have I not given you ample evidence of that? I have helped you several times, aye, and saved your large companion as well. But you do well to be wary, for there are many others of my kind who are a threat to you, and to humans in general."

"The one in the gold armor," I said. "Are you done being enigmatic now? Because all those guessing games of yours nearly got me killed last time you 'helped' me."

To my surprise, he chuckled. Like everything else about him, his laughter was beautiful. Possibly, quite literally, enchanting. "Impatient little mayfly. I will tell you a thing. My name is Torcion."

I nearly had a heart attack. The Folk never, *ever* tell us their names. As some of the old lore goes, if you know a thing's name, you can control it magically.

"Speak my name thrice, shepherd, and I will hear you wherever

I am and come to speak with you." His expression darkened. "But do not think to lure me into a trap with it. You shall not survive the attempt."

"I—wouldn't do that," I managed. And I knew in that moment it was a promise. He had never hurt me—in fact, he'd helped me. I didn't know why, but he had. And he had told the truth; he had saved Steel from certain death back at the first Barrier Battle.

His expression lightened again. He looked as if he was about to say more, but the radio crackled to life. *"Elite Joy, your ride will be there in five."*

"Roger, HQ," I said, and started to get up to plant the smoke flare, only to sit back down again. I wasn't sure how he'd take my getting to my feet—he might interpret it as a sign of potential aggression.

"Go," Torcion said, one side of his mouth quirking slightly. "We will speak again. Beware, there are those within your magic walls who serve only themselves, and would not hesitate to offer you up to the Alliance of Seven if it advanced their ambitions."

And with a gesture so casual it was almost absentminded, he opened a Portal behind him and stepped through it, leaving no sign he had ever been there.

By day's end, as usual, I was exhausted, but I knew that sleep was going to be hard to find. I finally brought Bya over as soon as I had finished my shower. *What do you think?* I asked him as I pretended to watch Apex News in bed, with Bya acting as a support and pillow behind my back.

He gave you his true name, Bya replied, but there was doubt and reluctance that mirrored my own. *I do not know what to think. Those of his realm beyond the Portal are enemies to me and mine.*

Huh. Two pieces of information about Otherside. That there were "realms" there, presumably separating types of Othersiders, and that there was fighting, or at least enmity, over there.

What do you feel? I asked instead of probing him about what he thought. I had always been able to rely on the Hounds' instincts. I was gambling I could trust them now.

My head says it is foolish to trust him, but my instincts say we can, Bya replied after a very long pause. *My instincts are seldom wrong. But... when they are wrong, they are very, very wrong. It means that the creature they are wrong about is clever and duplicitous enough to fool anyone, even me.*

What do the others think? I persisted because I knew there could be differences of opinion in my pack. I'd never interfered with that; Bya was pack alpha, and what he and Myrrdhin decided for the pack was what would be. But right now it might be a good idea to find out if there were any dissenters and hear them out.

There is no dissent. Myrrdhin and Gwalchmai favor this Torcion—perhaps because their realm is nearer to that of his people than ours. That surprised me so much I nearly jumped.

If that's the case... I wondered. *If they favor his people...*

I did not say that, Bya corrected, to my relief. *I said they favor* him. *They know more of his people than I. I think they are probably better judges than I regarding whom to trust in this situation.*

Well, all right, then. Even though it went against the grain, even though it went against *everything* I had been taught...I would trust a Folk Lord. For now, anyway.

I now had two people—or I guess you could say one person and one "creature"—who I was trusting despite certain misgivings. And with either of them, it was possible my trust was *wildly* misplaced.

Josh and Torcion. Either of them could land me in more trouble than I could handle.

I'd been exchanging texts and the occasional message with Josh after "making up" with him, but my schedule was giving me a reasonable excuse to keep interaction to a minimum. The only problem with that was—dammit, I was waffling. Half the time, I was dead certain he was telling me the truth, that Drift was about to take her ire out on him for protecting me. The other half of the time, I was certain he'd faked everything about being my boyfriend. I just didn't know him like I thought I did, and these fractional bits of contact weren't giving me any information.

And I hated, I absolutely *hated,* what I had become. I never used to be suspicious of people. I never used to even think about politics and all the garbage it brings with it. All this sneaking around and thinking of plots and counterplots was not *me.* It wasn't who I wanted to be.

Before I went to sleep, I got into my archived messages and called up every exchange Josh and I'd had since he ambushed me in the hallway. Fortunately we hadn't done too many face-to-faces, thanks to my insane schedule, so he just left messages. I studied what he said, and how he said it. And I honestly couldn't see any indications he was acting. He appeared genuinely relieved in the first message he'd left.

"Oh, remember that friend I told you about? Looks like things are working out for him," he said on the screen. Everything about his body language was indicative of relief; his posture was relaxed, as were the tiny muscles around his eyes. Josh's friend in the PsiCorps Admin must have told him he was safe again for the moment. "And Prefect Charmand is upgrading me to an office of my own," he said. I assumed that meant Uncle had gotten the same message—that Josh was safe for now.

The next several messages just reinforced my impression. But in the last one, just today, he was worried again. Not frantic but— "Office pressure sucks. I wish you could get a night off like we used to have." He must have been feeling impelled by PsiCorps to make real contact with me again. When I recorded a return message I would in turn "remind" him that I had bigger things on my plate than going Straussing, just to reinforce what he was saying.

If you keep studying those recordings you are never going to get any sleep, Bya reminded me.

Then he made himself all soft and cushy, instead of supportive, and I shut the vid-screen and the lights off and gave in. . . .

As always, morning came too soon. I'd been jarred awake by a callout around three a.m. last night because they'd needed me for my nets. We'd faced the biggest flock of Nightwings anyone had ever seen. Nightwings are what they sound like: flying black critters with no discernible body that feed by enveloping the victim. They are a lot smarter than you'd think, given they mostly look like those ocean critters called "rays." They know how to break windows or go down chimneys to get at their prey. The flock that had descended on yet another little town had been large enough to drain every Cit in the place twice over, if one of the creatures hadn't gotten a little too eager and rushed in before the rest. People managed to get themselves and their kids into basements or windowless rooms and called for help, and that was where we had come in.

Cielle's big power hadn't been of much use, but her winged Hounds were, and her nets were good enough to catch individual Nightwings. Meanwhile, those of us who could trapped them by the tens and twenties. The Hounds certainly ate well. If Nightwings couldn't envelop you, they were pretty well helpless.

I met Cielle at the door to the mess. We went and got our breakfast bowls and sat with Kent and Scarlet and their Hunter partners. Cielle looked as if she wanted to say something. Kent raised an eyebrow at her. "No, we've never seen a swarm like that before. I hope we've cleaned them out for a while."

"If they'd gotten into Apex..." Scarlet shuddered. So did I. I could just picture it, streets full of people out to have a good time, people who had no idea what those things were, didn't know to run from them—it only takes a Nightwing a minute to absorb someone, and they can "eat" a dozen or more adults before they are sated. Cielle's mouth formed an O.

"Well, it didn't happen. And now that we know they can

flock in those numbers, I've alerted everyone that can spot them *before* they get to Apex," Kent said firmly. "Bullets kill them very effectively, and a few helichopper gunships would go a long way toward thinning out the flock to a manageable size."

We're being reactive, not proactive, I realized in that moment—and I knew that Kent, despite his outward confidence, was probably thinking the same thing.

We needed to get a handle on this situation and start turning the tide.

Right. If only we could just figure out how . . .

WE'D SCARCELY FINISHED breakfast when we got the full call-out signal, which was for us *and* the night shift; we groaned but shoved ourselves away from our tables and headed for the landing pad.

As we all learned on the way to our rides, this one was for a city called Bastion that had wisely kept its physical walls and its artillery. And when we got there . . .

It was hideous. The walls had been swarmed by an organized army of Othersiders. It looked like a replay of the first Barrier Battle. We all bailed without waiting for the choppers to set down and summoned, quick and dirty. The enemy knew we were coming—choppers are not quiet—and we knew they were going to be at our throats in minutes at best. Portals to the Otherside popped up all along our rough line, and the Hounds came pouring out. By the time we'd formed up, the Othersiders had turned away from their attacks on the walls. They formed into rough groups of *Nagas*, Ogres, and Minotaurs and came after us.

But Bastion was not unarmed: they had mortars, cannon, RPGs, and other assorted goodies that they could, and did, fire at the back ranks of the Othersiders. The cannons on the west wall were mostly just keeping a Drakken pinned down, but that still meant we didn't need to deal with it just yet. Meanwhile all the smaller distance-weapons dropped lots of presents on the critters facing us.

"Form up on me!" Kent ordered, and we gathered in. "Steel, Hammer, Knight. I want a joint Shield on us, now! Hounds outside, us inside. Joy, you and your alpha coordinate all the Hounds."

If I'd had time to think, I would have been knocked sideways by that order. But I didn't have time to think; I only had time to act.

Bya, Kent wants us to coordinate all the packs—

There was not even a moment of hesitation on Bya's part. *Each one of the Hounds in your pack will take another two packs. Myrrdhin, Gwalchmai, Hevajra, and I will take four packs each. All will be well. Tell us what to do.*

I had to come up with something quick. Kent wasn't giving *me* any orders. *Hevajra, take the packs that can breathe fire. If there are more than four packs that breathe fire, Bya, take the others. Myrrdhin, Gwalchmai, take the packs of fliers. Dusana, take whichever packs that are left that have the biggest Hounds. The rest of you, work with who you know.* Thank heavens I could count on Byra and Myrrdhin to relay what I was saying to Hold and Strike. *Myrrdhin, are there any Harpies?*

At this point, the monsters had closed around us and were trying to get through our Shields.

There are Harpies, Myrrdhin confirmed. *We with the fliers will deal with them and anything else that flies. When the fliers are done, I will have them drop stones, or if we can get them, grenades.*

"Kent!" I shouted into my mic—the noise of us firing magic stuff at monsters, monsters beating on our Shields, and screaming was so bad you couldn't hear the person standing right next to you— "Contact Bastion Defense, and if they have hand grenades, give them to any flying Hounds that come to the walls." As I yelled to Kent, I thought what I was saying to him at my Hounds.

"*Roger that. Grenades for flier Hounds.*"

We heard, said Myrrdhin promptly.

You can see what you're doing out there better than I can. Do your best for us. I had to leave it at that because our Shields were beginning to bow inward from the weight of the Othersiders, weaponry, and rudimentary magic, and it was time for me to start throwing spells around.

Harpies streamed up into the sky from some spot to the north, where I guessed the Othersiders had a Portal. But they were met by our Hounds, who were more than a match for the cowardly Harpies. Myrrdhin and Gwalchmai were somewhere safe and concealed, presumably, where they had a good view of the skies from the ground and could direct their fliers. I trusted them; how could I not? My pack, individually and together, had saved my life more times than I could count.

Meanwhile, Dusana had grown to his biggest size, which was

roughly as big as a shed, and had gathered a pack of two Hounds the size of plow horses, one to either side of him, with the rest of the pony-size Hounds behind *them*. They rammed their way through the front lines of the enemy, about ten feet from the Shield, biting and clawing everything they could get their jaws on, cutting a path for the rest of their packs of smaller Hounds led by Shinje and Chenresig to follow. Those smaller Hounds, in turn, bit and clawed into the hordes to either side of that clear path. That kept some pressure off the Shield, and threw the front couple of ranks of Othersiders into disorder.

Where there were *Nagas*, the fire-breathing packs were wreaking havoc. As far as I could tell, all the rest of the Hounds led by Hold, Strike, Begtse, and Kalachakra were playing strike-and-run randomly along the back line, confusing the Othersiders when they found themselves attacked on two fronts. We Hunters couldn't use physical weapons across the Shield without leaving ourselves open to physical attacks, so all we could use was magic.

I already knew Othersiders had powerful senses of smell, so one of the first things I did was plant patches of skunk-spell everywhere I could. I had to be careful; too much and it would drift over to us, and then we'd be just as affected as they were. But the wind was at my back and in our favor, and by the number of Othersiders that were reacting sharply when the stink hit their noses, it was pretty clear my first efforts were a success.

I took advantage of their distraction by abruptly raising and dismissing tiny sections of Wall among them. Tripping and gassing the Othersiders served us just as well as cracking a Shield and delivering a levin bolt to the face. But I had to be careful not to trip the Hounds, so I made sure the bits of Wall were only up for seconds at a time.

Cielle didn't dare cut loose with her big power; she might hit the Hounds. So she was firing off lesser bolts, and whatever she hit went down and stayed down.

Dusana came through the lines a second time, and his team left screams of pain and death in their wake. A moment later, drops and drizzles of red spattered down on the Shield, then larger dollops. *The Harpies are over your heads*, Myrrdhin told me. *They are not faring well.* My gut churned a little, and I was glad that I was too busy to look up.

A moment later, dead Harpies began to fall out of the sky, hitting the top of the Shield and sliding down, leaving smears of red behind them. But they were already dissolving into air and dust the moment they hit the Shield, and by the time they were about halfway down, there was nothing left of them to land on the ground.

More of them—the not-quite-dead ones—were falling among their fellow Othersiders, further confusing the combat. *How are the fliers?* I asked anxiously, throwing up yet another tiny Wall and sending a cluster of three Minotaurs into one another.

Getting enough manna to heal themselves, was the terse reply from Myrrdhin, as Dusana and his accompanying brutes rammed their way through the fighting monsters a third time.

My Hounds clearly knew what they were doing. I only hoped I did.

Knight, Hammer, and Steel had kept the Shields up as long as they could, but eventually they had run out of physical energy to manipulate the magic, so they'd dropped our protection, and we'd gone to weapons. I thought for one fleeting moment that we were going to lose this thing. . . .

That was when the Hounds tore their way through the ranks around us and formed a defensive perimeter of teeth and claws and belching flames between us and the Othersiders. Unlike us, they were feeding off manna every time one of the enemy went down, getting stronger rather than more exhausted as they fought. Magic we had in full. It was pure physical energy we lacked now.

Then, at last, the close-air support arrived in the form of heli-choppers with their chain guns loaded with Othersider-specific ammo. They'd chased off the Folk Mages keeping the Portals open, cutting off the hordes of monsters that were replenishing the ones we had destroyed. That finally turned the tide.

The remaining Othersiders broke and fled when they realized there were no more reinforcements coming. My Hounds and I returned the packs to their proper Hunters, and we all went in pursuit, except for eight of us under the command of Kent who went after the last Drakken. I was so relieved to see that the Drakken was in pretty bad shape from all the cannon fire it had taken that I actually had tears running down my face. I don't think I have ever been so exhausted in my life, except at the end of the Barrier Battles, and there wasn't a one of us that was better off than I was.

It was another brutal fight. Eventually, thanks in no small part to Cielle, who managed to drag up just enough willpower and strength to fire off her mega–levin bolt, we brought the Drakken down in a hail of magic and bullets, and our Hounds dove in to feed off the manna.

And then, as the sound of chopper blades neared, I felt something like a cool breeze on my mind. My eyes flew open and I whipped my head around to the right.

And I saw him, for a moment. Staring at me from across the battlefield, standing all by himself. That Folk Lord, the gold one. Bya's head came up and I knew Bya could see him too. Beneath my hand, Bya's back vibrated with his sudden growl.

My Psi-shield wasn't on, of course. I couldn't have talked to Bya and the pack if it had been. All I had to keep me safe from the Folk Mage's psionics was concentration on my One White Stone. Was that enough?

The Mage caught my gaze with his molten-gold eyes. I couldn't look away. I felt as if I were a bird caught in the gaze of a snake.

Then he smiled sardonically, opened a Portal, stepped through it, and was gone.

We had some wounded on that run. We were going to be operating about a third light for a couple of days, and I could not have been more grateful for all our new partners if I had gone to each one of them and kissed their hands. I sent Cielle to the medbay—maybe there was something the medics could give her that would help her recover faster. In the chopper she'd looked as limp as a rag doll without stuffing. Me, well, I went to the lounge, since it was a lot closer to the armory than my room was, and flung myself flat on a couch. I wasn't the only one who'd had that idea either, and the vid-screens were blessedly tuned to random fractal patterns and soft, meandering music.

Had this been a test? It certainly felt like one to me.

My faint hope was that the Othersiders had overcommitted to this test and lost more than they could afford, at least for now. That might give us a couple days of respite—we'd had weeks of that kind of relief after the Barrier Battles.

As I lay there, getting my wind back, feeling the aches, the bruises, the cuts and bites and strains sort themselves out, I gradually began to wonder how *they* felt after this last engagement. The Othersiders, I mean. We hadn't lost anyone, but lots and lots of *them* had ended up dead. Did that even matter to them? It didn't seem as if it did. Getting injured enraged them, individually, and the adults with young that we had seen did seem to have protective instincts with regards to their offspring—but the deaths of dozens, hundreds of their fellows, right next to them, didn't seem to register with the still-living.

So what makes them keep fighting us? Individuals, even groups, yeah—prey drive would account for it. But these armies? It had to be something outside themselves, driving them. It had to be the Folk Mages, who were probably doing a lot more than merely opening Portals.

They don't have to be mind-controlling them the whole time, though, I realized after a long moment of weary blanking out. *The lesser Othersiders are probably set off with simple mind-controlling spells.* Now, *we* didn't have any magic like that, but there was ample evidence for it in legends and folklore.

"Hey," I said aloud into the quiet of the room. "Anybody got any clues as to *why* these motherless bastards keep throwing themselves on us like they are intent on suicide? This is not rational, thinking behavior. You saw what happened when I gave the Thunderbirds a chance to back out—so why don't the rest act like that?"

"They kind of always have." That was Defender, somewhere across the room. "At least, they always have when they attack in any numbers."

"Which is . . . when they have Folk Mages with them. . . ." That was Scarlet, clearly putting two and two together and coming up with the same answer I had.

Having started that particular conversation, I decided to keep my mouth shut and listen. They all had a lot more experience with Othersiders than I did; I just seemed to be a trouble magnet.

They were still hashing it out when lunchtime rolled around, and the discussion continued in the mess, where it soon involved every single Hunter that was there.

There was surprisingly little dissension—mostly people just recounted their observations. I'd have taken notes, except that I knew the vid-system was already recording everything. The thing is, yes, all this information *was* technically on the Hunting records—the ones made out in the battlefield. But the problem with those recordings was they were only that: pure recording of nothing more than what had happened on the field. Hunting is as much about observation and learning as it is about going in there with your powers and your weapons and killing Othersiders— the kinds of things we talked about when we analyzed ourselves in the lounge, for instance. What I wanted to collect wasn't on those tapes of the battlefield. It was in hunches, gut feelings—observation and deduction voiced out loud.

I sent a couple text messages to Kent, clueing him in on our discussion in the mess. Surely Hunter HQ had some techs who specialized in analyzing this sort of thing. I got back a terse but satisfying reply. *GJ. On it.* "GJ," of course, meaning "good job."

I had gotten the ball rolling. Maybe the techs—or the army Mages—could figure out how to block, or better still, cancel a controlling spell on the Othersiders. If we could get just some of them rebelling and fleeing, that would be a tremendous help.

And just as I thought that, my Perscom beeped. Small callout. Cielle and me, Knight and whoever he was paired with. Flock of Gazers moving in on a village; I could net them, and Cielle could blast swaths of them, while Mark and his partner sniped from afar at the nasty little Jackals, who had a symbiotic partnership with the Gazers.

I shoved off from the table; I heard chairs scrape as the other three did the same, and we all headed for the door.

There were three more small callouts, but they didn't involve me or Cielle. The Gazers proved a bit problematic out in the open, but with Cielle's and Mark's flying Hounds harrying them, we could keep them from turning their powers on us. Mark and his partner Sable set up on the top of a water tower, well out of Gazer eye-glare reach, and picked off the Jackals that half my Hounds and all of

Sable's herded away. While I netted Gazers, Cielle would blast the entire group, and the fliers would swoop in, suck up the manna, move on to the next group.

It was nearly sunset when we mopped up the last of them. By my count there had been over forty of the wretched things. The days when I was terrified by a single Gazer seemed a lifetime ago.

We managed to miss supper, but there was that little kitchen that used to be just for the Elite—everyone used it now, since it wasn't only the Elite that were missing the regular mess times. We all grabbed food, heated it, and wolfed it down, then said good night and headed for our rooms to let our showers try and wash some of the soreness out.

But when I got to my room, the message light was flashing. It was Josh. In guarded words, he told me that he was getting worried again, that he'd gotten warnings that Drift was impatient; she wasn't pleased about the fact that all we'd exchanged were messages. Uncle hadn't let me know that there was pressure being brought to bear, but Uncle didn't have a friend in PsiCorps Admin who kept track of the Psimons being sent into that . . . program.

Then again . . . I only have Josh's word.

Gah! It was *horrible* having to doubt people I should have been able to trust! For about the millionth time, I wished I was home. I wished I'd never met Josh. I wished that everything was simple again.

If only there was a way to test him!

And that was when it hit me. Because there *was* a way to test him.

If he was really, truly as afraid as he claimed, if all he actually wanted to do was to get as far away from Drift and PsiCorps as he could, well, there was a way for him to do that.

He'd have to ditch his Perscom, wear a Psi-shield, and go into hiding where PsiCorps never went.

Spillover.

Kent could probably help me arrange camping supplies for him; at this point Mark and I knew lots of places in Spillover where you could set up a pretty secure living spot. That old shelter where the three of us had met to talk about my bid for Elite status, for one. No one in PsiCorps would look for him there, because no one in PsiCorps would ever dream that one of *theirs* would subject himself to rough camping.

If he was that afraid, he'd grab that promise of escape with both hands and demand I arrange it yesterday. If he wasn't, well, he'd manage to find all sorts of excuses.

It seemed like a good idea, but I needed to get a second opinion.

I texted Kent. *Anything come of the discussion in the mess? Or did my brain go chasing a dekoi?* I figured he'd catch the misspelling and realize I needed to talk to him privately.

I was right, because I got a prompt text back. *Quite a lot. Discuss it with you in depth? Over fish?*

I sent back a *yes*, wrote a mental note of regret to my sore muscles, and headed for the koi garden. As expected, Kent turned up shortly after me, sealed the door behind him, and raised an eyebrow at me.

I explained my plan to him quickly. He nodded through all

of it. "It's solid," he said. "Your uncle and I can arrange for pretty much everything you need. You're unlikely to get in much trouble, even if he is trying to set you up in some way, if you just act like a stupid lovesick girl who is trying to help her boyfriend."

I grimaced a little at that. "Are you sure? I mean, I'd be helping him escape...."

Kent shrugged. "We're going to take advantage of some loopholes no one has ever thought to exploit. There's nothing forbidding a Cit of Apex from leaving and going to live in Spillover, probably because the only people who would are criminals. Your uncle will know if there are any regulations preventing Josh from quitting PsiCorps and walking—but you know, there probably aren't, because no one's even considered doing so before this. The only thing you could possibly be guilty of would be not telling PsiCorps that he was thinking of leaving."

Could it really be that simple? I dared to hope. "If that's *all* I told them, that he had told me he wanted to get out of Apex—"

"Misdirection, and do not tell them that you don't know where he is. Don't lie, just don't tell all the truth," Kent advised. "Besides, if he's telling the truth, well, this will get him away from Drift fast enough, and if he's lying, he'll make every excuse he can think of to get himself out of it."

"That's what I thought," I said, feeling suddenly doubtful. "But—"

Kent actually laughed. "Joy, he's a soft city boy used to having his meals on time and made by someone else, a proper bathroom, a proper bed, with all kinds of protections keeping him safe from Othersiders. Under normal circumstances, he'd never agree to live in the kind of conditions he'll find in Spillover. Trust me, if he's lying, there is not one chance in a hundred that he'd actually follow through on this."

I sighed. Well, Kent was probably right. Perversely, I found myself wishing Josh *would* try to make excuses, because then at least I'd know for sure where I'd stood with him from the beginning.

"I'll contact Charmand. You contact Josh. Meet him somewhere when your shift is over, tell him your escape idea, and we'll plan our next moves when we know his reaction." Kent rubbed his forehead with his hand, and I realized that he was just as beaten down as the rest of us. I was so used to him being the towering strength that held the Elite and the Hunters together that I had been ignoring all the signs that should have told me the constant battles were wearing on him as much, or more, than the rest of us.

I patted the curb around the pond with my hand. "It doesn't have to be right this minute," I said. "Or even today. Uncle would tell me if he was getting pressured to release Josh. And anyway, Josh is PsiCorps. He's not one of *us*."

Kent took my invitation and sat. "You seemed to like him well enough," he replied, with a sardonic tilt to his eyebrows.

"I did. . . . I—" I fumbled for words. "There are more important things to think about than how much I like a boy," I finally said, looking away, and I was glad it was dark enough here to cover my flush. "But he helped me a *lot*, and I owe him for that."

"Joy, look at me," Kent ordered, and reluctantly, I did, still feeling my cheeks burning. He put one hand on my shoulder, the way my Master Kedo used to when he was going to tell me something

• 87 •

important. "I am very pleased you have your priorities in order, but that doesn't mean you need to bottle up your feelings and never let them out. Got that?"

Now I was flushing even hotter. "I don't—actually know how I feel anymore," I stammered, and to my horror, I felt my eyes starting to sting. "I mean—he might have been putting on this huge act just so he could get inside my head!"

"And he might have been putting on a huge act for PsiCorps, to protect you," Kent pointed out. "Before, we had no way of proving which it was. If he *was* putting on an act to manipulate you, then I know you'll take the hit and keep going. But if he wasn't, well, you know you had a real, genuine friend you could count on, and that means a lot. And as for the rest, that's between you two, but"—he smiled slightly—"don't think that because things are hard right now you need to sacrifice everything, including your feelings. There is no official position on fraternization with PsiCorps personnel as long you take appropriate precautions—"

I choked.

"—to make sure Josh does not take unauthorized strolls through your skull." His grin broadened. "Or any other member of PsiCorps, for that matter. Why, Joyeaux Charmand, what did you *think* I meant?"

LUCK WAS KIND TO me the next day. The callouts were light, nothing Cielle and I couldn't handle by ourselves, but we ran late, jumping out of the chopper after the mess was already closed. So I had the perfect excuse to call Josh.

He answered immediately. "Hey!" he said, looking surprised, a little shocked, and maybe some happy thrown in there too. "I didn't expect to talk to you in person tonight. What's up?"

"Hey yourself. The mess is closed, I'm just off shift and starving, and I'm getting really tired of what's stocked here. Seems like this might be the only time we can actually get together. Do you know someplace quiet we could get something decent to eat?" I said, with some emphasis on "quiet."

"Do I ever!" He lit right up at that. "Take a pod to twelve-twenty-two Catalpa. I'll meet you there."

As soon as he hung up, I called a pod, then ran back to my room and threw on the first outfit in the closet. I managed to get out of HQ and into the pod without my Perscom giving so much as a chirp. One very good thing about our breakup—there weren't any cams following me anymore. Oh, my Perscom would register where I was, but the last several weeks of non-stop work plus the breakup had made me no longer news-worthy. I was just another of the Elite now, not someone who was trending.

Twelve-twenty-two Catalpa turned out to be a huge building, and I was afraid at first it was something like the Strauss Palais, or some sort of huge entertainment complex. But as soon as I got in the door, I knew I was wrong.

It was, essentially, a building full of shops and places to eat and drink. Like the main street of a big town, or a downscale version of the commercial part of the Hub. I waited at the entrance, and a few minutes later, Josh came in, wearing one of his beige-and-brown outfits. Good, he looked just like an ordinary, middling Cit. There was nothing to draw attention to either of us.

"Hey!" he said. "This is the building where I grew up. Apartments on floors three through ten, everything anyone needs on the two bottom floors, and a recreation center in the basement. Come on. I know a nice quiet place to eat."

There weren't a lot of people on this floor, but then, it was the supper hour, so I guess people were mostly eating in their own apartments. Josh led me to the middle of the place, then turned left, and we walked to the dead end of the corridor between shops.

There, on the right, was a little eatery with an illuminated sign that said, simply, NOODLES.

We went in. There were three or four people studiously working their way through big bowls of noodles. We took a booth at the back; you ordered from a vid-screen in the table. And that was all this place served: noodles in a glorious profusion of styles, mostly Asian as far as I could tell. My eyes went straight to a dish I hadn't eaten since I got here. Pad Thai. I stabbed the selection with my index finger, my mouth already watering as the screen registered my choice.

Josh nodded. "I think I'll have the same thing. This was my favorite place to eat when I lived here, because it was so quiet." I nodded too, understanding what he meant. Psimons are not only sensitive to thoughts; they can be sensitive to sounds as well.

Our meals came quickly, and we dug in with single-minded concentration. He was hungry, as if he'd been working hard all day and this was his first good meal. And I was starving as I always was. It wasn't until we'd finished, the noodle bowls had been taken away, and we'd gotten some sliced fruit to share that we started talking again.

"How *quiet* is it here?" I asked. "In the whole building, I mean." He raised his eyebrow, then closed his eyes a moment, putting two fingers to his right temple as he did.

"No one of any useful sensitivity in the building," he said. "And no cams in here except for the security system. Nobody famous ever comes here, mostly just people that live here. Most of them are salesclerks or office workers."

"Good. Because I think I have a plan." Quickly I got him up to speed on what Kent and I had worked out so far.

He stared at me for a moment in disbelief. My heart started pounding. I tried not to hope. . . .

"How soon can you get me out of here?" he whispered urgently.

We spent more time talking than I had thought we would, to the point that he ordered more fruit and drinks for us out of politeness to the shop owner. Now that he had committed, I wanted to be sure he knew exactly what he was committing *to*—the dangers of Spillover, the primitive conditions he'd be living under, everything. I went into great detail about the bugs and vermin, about the heat and cold, the weather—what storms would be like for someone living in an old building—about the damp, about everything.

He didn't care.

And I wanted to get up and dance.

"Josh," I said, taking hold of one of his hands and making sure he was looking right at me. "I don't know how long this is going to last. I don't know if it will ever be safe for you to come back to Apex. You might be living out there for a lot longer than any of us guess. Right now, all you'll have to contend with are the bugs and the weather and the Othersiders—but fall is around the corner, and winter will be far worse."

"I'll take that chance," he replied firmly. "But will this get *you* in trouble?"

"When you disappear, I'll be either in my room at HQ or out

Hunting, well away from Spillover, and my Perscom will show that," I promised. "And if someone comes and asks about where you are, I'll just get frantic and worried about you, and maybe hint tearfully that you might do something stupid. And that will be the truth, because I actually will be frantic and worried about you."

He smiled faintly. "And I do stupid things all the time. You won't have to lie about that, either." He turned over his hand and held mine. I got butterflies in my stomach. "Thank you," he said fervently.

"Thank me when you're out," I retorted, though I didn't take my hand away. I reminded myself that this was no time to think about romance. "This is going to take some careful planning, and that will take time. You're going to have to be patient." I thought about what else he could do to prepare. "You can start watching the older Hunting vids, especially if you can get uncut stuff from Mark Knight's Spillover Hunts. But mix them up with other vids so you don't give away where you're running to. If you've got a way to look up some of the old pre-Diseray survival manuals, you probably ought to."

For the first time he registered hesitation. Had he been faking this? Was he about to try and back out now? Had he just been stringing me along all this time? My heart fell. "Reading and watching vids isn't going to give me *skills*," he pointed out after a long moment, biting his lip. "If I start fumbling around, I could get myself hurt or worse. Maybe I can talk Mark into letting me take it from his mind? Then I'd have actual physical skills, the way I learned Straussing...."

Oh boy. *That* was absolutely not going to happen. Mark knew about the Mountain and the Monastery, and there was no way in hell I was going to let any Psimon, not even Josh, play around in his head, even if Mark was willing.

"Mark's people live in proper houses; they aren't camping," I said, giving him a little bit of stink-eye. "They have electricity, Perscoms, trucks, indoor plumbing, bathrooms, high-efficiency woodstoves, and running water. Same for my people. Just because we're turnips, it doesn't follow that we're camping out in caves and cooking dead squirrels on sticks over open fires."

"Oh...uh, sorry," he said, shamefaced. "I didn't mean..."

"Don't worry. I'll find ways of making sure you know what you'll need to know," I promised, though I hadn't the faintest idea how I was going to do that, much less what information he'd need.

My Perscom went off—it was an alarm I'd set. We both looked at it, and he must have read the time, because he made a face. "You need to go back, don't you?"

"My shift starts at seven a.m.," I reminded him. "And it goes for twelve hours. Sometimes more."

"Then I'll be grateful for every minute I got," he replied. He lifted my hand and kissed my knuckles. I blushed, but I didn't take my hand back. "And more than grateful for your help."

We walked out together, and we held hands until our pods came. It didn't feel like we'd erased all that stuff that had come between us, but it *did* feel like we were starting over, which maybe was better.

"Listen," I said as the first pod rolled into sight. "If things suddenly go bad, send me a message, mark it 'urgent' so my text alarm goes off, but just say, 'Do you like roses,' okay? Then go to Uncle.

Maybe he can hide you in a storage closet somewhere." I was only half joking with that.

"I will," he promised. My pod had arrived, so I stepped into it and left him standing there all alone on the sidewalk.

I looked back at him as the pod drove away, knowing he couldn't see me through the darkened glass. He stood there with his arms crossed over his chest. Everything about his posture told me he was scared. And as the pod turned the corner and he was lost behind the building, all I could think of was the great big reason for why I felt so guilty about him.

This was *my* fault. If I'd never turned up, he'd never have gotten in trouble for not getting into my head.

Kent strode into the mess looking like he'd gotten a decent night's sleep. Actually, everybody but me looked that way. I'd tossed and turned, worrying about Josh, feeling guilty about Josh, wondering what Josh was going to do after we got him out, wondering where we would actually put him so he didn't end up in worse danger than he was now.

At least we hadn't gotten a callout.

"All right, Hunters, we may not have much time before a callout, so I want you to pay attention, especially any of you that are going out into Spillover. Watch the monitors."

A map of Apex came up, and that's when I realized, somewhat to my surprise, that Apex was *not* a series of nicely nested, neat circles within circles. The main part of the city, where most of the population lived, was a mathematically laid-out grid of streets inside a rough oblong. But after that, things got messy. Each successive layer got more and more amoebalike, with protrusions and indentations.

Spillover was a sort of kidney-shaped thing just outside the last Barrier, an area that butted up against the enormous army base in the south, and an area marked "uninhabitable" in the north, complete with the signs for radiation and poison. That kidney shape that represented Spillover was what the armorer zoomed in on, until landmarks showed on the map.

"About fifteen years ago, the then armorer and I had a project in Spillover," Kent continued. "We were hunting out all the emergency shelters that were still sound, cleaning them out, restocking them, and putting new locks that responded to Hunter Perscoms on the doors. The idea was that if you were caught by a storm out there, you'd have a safe place to hole up for as long as it took for the storm to pass. As it happened, storms have never moved in so fast that we weren't able to get people back, so we never needed them, and people have forgotten them. But," he continued, looking sober, "as you know, Hunting the Othersiders itself has changed. If we get a major incursion in Spillover, we may need a safe place to store the injured until they can be evacuated. Or if you're Hunting Spillover and bite off more than you can chew, you'll have a safe place to take cover. That's why I'm updating all your maps with the locations, and I sent out restocking parties today. Any questions?"

Well, *I* had one, but it wasn't one I could ask aloud. Nobody else had a question, though—and that was when we got the callout.

Cielle and I were paired up with Kent and Raynd; we got to the target just in time to keep a Gog and Magog from destroying a set of grain storage silos. Cielle was pretty exhausted and fell asleep on the way back; then my Perscom vibrated. I looked down, and Kent was texting me.

I've added one shelter to your map. That's where your friend will go. And Scarlet's in on the plan. Well, that would make one thing a lot easier—establishing *my* alibi.

I flashed Kent a relieved smile; he gave me a wink, then leaned back in his seat. I felt as if half the world had been lifted from my shoulders. Poor Josh wouldn't have to try and survive in one of those ruined buildings, constantly watching for Othersiders and the "rebels" that were still out there, who were little more than bandits. He'd be in a safe, secure place stocked with everything he'd need. It wouldn't be *fun,* and he'd probably be a bit less than comfortable, but this was something an Apex-bred boy could cope with.

I had just sluiced off the several pounds of yuck and sweat in the shower and was reaching for a robe when my Perscom went off. With a groan I didn't even try to suppress, I reached for it—and the message on it woke me right up. *Report to my office. Senior Psimon Abigail Drift requires your presence.*

I tried not to panic. Because, of course, the first thing that sprang into my head was that Drift had discovered we were trying to help Josh escape from her claws. Or rather, that *I* was. And the second thing that sprang into my head was that Josh had been a much better actor than I had thought, had been stringing me along all this time, and *he* was the one who'd turned us in.

I hated this. I absolutely hated this. I was a Hunter. I should be worrying about Othersiders. I should not be looking over my shoulder, waiting for someone *who was supposed to be on my side* to stab me in the back!

I dressed with precision and care, going for a Hunting outfit, the one that looked most like armor. Only when every hair was in place, every seam precisely aligned, and my Psi-shield turned on did I head for Kent's office.

I tapped on the door, which opened to let me inside. Drift was there, her white-blond hair slicked back, looking more like a ferret than she had the last time I saw her. "You requested me, Senior Elite?" I said politely to the armorer, ignoring Drift. Tonight she wasn't in PsiCorps HQ, or in my uncle's office. She was in *Hunter* HQ. And if she intended to play power games, I wasn't going to just go along with it. Stupid, maybe, but I was more than tired of Abigail Drift.

Kent's eyes crinkled a tiny bit at the corners, but his mouth stayed sober. "Senior Psimon Drift wishes to ask you a few questions, Elite Joyeaux," he replied. Since I had not been told to sit, I didn't. Sometimes sitting puts you in a position of power, but sometimes it doesn't, and I preferred to be at eye level with Drift. What I *did* do was go into a relaxed "parade rest" stance. Damn if I was going to give her the deference of being at "attention."

"Very well, Senior Elite," I said, and waited for Drift to get on with it. She frowned, clearly not caring for my attitude.

I concentrated on my One White Stone. I might be angry and scared, but I wasn't going to let her see me sweat.

"When you first arrived here, you were frequently seen in the presence of a Psimon, were you not, Hunter?" Drift said, her tone as cold as the frozen Mountain in midwinter. Well, now I knew for sure this was about Josh.

"Psimon Josh, yes, Senior Psimon," I replied, keeping my own tone as bland as unflavored oatmeal. I wasn't going to let her intimidate me, but I also didn't dare antagonize her. *Don't offer any information,* I reminded myself. *Only answer exactly what she asks.* I probably should not have even said Josh's name, but it was too late to go back now. It was really, really tempting to point out that *she* was probably the one who had set us up for that initial date in the first place. It was equally tempting to point out she had known damn well we were seeing each other and if she hadn't liked the idea, she should have said something after the first date.

But that was volunteering information. *Don't volunteer information.*

There was a lot of mistrust of PsiCorps by the Cits, which was only to be expected, given that there was absolutely nothing keeping them from sifting through the average person's thoughts on a whim. But there was even more mistrust and animosity between the Hunters and PsiCorps; I had to wonder how much of that was due to Abigail Drift herself. She surely did not like Hunters—the way we were idolized by the Cits—at all. And she hated my uncle. I was certain she figured him for being the one thing standing in the way of her gaining more power with the premier.

"Recently you had a falling-out with him," Drift continued, glaring at me.

"Yes, Senior Psimon," I repeated. Good gods, if she was going to beat around the bush like this, her interrogation was going to take all night! On the other hand, if I kept dribbling information out in bits and pieces, maybe she'd get impatient and give up. Not likely, but I could hope.

"And what was that falling-out about?" Drift demanded.

"With all due respect, Senior Psimon, that's none of your business." That, I thought, was what the answer of someone who was totally innocent of chicanery would be. "It was personal, and had nothing to do with my status and position as a Hunter, or with PsiCorps."

Just a tiny little fib, not quite a lie. And, well, when you dissected everything down to basics, the reason I'd sent Josh packing *was* completely personal. I was trying to protect him. And not from PsiCorps. From Drift herself.

"So long as her personal life does not interfere with her duties, she's not required to answer any questions about it, Senior Psimon," Kent said.

"Well, the falling-out certainly affected my Psimon's ability to perform his duties!" Drift snapped.

"And with all due respect, that is between you and your subordinate, since I have seen nothing to complain about in Elite Joyeaux's performance," Kent replied, with a face as calm as one of the Masters'.

If Drift was supposed to be the prime exemplar of the impartial, emotionless Psimon, she was certainly doing a bad job of it. Then again, she had all but promised Premier Rayne that the PsiCorps was going to be the salvation of Apex and the whole country, and so far, she hadn't been able to come through on that promise. I wished Uncle were here. He'd have known what to do to turn the tables on her. I'd just have to hope I could stay a step ahead of her.

I concentrated on my One White Stone. It was an actual stone, one I had selected from among the thousands in the bed of Troublesome Creek, where it ran down between the settlements of Double Mill and Graeme's. As Master Kedo had instructed me, I had picked out the first stone that caught my eye and attention. I think it was quartzite, the stuff that sometimes has gold in it. This stone didn't have any gold, but it attracted my eye because of the way it caught and held the sunlight; it had been rounded and tumbled by the waters of the creek for hundreds of years, probably, and fit perfectly in the palm of my hand. I studied it over the course of an entire day, from midmorning until sunset. And then I put it back in the creek. The point was not to physically own it; the point was to *know* it, and know it so thoroughly I could occupy my mind with it for as long as I needed to.

I think maybe it was a good thing I was concentrating on it at that moment, because she seized me by the chin and stared into my eyes. Hers were like two gray marbles, the pupils contracted down to pinpoints. I thought about my Stone.

Whatever she was expecting to get from that gesture, she was disappointed. After a moment, she let go with a snort of disgust. Kent said nothing, and neither did I.

"You renewed contact with the Psimon," she said into the silence. "Why?"

A flash from Kent's eyes warned me to tread very carefully, as if I had not already known that. "Three reasons, Senior Psimon Drift," I said, finally. "First, he was unhappy that I had broken things off, and I didn't like thinking about how I'd made him feel. Second, I realized that I was the one who was in the wrong, so I needed to apologize. And third, I missed his company."

All true. All absolutely and completely true. So true she could have probed my mind at that moment and seen it herself. I stated them in a matter-of-fact tone, not a defiant one, and prayed that was the right play to make.

Kent chuckled, an unexpected sound in the tense silence. "Come now, Senior Psimon. My Hunter and your Psimon are both youngsters. The young are going to have emotions and hearts to break whether you like it or not."

Drift pulled her attention away from me and leveled another frozen glare at Kent, who seemed utterly impervious to it. He just smiled and shrugged.

"My Psimons are expected to know better," she said coldly. "My Psimons are strongly discouraged from forming personal attachments."

"Then you were a fool to encourage your Psimon to escort Joy on dates," Kent countered, and she went rigid. "Oh come now, the control you have over the Psimons is well known. He wouldn't have been permitted to breathe in Joy's presence, much less take her Straussing, if he hadn't had your permission and encouragement. And I agree, seeing a handsome young Psimon escorting a pretty, charismatic, trending Hunter was a good move on your part. It put a softer, more acceptable face on PsiCorps. But you took a risk when you did that, the risk that the youngsters would actually *like* each other. They did—you lost—so move on and let them handle the situation themselves. Your Psimon will be a great deal less distracted if you just let things take their natural course without coming here to bully his girlfriend."

Drift stood there with her mouth agape for a full minute, I swear. Of all the things she expected to have said to her, I reckon Kent's speech just then hadn't even appeared on the list of possibilities.

Finally she just turned on me again and pointed a long white claw at me. "No more upsets!" she ordered me.

Kent laughed out loud. "I don't think that's anything either of us can control," he pointed out. "And it's not in *their* control, either. Let it go, Senior Psimon. You'll just have to accept there are some things no one short of a god can do anything about."

Well, if his previous statement had left her without a word to say, this one gave her a mental meltdown. She opened her mouth and closed it, then drew herself up and looked down her nose at him. Which was *hard*, since she was a lot shorter than he was. "I'll take it under advisement," she said icily, and walked out.

We both looked at each other. I sat down hard, without waiting for permission.

In the next moment, Kent took the chair behind the desk. "Well, we dodged that bullet," he finally said and then looked at me. "You do know she was trying to get around your Psi-shield, right?"

"I didn't know, but I guessed," I replied, and sagged in the chair. "Do you think she had..." I left the end of the sentence dangling.

But he shook his head. "I think that her little experiment with her Psimons isn't going as well as she promised the premier. I think she wants to find something to take her frustrations out on. You and that boy made a good target of opportunity."

I wasn't at all sure of that. But she had definitely left disappointed, so whatever she was looking for, she hadn't gotten. "Can a Psimon get past a Psi-shield?" I asked, pursuing the previous thought.

"That's the rumor." He rubbed the back of his neck. "You have to be something special in the way of a Psimon, they say, and you have to have physical contact. Of course, she might just have wanted to make you feel about four years old."

"She managed that," I admitted.

After a little more conversation with Kent, I went back to my room. But I wasn't at all sure that his conclusions were right. I didn't think that Drift was looking for someone to terrify—she had plenty of her own Psimons who were afraid of her. Maybe, just maybe, she had been trying to send a message to my uncle that she could exercise her power over me anytime. Kent had blocked that particular move, making it clear that I was a Hunter, first, last, and in between, and he would stand by me.

Maybe she was trying to see if Josh had told me anything that she didn't want to get out. Like details of her experiment, and how many Psimons it was devouring.

Or maybe she was just fishing for anything she could find. Anything at all.

It was all making my head hurt.

This did make one thing very clear, however.

When Josh escaped, I had to have an ironclad alibi. I had to be somewhere else. Preferably with a record of the fact.

I wished I could grab Mark at that moment and just talk his ear off about it. I really, really missed having a friend who was in on most of my secrets. Cielle would have been ideal, but I didn't dare let her know what was going on with Josh. But Mark was safe. . . .

No, that was me being selfish again. There was no good reason at all for me to drag him into my troubles, and every reason to keep him out of them. The fewer people who knew about what we had planned, the better.

FIRST, A STORM—A SHORT one, only half a day—which was exactly what we needed to recuperate. Then as soon as the sky cleared, another (thankfully) disorganized raid on the part of the Othersiders: this one, providentially, in Spillover. Also exactly what we needed. I tried not to get excited, but it looked as if the stars were aligning perfectly.

The Othersiders must have been thinking that the storm would lock us down for longer than it actually had, because their target was a bricked-up tunnel that ran under the Barrier. It was led by a single Folk Mage, one of the feral ones.

Kent, Cielle, Raynd, and I managed to run the Folk Mage off pretty quickly, and the gang of motley Othersiders he had been leading evaporated. We Hunted out the whole area and didn't find much except mud. "I'm going to check on something," Kent said as we gathered at a good landing spot to wait for our ride back. "Tell the chopper pilot we might be five coming back."

He strode off into the jumble of ruined buildings before anyone could say anything. This was the chance we had been waiting for.

Now. Follow Kent, I thought to Bya.

Cielle and Raynd gave me quizzical looks. "I have no more idea than you do," I replied, doing my best to sound baffled. "Let's send the Hounds back. The chopper will be here any minute."

Nice thing about having so many Hounds, and half of them *Alebrijes*: in the flood through my Portal when I opened the Way, what with all the milling around and all the crazy colors and patterns, the other two didn't even notice I was one short.

The chopper arrived shortly after that, and I told the pilot that we were waiting for Kent and maybe a passenger. A few moments later, Kent came running toward the craft through the weeds and bushes with someone following him.

They both jumped in and fastened down, and the chopper took off before they got all their straps cinched. Between Othersiders and the rebels who were still somehow operating out here, pilots didn't like to linger.

Cielle and Raynd gave the newcomer the hairy eyeball. He looked like a typical denizen of Spillover: weather-beaten jacket, shabby brown "utility" tunic with a heavy belt, and darker brown pants with boots much the worse for wear. There was not much to be seen of his face under the heavy growth of dirty blond facial hair. He had blue eyes, and as you might imagine, the hair on his head looked as if any barbering he'd had in his life had been done with a knife.

The only thing he had on him was a very old-fashioned and heavy Perscom. I caught Cielle and Raynd both trying to give Kent silent signals of *What the heck is going on?* without being too obvious about it.

"*Informant*," Kent said over the radio, since the noise of the chopper motor made ordinary talking impossible. "*Needs to report to Charmand in person.*"

Raynd's and Cielle's eyebrows went back down, and they nodded. This made perfect sense, of course. Although no one had ever said anything officially, everyone knew there had to be informants among the rebels. Uncle would have been insane not to try to plant them out there, especially after Knight and I were ambushed, back before we were both made Elite.

We all settled in for the short ride back to HQ.

Well, Bya said with amusement in my head. *Will I do?*

I suppressed a smile. *Just don't pant. Or try to drink from the toilet.*

Bya's snort of derision was purely mental. Actually, he'd been practicing taking human form for days, and he'd gotten really good at it. Kent and I had both been impressed when he showed us the end result.

When we arrived back at HQ, Raynd paused at the door, and of course, so did I.

"Do you need help, Armorer?" he asked, giving Bya another

dubious look. But Kent and Bya both laughed. Bya did an excellent human laugh.

"No. Al here is an old friend of mine," Kent replied, with a slap on Bya's shoulder that made dust rise from the jacket and tunic.

Nice touch. Did you roll in the dirt before you got on the chopper? I asked.

Of course I did. Part of the disguise. Also a reason for Kent to get me real clothing. Because the "clothing" he was wearing right now was actually his own hide, and he'd need real garments for the next part of the plan.

"Bloody hell." Kent coughed, waving his hand in front of his face to dispel the dust. "I'd better take you to my quarters and get you cleaned up before I take you to Charmand, Al."

Bya shrugged. It wasn't quite a human motion; it was too fluid, more like a ripple of the shoulders than the up-and-down motion of a shrug. But Raynd wasn't paying as much attention to "Al" as he was to the dust, which was going everywhere and making him cough slightly. "In that case, sir, I'll go wait for the next callout," Raynd said.

"You do that," Kent replied, and motioned to Bya to follow him. I headed for my next position—Scarlet's room, where she was waiting for me.

Scarlet had a suite of rooms that reminded me so much of the Monastery that I was overwhelmed by waves of homesickness. Her personal colors of red, brown, and gold could so easily have been gaudy, but instead, due to the spare simplicity of her furnishings, everything in these rooms had a distinctly Eastern, minimalist flavor to it.

"You're sure you want to go through with this?" I asked nervously as we exchanged clothing. We were very nearly the same size, and I'd copied several of her Hunting outfits, so we already had sets of Hunting gear that were identical in cut and only differed in color.

"Of course I do," she chided. "Seriously, Joy, you need to stop asking that. You're not just my fellow Elite, you're my friend. That's the only reason I need."

I swallowed around the lump in my throat—a lump composed of equal parts fear and gratitude. I still could hardly believe Scarlet of all people was going to be not only an active part of this insane plot, but an eager one.

Of course, if we got a full callout, this whole business would fall completely apart. It all hinged on the fact that we'd gotten a heavy half-day storm, and so far we'd never yet gotten a full callout in the first twelve hours after a storm.

At least now the waiting was over.

Once we'd completed our clothing exchange, Scarlet and I hugged, and under cover of that hug, exchanged Perscoms as well. The software would be unable to tell that we'd made the exchange. Now, as far as the system was concerned, Scarlet was me, and I was Scarlet.

Scarlet gave me a wink as we broke apart, and put her hood up to shield her face—something I did a lot anyway, so no one would think twice about it. Then she left. She'd go to my room and wait for her next signal on my Perscom.

Meanwhile I waited in her room for mine.

About ten minutes later I got a text from Kent. *Prefect Charmand wants a debrief on our observations while we've got a few hours of clear time. Helipad, now.*

I confirmed with a *five-by-five*, which was what Scarlet would have replied, rather than a *Roger*, which was my usual response. I put the hood of Scarlet's outfit up and headed for the helipad at Scarlet's rapid, long-legged pace rather than my own trot. Of course, if anyone ran motion analysis on either of us, we'd have been busted for sure. But the point of all of this was to obfuscate everything so that no one would bother to investigate the Hunters once I was superficially cleared. And while all this song and dance of switched identities felt contrived and stupid, Uncle and I were both pretty sure that if I wasn't directly involved with the rescue, Josh wouldn't go along with it. If he was being straight with us, Uncle didn't think he'd really trust anyone *but* me. And if he wasn't, well, he'd want me along to make sure to cement my guilt, but he wouldn't know Scarlet and I had switched Perscoms as well as clothing.

Kent and Bya nodded at me as I got into the chopper, which took us to the pad on top of the Admin building where Uncle had his offices. Bya was cleaner and wearing real clothing rather than the stuff he'd manufactured out of his own hide.

The receptionist wasn't at her desk; Uncle had messaged her that she was to take the day off when the storm moved in. Again, this was usual for a storm day. Also no different from any other storm day was that Josh had already been at the office, and aside from not being able to move about the city for those few hours, his workday had proceeded the way it always did.

Kent and I went down to Uncle's office, where we stayed talking for about an hour. Kent reported some unverifiable stuff about the rebels in Spillover—mostly that thanks to all the Othersider activity, they were taking a lot of causalities. Bya mostly nodded rather than talk, but he did put in an occasional word or two. Then Kent reported the fact that the Othersiders had started to target Apex's food sources in their raids. I nodded or occasionally shrugged. And here was the first level of uncertainty; would anyone notice this was slightly out of character for Scarlet? Well, we hoped not.

Eventually, Bya cleared his throat. "Need to take a break, sir," he croaked. I tried not to wince. His voice really did not sound quite right.

"Of course. My aide will escort you," Uncle said, and Josh got up and led Bya to the bathroom.

And there, in the one place where cameras would not be, Josh became "Al," and "Al" became Josh.

Most important of all, they exchanged Perscoms.

That was the reason for the heavy growth of facial hair Bya had sprouted. It mimicked the fake beard Uncle had gotten for Josh, a beard that effectively erased any chance that facial recognition software would pick him up as himself.

When they came back out, Bya looked *exactly* like Josh. I was amazed. His human mimicry had improved beyond all recognition. . . .

But there were stories about that, in the pre-Diseray folklore, about creatures that could so accurately mimic a person that their own spouses could not tell the difference. "Shifters" did not always change from man to animal. Sometimes they changed to *specific* people. *I think I had better talk to Bya about this. If there are more Othersiders that can do this . . . they might be walking the streets of the city this very minute!*

Of course, that was what the Psimons were *supposed* to be looking for, but I no longer trusted that they were.

And there was something else hidden in all that hair on Josh's face: a voice-distorter, one carefully tuned so that "Al's" voice wouldn't register as manipulated, but also wouldn't match Josh's voiceprint.

Now "Al" did a lot more talking, and I was actually kind of impressed with the stuff Josh was making up. I wasn't sure where he was getting it from, and I don't think *I* would have been able to be so glib. But then again, he'd probably been given access to Uncle's files on the rebels and was using them as the basis for his "report."

We kept this going as long as it seemed feasible, then just when I was beginning to think we were pushing our luck, our Perscoms went off. That is, mine and Kent's did. Not with an actual callout, but with the request to run our Hounds and eyeballs over another site in Spillover, since all the on-shift Hunters but us were otherwise engaged.

"Just drop me off there," said "Al." "I'll make my own way home."

"Unarmed?" Uncle said, looking just enough concerned to be plausible.

"Al" laughed. "Been running Spillover for twenty years, I figure I know how to get around by now, armed or not."

So we three headed for the roof, where the chopper picked us up and dropped us off in an area of Spillover unfamiliar to me in person—though I knew from my map this was where the shelter Kent had picked out was. We made a show of poking around, but we only stirred up a couple of Goblins.

Then Kent ducked inside the wreckage of what looked like some sort of "official" building. There were carved stones that had fallen from the facade that said P and ICE, so I guessed "Post Office." We headed down a long set of cracked and overgrown cement steps. It smelled of damp and crushed moss down here. Kent gestured to Josh to put his antique Perscom up against the lock on the door. He did; the lock recognized it, and clicked open.

The door was massive. So were the walls. Kent shook up a chem-light, and we went in.

Once inside, he found a hand-lamp, lit it, and closed the door. We were standing in an entryway that led to a second massive door, this one standing open. The wall must have been a good foot thick. We went in and found ourselves in an enormous open room.

"Wow," Josh said, pulling off the beard. "This is bigger than I thought."

"Government shelter from the Cold War days," Kent said. Josh looked baffled. "Never mind. It's probably as old as the building, decades before the Diseray. It was meant to hold a couple hundred people. This would have been the space where everyone spent their waking hours."

We walked through the shelter, which was cleaner than I had expected. There was the entrance room; the one big central room; a long room that was obviously a bathroom with sinks, showers, and toilets on one side of the central room; three smaller rooms including a kitchen on the other side; and a room full of bunk frames at the rear. The bunk room was pretty useless; the frames had been bolted to the floor, probably to keep them from going over during a bomb blast, and they had rusted and buckled into a tangle of dangerous metal. Somehow the bathroom still actually worked, maybe from cisterns somewhere that were still fed by rainwater, though I sure wouldn't trust that water to drink. The kitchen was also useless—the big stoves had turned into single chunks of rust, and the refrigerator doors hung askew on fused hinges—but the two remaining small rooms had been cleared out, one turned into a storeroom, the other into a place to live.

The air moved, ever so slightly. By now whatever filtration system had been designed to remove the radioactive fallout was long gone, but something was bringing fresh air down here. Maybe back when these shelters had first been cleaned out and stocked, the ventilation system was opened up. Again, there was a scent of damp and cold concrete, but nothing musty or redolent of mildew down here.

And I was impressed by how well it had been stocked. There were cartons of Basic Ration Biscuits, enough to last a year, a good supply of clean packaged water, and plenty of other supplies I didn't examine. In the living area were foam mattresses and sleeping bags, a bicycle-style battery charger, cartons of batteries, a basic rifle and pistol and plenty of ammo, a bookcase full of books, lanterns, and cartons of the same standard clothing Josh was wearing now, warm- and cold-weather versions.

"If you lock the door into the kitchen, you lock access to all three rooms," Kent said. "And if you think you hear someone trying to break in, I suggest you do that, then douse your lights and stay quiet, just in case they brought something that can get them past the blast door. Don't leave anything anywhere else in this place that suggests there's anyone staying here." He spread his hands. "Other than that, it's yours to do what you want. If I were you, I'd set up targets in the big room and use it as a shooting gallery."

That was Kent's delicate way of suggesting he didn't think Josh knew how to shoot well enough to protect himself. Josh nodded.

"You're far enough underground and sheltered enough by the blast walls that you should get the 'cave effect,' meaning it shouldn't get colder than about fifty-five in the winter. If you're here that long, we'll have to figure out a way to heat your small room, at least." I'd wondered about that. "I advise you to do some careful exploring around here; your Psi-powers should warn you if anything or anyone is coming close. And if they do, retreat and close and lock the blast door to the outside. Then do the same with the inside one."

"Ah," Josh said, speaking at last. "I can open the door from inside, then?"

"That Perscom you have now will unlock it from either side. It also has a Psi-shield on it," Kent continued. "There's a stud on the side that activates it. So if you suspect there is something or someone looking for you with psionic powers, use it. Don't use it for anything but passive listening, reading, or watching what's loaded in it, though, unless it's a complete and total emergency. It's an old Hunter model, but if you show up on the network people will wonder why it's still active. I'll give you a contact number you can use if it is an emergency, but normally we'll contact you, not the other way around."

"I think I'd have to be bleeding to death before I'd call for help," Josh said with a shudder. Then he seized Kent's hand and began pumping it, repeating his thanks and his gratitude so many times I began to wonder if he was stuck in a loop. Kent rolled his eyes at me but seemed pleased enough. I certainly was. Josh had gotten his up-close look on how he was going to be living for the foreseeable future, and if he'd been faking all this, now was the time for him to back out.

But he wasn't. We'd removed him from home and comforts, we'd completely severed him from PsiCorps, and he was *grateful*. So there was my answer. He hadn't been faking any of it. Maybe I should have been ashamed of myself for doubting him, but I wasn't. I was too busy feeling relieved.

And about that time, our Perscoms went off. This was a call-out. A real one.

Kent called in for "me" to meet us at the chopper. Then he made a second call to Tober, Raynd, and Cielle. "I want you three in a chopper now, and get me an on-site assessment," he said as we sprinted across the empty expanse of the big room. "We'll be about ten minutes behind you. Don't engage unless there are lives in danger." We ran up the concrete steps, and Josh shut and locked the blast door behind us. Our chopper was coming in, and we jumped for it.

In five minutes we were back at HQ, and as soon as we set down, "I" ran out and jumped into the chopper. I've been in too many communal hot tubs to have been embarrassed by stripping down in front of Kent and exchanging clothing and Perscoms again with Scarlet, but doing so in a moving chopper was...an adventure.

"Team TRC to Kent."

"Go, TRC," Kent replied, as Scarlet and I lay on our backs and kicked our legs in the air, pulling our pants on as quickly as possible.

"Get here as fast as you can," Tober said. My blood ran cold. *"It's something new."*

"HQ, can you ID?" Kent asked as we raced toward the ag-station. This one had been in harvest mode, up and running at full capacity, which meant it was completely manned with at least a dozen ag-techs. The electric fences were down, the solar arrays destroyed, the wind generator lying on the ground in a complete state of wreckage. There was an open Portal about a hundred yards away, just outside of the remains of the electric fence.

But that wasn't the worst of it. The worst was that one of the big cargo doors to the loading area was torn off its hinges, and the Othersiders were inside. Now there was just one door between them and the inside of the station where the techs were.

Othersiders that weren't like anything I had ever seen before.

Before the Outsiders spotted us, we dove for cover beside the rest of the team behind a harvester that had been turned off and left in the field when these things attacked. We all took time to size the situation up.

These things were just *wrong*, in a way that nothing I had seen before had ever been. Like someone had taken three different critters and mashed them together. Not at all like the Minotaurs, who gave the impression that cattle had managed to evolve into bipeds. Even the *Nagas* had a certain symmetry to them, once you got a closer look.

But these . . .

Let me just start with their size. Big. As big as the average farm truck. Sand-colored, furry bodies, and bushy dark manes like a lion, but that is where the comparison broke down. They had tawny humanoid faces, faces that were just human enough to slingshot them into the uncanny valley, with big flat noses and upper and lower fangs protruding over the thick lips. It just looked . . . wrong. Like something had carved off the lion's head and stuck an almost-human face there. A demonic face, maybe.

Then there was the wrongness at the other end, because instead of lion tails, they had fat, segmented, chitinous tails curving up over their backs, exactly like a scorpion's, complete with wicked stingers. And just to mess things up some more, their feet were scaled instead of furred, and looked like they'd been yanked off a giant reptile.

"*Folklore says Manticores,*" HQ replied promptly. "*Seen in Eurasia, not here. At least, not until now. Sting carries a toxin.*"

"*Because of course it does,*" Kent muttered.

"*Claw strikes are lethal, bite is lethal, sting can be lethal or narcotic. Reports are they can control the amount of toxin.*"

"*Of course, if that stinger goes in the eye or the heart, the amount of toxin won't matter,*" Raynd pointed out. We were all subvocalizing through our headsets to avoid being heard by the monsters.

"We're Hunters. We'll figure it out. More Hunting, less talking," said Tober impatiently. And he was right. Those things were trying to enlarge the door into the station itself, and if they succeeded, they'd be a lot harder to attack without putting the staff in danger.

"Bullets work," HQ said helpfully. *"They don't Shield."*

"That's what we need. Kent out." The armorer unslung his assault rifle. Cielle and I did the same. Until we killed a couple of those things, Cielle was more use as a markswoman than using magic.

The guys had already brought over their Hounds; in the shelter of that enormous red harvester we opened the Way and brought over ours. Bya, of course, was still not among them.

They packed up around me, looking at me in expectation. *Myrrdhin for now is pack alpha,* I said to all of them. Then to him, *Use your best judgment.* I was just grateful Myrrdhin was as competent as he was. I couldn't have asked for two better pack leaders than Bya and Myrrdhin.

We all moved on the building as a group, staying below the tips of the crops and creeping along slowly, with the Hounds between us and the Manticores. The Othersiders didn't seem to notice us; they had managed to pop the door out of its frame, and now they were trying to enlarge the hole where it had been. All the ag-buildings out here were reinforced 'crete, hard to break or dig into, but there were a lot of the Manticores, and they were powerful and determined.

Just then one of those stinger tails lashed forward to strike something I couldn't see.

"Kent!" I shouted, as the Manticore lunged forward and then spun around and dashed out of the cargo bay, a limp human in its mouth. But Kent had already seen it, and so had Cielle and Scarlet.

The beast tried to make for the Portal, but Scarlet's and Cielle's Hounds harried it from the air, and half of mine cut it off from the Portal. Kent, Cielle, and I let loose with a volley of shots, aiming for the body. We didn't dare shoot at the head, not with a victim in the thing's mouth.

It tried to fight through the Hounds, but there were too many of them, so it turned to face them. It moved as fast as a regular scorpion, and although its mouth was encumbered, its tail and forepaws were not. The Hounds worked together like a well-oiled machine, dashing in and out, keeping it confused with a multitude of targets, until we finally got enough bullets into it to drop it. Dusana dashed in and picked up the limp body of the man the Manticore had stung. *Get him somewhere safe and guard him!* I ordered, and as I heard his wordless assent, turned my attention back to the Othersiders still trying to get into the building. Our assault on their companion had gone unnoticed, so they must not have had any psychic links. They might be like Minotaurs—once they got focused on something, it would take a grenade to pull their attention away.

Grenade!

"Kent, do we care about the stuff in the dock?" I shouted over the radio.

"*Hell no!*" came the reply.

"*Good!*" Tober snarled, as if he had read my mind. "*Fire in the hole!*"

And with that, he brought up the RPG launcher he was carrying and fired into the loading dock. Before I could blink, the loading dock vanished in smoke and a flash, and the heat and shock wave of the blast struck us.

When the smoke cleared, the trailers that had been unloading there were in bits. There was vegetable pulp everywhere. And there were a couple dozen pairs of flat, golden eyes staring at us angrily. A couple of the Manticores opened their mouths and roared at us, and the rest charged.

The Hounds wove a gauntlet of protection between us and the Othersiders as the beasts did their best to get within striking distance, and we unloaded bullet after bullet into their hides. But as we had seen with the first one, these things took a *lot* of damage before they went down. Those wicked stingers lashed out again and again, fast and deadly, and I felt them just skimming past my Hounds' hides as they danced with death.

If they got as far as us . . .

But they didn't. The Hounds saw to that.

And once we'd killed three or four, Cielle's Hounds were able to feed her magic energy, and she was able to open up on them. *That* was something they weren't able to shake off.

I didn't know she was powered up until suddenly the Manticore I was shooting at lost its face.

"Holy—!" I exclaimed, startled. The thing had dropped in its tracks, of course, and a second later I was shooting at another, but

I hadn't been prepared for how vulnerable these things were to Cielle's blasts. If bullets worked, magic seemed to work better! So I dropped the muzzle of my rifle and let it dangle from the sling while I unloaded a levin bolt of my own.

It was nothing like as powerful as Cielle's, but this Manticore dropped too, with a massive hole where its eye had been.

Seeing our results, the others did the same, and after another four went down, the Manticores suddenly realized that we were mowing them down. One of them roared, and they all turned tail and ran for the Portal.

The Hounds chased them all the way there; the others followed, but since we had them on the run, I headed for Dusana, where he was standing guard over the tech we had rescued.

Dusana had blown himself up to his full height and planted himself right over the man's unconscious body. I didn't doubt that Dusana could have held his own against any Manticore that had wanted to recapture its prize.

How is he? I asked as Dusana moved aside so I could examine the man.

Unconscious, Dusana replied. *But as far as I can tell, no worse.*

"Kent," I called into my radio, as I knelt beside the poor man. "I have the victim. He's still unconscious." I felt for a pulse, and got one. "Pulse is fast, he's twitching and drooling and sweating. Anything I should do for him?"

"I'm on my way with the field kit." Kent had way more experience than I did in treating things in the field. I didn't touch the man except to make sure his airway was clear. Kent was there within a minute and took over from me.

"For the future, this is anaphylaxis, combined with something else. I'm treating the former," the armorer said, administering something in a blue color-coded pen-syringe. "HQ, this is Elite Senior Kent. We have a civilian down with a Manticore sting and need immediate evac for him."

"If you need someone to stay behind, I will," I volunteered. "I can interview the Cits while I'm here."

"Good, thanks" was all Kent said as we heard our chopper coming in.

So that was what I did—which gave me almost two dozen witnesses who could say where I was while Bya was making Josh "vanish."

There wasn't much they could tell me; the Portal had opened while they were offloading the harvested squashes from the trailers, and their supervisor had the presence of mind to get them all into the building and get the outer doors barred before the Manticores tore down the electric fence. That gave them time to get into the building itself and reinforce the locks on the doors with a big physical bar.

Unfortunately, that didn't hold, and one guy—our victim—had been caught alone when the Manticores tore the door off its hinges. He panicked and tried to sprint across the hallway to the rejoin the rest, and that was when the Manticores stung him and dragged him out.

They were more than rattled, so I promised that the Hounds and I would not leave them until a repair crew arrived with a better answer for their protection than the simple electric fence and flimsy outer doors. I had kept the mic open to HQ as they spoke; I wanted to make sure HQ heard directly from them, because what they had to say was disturbing, to say the least.

It appeared that Apex took their plight seriously, because what arrived was not just a repair crew but army troops and engineers, and reinforced doors for the cargo bay and building. By the time I left, repairs and improvements were well under way, and the army had established a defensive perimeter to make sure everyone stayed protected until the repairs were complete.

I climbed into one of the cargo choppers for my return trip, after sending all the Hounds back. It was a little strange, riding in this big, empty thing that didn't have an open door to look out of.

I called in once I was strapped in and the chopper had lifted off. "Elite Joy to HQ."

"Go, Joy."

"Inbound on cargo chopper. Any orders?"

That was good. Kent must have taken care of the debrief. Although the attack of these Manticores was not an important one, at least on the surface of it, I knew it was a lot more serious than it seemed. The Manticores hadn't been there simply to wreck things and kill people. They'd been there to take humans prisoner.

Just as I had wondered . . . except now we had direct eyewitness proof of it.

I'd had plenty of time to examine that poor man, as well as take the eyewitness testimony; he'd been stung in the arm, and he hadn't taken in enough poison to kill him. As Raynd had pointed out, if he'd been stung in the chest or the eye, he'd have been dead regardless of how little poison was pumped into him.

So they had intended to take prisoners, and with that many

Manticores involved in the attack, it was clear they'd intended to take more than one.

As far as I knew, this was the first time—ever—we had actual proof that the Othersiders had attempted to take human prisoners. I had no doubt it was on orders of the Folk.

Which begged the question that was likely on the minds of everyone in the know: What did they *want* with prisoners?

FINALLY, THE MENTAL CONTACT I was waiting for came. *Are you in your rooms?* Bya asked politely.

Yes! I said, and before I could say anything else, Bya *bamphed* into my bedroom. He was in the form of a house cat, but before I had taken another breath, he had expanded to his normal form.

Well! That was entertaining, he said genially. *Shall I show you?*

I didn't need to be asked twice. He jumped up on my bed, and I joined him, putting a mindless drama-vid on. He cuddled up next to me while we pretended to watch.

But what I was really watching was Bya-memories.

The first part went pretty much as I had expected. As Josh, Bya had puttered around the office until Uncle sent him home. Part of the puttering had been to make sure Josh's Perscom could guide him to Josh's apartment; I'd shown him how mine worked, so he was familiar with one. I had expected some worry or trepidation over this on his part, but instead I sensed only excitement. This was all new to him; he had experienced HQ and the Monastery, but no other human buildings in Apex. So he enjoyed his stint pretending to be Josh, and he enjoyed the "going home" part even more. Elevators were fascinating for him—I felt the things he had felt, and he had a way of sensing not just motion but direction. When the doors opened on the ground floor and he stepped into the lobby and out onto the busy street, he was alert and fascinated. All of it was intriguing to him, all of it worth paying attention to. He'd walked to Josh's apartment building—it wasn't far, and he was much too fascinated by the buildings, the people, and eventually the shop windows to take a pod.

I had to smile at his reactions. He was just like a kid seeing new things, or a turnip seeing a place bigger than a village for the first time.

He managed to use his Perscom to navigate without being obvious about it, and when it registered the building Josh's rooms were in, I felt his disappointment. Before going into the building, he stopped at a little pocket-park nearby—not much, just a couple hundred square feet of trees, grass, and bushes. Josh had recently gotten into the habit of sitting there for a while before going home. It had the advantage of being overlooked by just a single security cam. Bya took a seat and surreptitiously examined a spot under some bushes, out of sight of the security cam. A human couldn't have hidden there, but there was plenty of space for something considerably smaller.

Once Bya had been sure he knew the spot he had chosen down to the smallest root and pebble, he entered Josh's building, took the elevator to the fourth floor, and presented Josh's Perscom to the door lock as he'd been instructed.

Once it opened, he went in, turned on the vid, ate a prepared meal—which was a surprise to me because I didn't know he could eat like a human—and after a very little bit, went to bed. Josh had told us that was not unusual for him lately.

He left the Perscom on the bedside table when he did that.

But of course, as soon as the lights were out, Bya transformed into a house cat, leaving behind the pajamas and the Perscom, and *bamphed* himself down to the spot at street level and sauntered away. From there, he got to HQ in a series of *bamphs* and ended up in my room.

I expected something much more exciting, I told him. *You turning into a snake and slithering into the ventilation ducts, maybe, or a gargoyle and flying out the window.*

He nudged me with his nose. *How many times did the Masters tell you "simpler is better"? No one looks at a stray cat. They would have reacted poorly to a gargoyle flying overhead, or a snake coming out of a vent.*

I petted him. *You are wise,* I said. *I'm sorry you missed out on the manna from the Manticores.*

There will be more tomorrow. The program ended and he got up off the bed and stood there looking at me expectantly. I cast the runes, opened the Way, and he went back "home."

So . . . assuming that Josh's Perscom didn't send out an alert when there wasn't someone wearing it—which would be kind of stupid since lots of people took theirs off when sleeping—he wouldn't be missed until tomorrow morning, There were dozens of security cams that now had vid of Josh behaving normally right up until the moment he entered his apartment door. Josh hadn't mentioned any cams in his apartment, but I hadn't wanted to leave that to chance, which was why I'd asked Bya to go through the whole sham of eating, viewing, and going to bed. The only possible glitch in all of this was if there were cams that recorded heat signatures—there would be a moment when "Josh" suddenly shrank, then vanished. I didn't know what the authorities would make of that....

But we just had to take that chance. This had been the simplest—and we hoped the best—way of getting Josh out and leaving behind a puzzle that the authorities would have a hard time unraveling, and an even harder time linking to Uncle *or* the Hunters, particularly me.

So now I had to act normally. Tomorrow Josh would fail to turn up, Uncle would "try to reach him," and when calls went unanswered, would report his absence to PsiCorps. And then... we'd see what happened.

I crawled into bed, feeling the adrenaline that had kept me going drain out of me. And the relief I'd been riding on, now that Josh was safely away, gave way to more worry. Sure, Drift couldn't get her claws in him, but now what were we supposed to do with him? Leaving him in Spillover wasn't an option.

At least, I didn't think it was.

I wished it was possible to send him to the Mountain. There, the problem of how the heck he would keep himself fed simply wouldn't come up. He could go to the Monastery, he could use his

Powers to help the Hunters, and he could probably train anyone who had psionics under the supervision of the Masters. But that just was not an option. Not while there was a chance PsiCorps could trace him there.

The best thing would be to somehow get him on a train and get him far enough away from Apex that PsiCorps would be unlikely to find him again. But that led to two more big problems: how to get him on a train in the first place, and how to get him some set of skills that would let him eat. He hadn't seemed all that enthusiastic about plucking the knowledge of a mechanic out of someone's skull, I guess because he just wasn't enthusiastic about becoming a mechanic in the first place. I couldn't really blame him, but what else could he do? I was pretty sure he wouldn't like farming, and anyway, he didn't have the strength for it. He could probably teach kids, especially if he pulled skills out of a teacher, but would he like it? It didn't really fit with what I knew about him.

I tossed and turned as I tried to come up with a solution and pretty much came up empty-handed.

I guess I just don't know him. . . .

That was the thing that kept occurring to me over and over. Every time I tried to match Josh up with something he could do *besides* be a Psimon, I couldn't make a fit, mostly because I didn't know how he'd react to the idea.

Heck, I had a better idea of what my old friend Kei or even Mark would consider a reasonable way to make a living than I did of Josh! Mark would farm or hunt or both, obviously. Heck, I knew what Cielle would do; she'd probably design and fabricate clothing. But Josh? I hadn't a clue.

Which was pretty sad, really. You would think I'd know more about a guy I'd spent a lot of time kissing, wouldn't you?

I guess I should have spent a lot less time kissing and a lot more time talking, I thought as I turned my hot pillow again. *Guess I'm not as savvy as I thought I was.*

My day started early. I was just back from an eight-man callout (more Manticores, plus Minotaurs and a couple Ogres, all on another raid on an ag-station) when my Perscom went off with an unfamiliar ID. I was glad that I was in armory getting resupplied at the time; it would be a very good thing to have witnesses.

I accepted the call, and the face of a cold-looking Psimon—a Senior Psimon by his discrete badges—came up on my screen. In fact, I knew this guy. He was the one who'd given me such a hard time after I found the first body of a dead Psimon down in the sewers.

"How can I help you, sir?" I said politely.

He launched straight into it without any warning. "Have you had any contact with Psimon Josh Green today?" he barked at me.

I blinked several times but responded immediately. "No, sir, I've been busy since I came on shift. Is there a problem?"

"What about last night?" he continued, glaring.

"Night before last, sir. We don't talk every day." Which was true. We'd been very carefully keeping things to every *other* day, at most. "I just don't have time—"

"Do you know where he is?" the Psimon interrupted, startling me, which was good, since my reaction to his rudeness was pretty much the sort of way a perfectly innocent person who *hadn't* just helped their Psimon escape would act.

"At Prefect Charmand's office at this hour," I replied—by now I'd gotten a small audience. Cielle, of course, and Kent, and Mark Knight. "If he's not there . . ."

"He's not there," the man stated flatly. "The prefect is concerned. Do you know where he could be?"

Voice-stress analysis, I reminded myself. "Do *I* know where he could be?" I said, repeating his question. And then I thought extremely hard about Josh all alone in that shelter, and all the ways he could manage to hurt himself because he didn't know how to take care of himself there the way a Hunter would have. "Could he have had an accident?" I asked. "Have you checked with a hospital?"

"That will be all, Hunter," the Psimon said, cutting me off. And then he hung up on me.

"Was he talking about your boyfriend?" Cielle asked, half concerned and half bewildered.

"Josh, yeah," I said. "I can't imagine what could have happened. Maybe he fell over something and hit his head and he's lying on the floor unconscious. . . . Does that even happen here? It does at home. I—"

No one had a chance to answer me, because Uncle called next. "Joy, did Josh talk to you last night?"

"No," I replied, thinking hard about all the ways this could go wrong. Genuine stress entered my voice again. "And PsiCorps just called me asking the same thing! What's going on?"

"I don't know," he told me. "Josh didn't call in this morning, and I got no answer when I called him. Don't worry, we'll get to the bottom of this."

And *he* hung up on me.

Before anyone could ask me anything else, we got a callout. I never thought I would be grateful to Othersiders, but their timing could not have been better.

Uncle called me back later when I was off shift, giving me the story we had agreed on. That Josh had gone home and apparently disappeared from there. That at least he hadn't been found sick or hurt, and that I was not to worry. Which would have been a really stupid thing to say to me had I not known exactly where he was.

PsiCorps called me immediately afterward—that same cold Psimon, informing me that Josh's disappearance was a matter for internal security now, and I was not to say anything to anyone about it.

"Yes, sir," I said meekly, doing my best to look terrified. I must have convinced him, because he finally got an expression on his face. Smugness. So smug I wanted to slap him. Then he hung up.

Which was just as well since I'm not sure I could have kept up the act much longer.

"Internal security"—what could *that* mean? Did they think he'd run, or did they think he'd been kidnapped? I'd never heard of someone being kidnapped right out of the heart of Apex, and with all the security cams around, I wouldn't think it was possible. Unless...

Unless a Folk Lord could do it.

And that was something they wouldn't want even a Hunter to know.

Ah, more likely than not, it was just that they figured he'd run (which he had!) and they hadn't been able to deduce how he'd done it. With any luck, they never would.

The next morning, Kent signaled to me as I checked out my weapons in the armory. Obediently, I slipped through the rest of the Hunters and moved toward him. "Joy, I want you to run a sweep of a sector of Spillover I'm concerned about. Cover as much as you can," he said. "You're the only one with enough Hounds to do so effectively."

"Yes, sir," I said, but he wasn't finished.

"There's a prediction of weather today, but now that we've stocked all those shelters, if you get caught too far from the Pylon, there ought to be at least one within running distance, since you can ride one of your Hounds," he told me. He raised one eyebrow at me. It took me a minute, but then the light went on in my head.

"Yes, sir," I repeated, and raised my own eyebrow. "I'll take a pod out. Too bad the rest of you won't have that option."

"Well, if the storm looks bad enough, we'll call in evac," he replied. "And if it's not, it won't be worse than we faced at the Barrier."

And just then, we got a callout; he assigned a team of four to it, and I called a pod.

While I was in the pod, I took the time to check out the storm that was moving in—how fast it was coming and where it was expected to hit first. The general projection was that it was about three hours away; I made a rough guess how far three hours of sweeping would be from Josh's shelter, and sent the pod to that part of the Barrier.

This was another spot I hadn't been to before, and I could see why Kent had a valid reason to be worried about what this part of Spillover might hide. On the Apex side of the Barrier, it was all warehouses. On the other side, though, it was nothing but tumble-down ruins overgrown with trees.

A forest? Where almost anything could be hiding, from rebel humans to *large* groups of Othersiders? Right against the Barrier? This was insanity!

Or hubris. The "nothing ever came from there, so nothing ever will" attitude that Cits and those who should have known better both seemed to share here. *Well, we're going to do the most thorough sweep of this area it's ever had,* I decided. I couldn't get to the other side of the Barrier and open the Way fast enough. Once the Hounds came through, they shared both my astonishment and my outrage. Pretty soon they were formed up in a line on either side of me, and we began our sweep.

It wasn't easy because this wasn't easy ground to walk over. There had been a lot of buildings here originally, and now there wasn't a wall that was more than knee-high. Dust, dirt, and debris had all settled in here, and the forest had seeded itself in the pockets of dirt and grown undisturbed. Now the trees were as tall as anything on the Mountain, but the ground underneath them was still rubble. The only good thing was that ground like this merely supported sparse grasses and weeds, so there weren't fifty million wait-a-minute bushes to have to push through.

There were plenty of Othersiders here, as expected. Acres to hide in and right on the Barrier itself? The only thing that was surprising was that there weren't entire colonies of the big, dangerous kinds. We hadn't gone half an hour in before the Hounds were full to bursting with manna, and I had taken to using magic to burn the excess they were passing me. It was all little stuff: Piskies and Goblins, a Redcap or two, Willow Wisps—stuff that I used to Hunt at home without too much trouble.

At the end of an hour and a half we came out of the forest and into the sort of ruins I expected for Spillover. We stopped for a brief rest then, since I was pretty tired of stumbling over piles of rubble that never seemed to end. I braced myself against a tree trunk and had a look around.

After going into Spillover so much with Mark Knight, I'd gotten to know the kinds of places where the people who inhabited Spillover were likely to try and live, and this wasn't one of them. Looked like this area was a bit marshy, probably a breeding ground for mosquitoes and all other kinds of bugs; I could pick out the wet spots by the presence of cattails. The walls of long-gone houses were few and far apart. But *big*. I reckoned they'd been very fancy in their day, with property that was measured in acres rather than feet. Maybe this had all been an area for very rich people, nicely landscaped, with pretty little ponds and a stream or brook linking them.

At least I was wearing good waterproof boots. I was in for a slog.

Not surprisingly, the only things here were wildlife and a few Willow Wisps that we startled up out of their rotten logs. They didn't look like much, just glowing globes, but they could hypnotize you and hold you until something more lethal came along. A levin bolt took care of those, if one of the Hounds didn't snap it dead first. The worst of it was the sucking mud, if I made a misstep, and the *smell*. Ugh. Stagnant water, rotten vegetation, and whatever was festering down in that mud. And as I had feared, mosquitoes. Lots and lots of mosquitoes. I was reduced to putting up a light Shield to keep them off, or I would have been sucked dry.

My Perscom went off with a warning just as we got out of that area; I looked up and to the west, and sure enough, there were the tops of the storm clouds. The radar feed I pulled up showed it as mostly orange with some angry red spots. Unfortunately, we were a lot farther from Josh's hideaway than I had thought we'd be when I entered the forest. I called in the Hounds, who circled around me, looking from me to the sky.

"Yeah," I said aloud. "I think we're going to have to make a run for it. Any of you want to go back Otherside?"

Hold and Strike—who couldn't *bamph*—pushed to the front of the pack and looked at me hopefully. I opened the Way for them, and they jumped through. So did Gwalchmai; Myrrdhin, however, elected to stay with the rest of the pack. I swung myself up on

Dusana's back and looked down at them. "All right, pack. Time for a race." I pointed in the direction of Josh's shelter. "That way."

And we ran. As soon as Dusana launched, I put my head down along his neck and put my wrist up to my mouth. "Elite Joy to HQ," I called in, a little breathlessly. "I've been caught by the storm. I'm seeking one of the shelters that is right near me."

"Roger that, Elite Joy. Stay safe out there."

"Will do. Roger, out."

Well, that took care of things. Now no one would be mounting a search for me if I fell out of touch for a few hours.

The Hounds all kept close to me; this was no time to go scaring up something we might have to fight. Thunder growled off to our left, and the light slowly dimmed as the tops of the anvil clouds reached out and overshadowed us. When we were about halfway to Josh's hiding place, I checked the radar again. Sure enough, the storm was bigger than before, and more of it was red. I made myself as small on Dusana's back as I could, and I felt him put on more speed.

But I wasn't frightened; if anything, I was getting a big rush out of this. Honestly? It was *wonderful.* The ground streamed by underneath us, and what wasn't running away from us was just heading for shelter itself. Dusana ran far faster than any horse I had ever ridden, and much more smoothly. For just these few minutes, I wasn't Hunting, there was nothing threatening the city worse than a little bit of weather, and I was completely and totally free. The wind tore my hair out of its tail, and my nostrils were full of the smell of green things and that scent that means rain is about to hit.

If only we could have run like this forever, it would have been heaven.

Drops began to patter around us. *Shields up!* I ordered. The Shields would guard us from rain and probably from lightning, unless we had a direct hit. And we wouldn't; I knew how to dissipate lightning skyward by making connection with the Shield, something every Hunter learns on the Mountain.

We finally reached the building where the shelter was hidden. Dusana stopped and knelt at the staircase so I could tumble off his back; we all collapsed our Shields. I stumbled down the stairs and presented my Perscom to the outer door lock. It accepted me and popped open; I held the door open for the Hounds, who poured through, and I got inside and slammed the door shut just as a torrent of water dropped down out of the sky.

It was pitch-black down here. The Hounds could see in the dark, but I didn't have night-vision goggles with me. No worries; on the Mountain, one of the first things anyone with magic learns to do is make a light. I spun up three mage-lights and sent them to hover above my head. The second door was closed and probably locked; I presented my Perscom to it too, and it unlocked with a faint click. I sent the mage-lights ahead of us, into that big common room. There was absolutely no sign of life there.

Exactly as it should be.

While the Hounds sniffed around, I went to the door that led into the kitchen. I tried it; it was locked.

Exactly as it should be. In the back of my mind I had been worried that Josh hadn't taken Kent's instructions to heart—or worse, that he'd meet us at the door with a gun, drawn and ready, that he didn't really know how to use. Instead, he'd been smart. He probably kept the inner door locked, and when he heard the outer one go, he'd gone to ground.

So I knocked on the door. "Hey, Josh, it's us. I mean, it's me and the Hounds."

I heard some furniture scraping the floor on the other side of the door, then the sound of a bolt being thrown. The door opened and Josh peered cautiously around the edge of it. He smiled hugely when he saw me. "Joy! I didn't expect to see anyone so soon." He pulled the door open wider. "Come in here, it's a lot more comfortable. Aren't you going to be missed?"

I followed him and the mage-lights followed me, floating just above my head like a halo; the Hounds were still investigating the shelter. The kitchen area didn't have anything except a water-purifier operation going, but then, the supplies Kent had stocked this place with were Basic Ration Biscuits, which didn't need any prep. Josh had cleaned the kitchen up, though, which was probably wise. I didn't want to think about how many rodents had probably run over those counters.

"Nobody's going to miss me. A storm just moved in, and I let HQ know that I was seeking shelter," I said as we left the kitchen and entered the storage room. "Oh, hey, I like what you've done with the place."

This room had been meant to store supplies for several hundred people for several months, so even with all the stuff Kent had ordered to be stored here, there was plenty of space. But Josh had constructed a false wall of wreckage about halfway down the room, backed by the boxes of supplies. Once we had squeezed through to the other side, where he had a single light going, I saw he'd made himself a pretty cozy living space. On one side was the bicycle generator and the battery holders, ready for charging. On the other, he'd taken a table and put two of the mattresses under it, one across the back between the table and the wall, one on top, and piled the rest along the sides, leaving one he could pull across the front after he closed himself inside. It was a very cozy little "cave" that his own body heat would keep warm. That had worried me; he was far enough belowground that in winter the place probably wouldn't get anywhere near freezing, but it would still be uncomfortable, and hard to sleep.

"There's plenty of water," he said. "Wherever that cistern is, it's full. I've figured out how to wash clothing in the showers, and I just leave what I've washed hanging in there to dry." He shrugged and smiled wryly. "This is better than I thought it would be, and camping out in the ruins would *still* be better than whatever it was Drift had planned for me."

"About that," I said. We made ourselves a comfortable place to sit on a couple spare mattresses while I told him about what had happened after he "disappeared."

When I told him what Bya had done, he looked thoughtful. "I wonder how they're going to take that," he said. "There are folk tales about people—people with Psi-powers—vanishing out of their beds. Drift hates those, and any other stories like them, that imply anyone with psi can do . . . well . . . occult stuff."

I raised both eyebrows. "Do you think they might actually believe you—what?—vibrated yourself into the ether?"

"If they can't find any other explanation, they might," he

replied. "Drift really does try to put fear of anything superstitious into her Psimons. Back in school, if our teachers found out any of us were participating in anything remotely religious, the teachers would make fun of us unmercifully. As for all those old occult and psychic things people supposedly used to do before the Diseray, well, you'd get *days'* worth of lectures on how they were danger-ous practices that would drive you mad, or worse, open you up to manipulation by Othersiders."

"And disappearing out of your bed would qualify as worse, I guess," I hazarded. "Well, I hope that's what they decide on. Anything that unsettles them is something I highly approve of." I paused. "Do you think Drift might decide that opening yourself up to Othersiders would include being stolen from your bed by them?"

He shrugged. "I have no idea. How would they get to me in the first place? The Barrier is pretty effectively keeping them out. I mean, unless they had some way of taking over my mind and somehow empowering me to make a Portal. Ace certainly was affected by the Othersiders while he was inside the Barrier. For all I know, Drift's figured I was too."

He was right. There was no telling what Abigail Drift had decided. I just hoped she had eliminated Uncle and me from being the probable causes.

ABOUT AN HOUR WENT by as Josh showed me what Kent had left him, and what he'd improvised on his own. I looked through the bookcase of books. Kent had been ... very practical about what he'd left here. Every single one of those books was some kind of wilderness survival manual—from how to make fire, shelter, and clean water with minimal supplies, to how to snare, kill, clean, and cook game over a fire. Very useful, of course ... but not what I would call entertaining. It looked from the books with bits of toilet paper stuck in for markers that Josh had tried to make a start on some of them but was finding them heavy going. I already knew there was nothing on the Perscom that Kent had given him other than the barest of basics—the kind of vids and books that came preloaded on every Perscom—because I'd looked it over after Kent got it for him.

I dropped down on a "couch" he'd made out of mattresses covered with an opened sleeping bag. Josh started to make tentative little moves toward me, taking one of my hands and putting his arm awkwardly around my shoulders, that suggested he wanted to do something other than just sit there and talk. And while part of me wanted that too—a *lot*—I reminded myself what I'd determined. I really didn't *know* him—not enough to trust to send to Anston's Well, much less Safehaven and the Mountain. So much as I wanted to hold hands and kiss and all that . . . I needed to figure out as much as I could about him in the few hours the storm was going to give us.

"So besides charging batteries and rearranging boxes, what are you doing out here?" I asked.

"Well . . . mostly that," he replied, taking the hint and removing his arm from my shoulder. "I've done a very little bit of exploring around the building this shelter is under, and I found a few little odd things, but I haven't done much else." He made a face. "I had no idea how much I depended on vids and games until I lost access to them. It's almost impossible to play anything for any length of time on the Perscom screen, and there's nothing but a couple of nature vids on it anyway."

"You could read," I replied with envy. I had downloaded *so* many books into my Perscom since I got here . . . and no time to even look at any of them unless there was a storm.

"Uh . . ." He flushed, embarassed. "Yeah, I suppose I could if I had anything I might like. Those survival manuals aren't exactly something you breeze through for fun, and there's not much else down here."

I tried not to goggle at him. "You don't read?" I couldn't imagine it. When I thought of all the winter nights I spent tucked up in my bed reading one of the real paper books from the Monastery library while a blizzard howled outside, a hot brick wrapped in towels at the bottom of my bed under the covers to keep my toes toasty...I'd have gone insane with boredom if I hadn't had that library to dive into.

"Not much," he admitted, flushing more. "It's just so much easier to watch a vid...."

"Well, I have a metric ton of books on my Perscom," I said firmly. "Let's figure out what you might like. I've been reading some that were like that game we were playing, remember? Magic, and set in the same time, pre-Diseray. Let's look at those first."

We put our heads together over my Perscom and started looking at first chapters. Pretty soon we had a good idea of what he might like, and I linked our Perscoms and transferred copies to him. You can tell a lot about someone by the kinds of stories he likes, or more tellingly, the kinds of characters he likes. In a couple of hours I had learned more about Josh than I had in weeks.

And it was shocking. Shocking to discover how much had been kept from him as a Psimon, even though he'd had a "relatively normal" childhood. But at least I didn't learn anything that would change my mind about how I felt about him.

The Hounds settled around us, listening as we talked. He was more than a bit self-conscious at first, with all those eyes on him, but after a while he got used to it. Once in a while Bya would suggest a book I'd forgotten I had.

Every so often, I'd go to the door to check if it was still raining, since my Perscom got no reception down here. When we'd loaded about fifty books onto his Perscom, I decided to see if there was something to be done about the lack of reception.

"You know, I can't believe they'd have a shelter without a radio," I said at last. "I mean, that would be the one way they could find out if there was anyone else left, right?"

"I . . . guess?" Josh replied, looking a bit bewildered, which made sense now that I realized he knew very little about pre-Diseray history.

"So the radio is probably long gone, most likely taken when this place was looted for the stores, but the external antenna should still exist," I explained. "And that will give us a way to get reception down here for our Perscoms." I got up. "I'm going to look for it."

I took two of my mage-lights with me and went into the big common room. Since Josh trailed after me, I decided to think aloud. "You'd assume the radio would be *here*," I said as I scanned the walls for something like a conduit that would lead to the building above. "Because everyone in this place would have wanted to know if there was any contact with the outside world, and even find out if friends and relatives had made it into shelters themselves."

I didn't see anything like a conduit, so I tried to put myself inside the heads of some of those pre-Diseray authorities. Who were . . . authoritarian. "Now, the people who built shelters like this, though, probably wouldn't have been too pleased about the Cits crowding around the radio, every single one of them wanting to do something with it. So . . . that means they'd want it under their complete control. And the one room in the entire shelter that would absolutely be under the complete control of whoever was in charge would be—"

I turned back around and pointed at the kitchen door.

"—the supply room!" I went back into the room Josh was using for his living quarters and went all the way to the back wall. There were boxes stacked there all the way to the ceiling. Because of course there were. And there was a rolling ladder here that actually still worked—more like a rolling staircase, really—so I climbed up and began moving the top boxes away from the wall until I found what I was looking for.

It was a conduit coming down out of the ceiling along the wall, just as I had thought. And it wasn't connected in any way with the electrical conduits.

I won't go into all the work we had to do, but in about an hour or so, the supplies had been restacked and we had a functioning antenna to the outside of the bunker. Josh was baffled as to how this was supposed to work, but I did some trial and error with a length of wire and discovered we got decent reception by attaching one end of the wire to the metal wristband of the Perscoms. A little more rearranging of supplies and mattresses, and Josh had a nice comfortable spot he could use to check feeds and watch anything being broadcast.

"Don't do *anything* active," I warned. "I mean, you know not to make calls unless it's an emergency, but don't download anything or even connect to a database. All that stuff is recorded, and if a Perscom out in Spillover starts downloading vids, *someone* is going to take notice and maybe investigate."

"Don't some people in Spillover have Perscoms?" he asked. "I mean, some of them used to be Apex Cits, after all."

"You can bet that every one of them has its ID number on record," I replied. "You can't handshake an active feed without a Perscom ID. Watch," I said, and showed him how when I connected to the active feed for Hunters, my Perscom logged in for me. His face fell. "But, look, whenever I'm out here, I'm *supposed* to be out here. I can handshake and download, then transfer to you. The rest of the time, just watch the passive broadcast stuff." There were four channels from all the ones available in Apex via 'net that were on broadcast, for the benefit of the towns and villages around Apex. The signal traveled quite a distance. It wasn't the hundreds of channels you could get if you were in Apex and connected to the wired 'net, but it was better than nothing. At least now Josh wouldn't be quite so cut off.

"It's time," I said, when the radar showed the storm was a good half mile downrange of us. "I'll find a way to get back here, but the weather probably won't cooperate, and it probably won't be for as long—"

He interrupted me with a kiss and a hug that practically took my breath away, and it was absolutely *the* best kiss I had ever had.

"You've already done so much," he said, when we both needed air. "And I can never repay it. You're amazing, I don't deserve you, but promise me that somehow we're going to manage to stay together long enough to find out if . . . if we can stay together? I mean, regardless of what's going on outside of us?"

I shook my head. "I can't predict the future. But I promise if we don't, it will be because what's outside of us made that impossible."

"That'll do," he said, and kissed me again. That kiss just made me tingle all over, put flutters in my stomach, and made me hyper-aware of every inch of my skin—and every inch of my skin wanted him to touch me.

It was really, really hard to break off, gather up the Hounds, call in my mage-lights, and go out that door. Hearing the heavy blast doors closing felt like I was closing my own heart into a little dark box. And on top of that, I knew that *he* was being closed into a dark box . . . even if it wasn't a little one. He was going to be all alone out here, and although he was used to being alone, he wasn't used to being this isolated. It was awful. I wanted to run back in there and tell him I was going to find a way to send him to my home. Or tell him we'd find a way to hide him in our HQ.

I picked my way through the half-destroyed building, using all my skills to keep from leaving a trail, and got out, not looking back. Because if there was a cam up that I couldn't see, I didn't want anyone to think that I'd done anything differently than I'd reported. I'd just used one of the shelters, whiled away the hours, and now I was back on patrol.

Right there on the steps of the building I opened the Way for Hold, Strike, and Gwalchmai to come through and rejoin the rest of the pack.

Is there an Eye? I asked Bya, who was supersensitive to the presence of cams.

He shook his head. *There is no Eye. Why?*

Because I want some bloody answers, I replied, settled my One White Stone in my head, and turned on the Psi-shield on my

Perscom. Nervous and marveling at my own hubris, I called out loud: "Torcion! Torcion! Torcion!"

I felt the rough caress of a *lot* of power on my skin, and I clamped down hard on my fear. As the Hounds closed in around me, a Portal opened in the middle of the ruined, cracked, and potholed street in front of us, and the lavender-robed Folk Lord I now knew as Torcion stepped through.

He looked just the same, so far as I could tell, except he was walking on his two feet rather than floating high in the air. "I was wondering when you would find an opportunity to call upon me," he said, his eyes alight with both interest and what I thought was amusement. "It was longer than I anticipated."

"Well, it's not as if you aren't one of mankind's deadliest enemies, after all," I retorted. "And it's not as if—" I was going to say *Not as if I have a reason to trust you*, except that was wrong. He'd helped me, or people near me, several times already. He'd offered reasons to trust him. And I had already lost control of this conversation. "—as if I haven't a reason to think you might be setting me up for a trap," I said instead. "You could have given me the way to summon you just so you could get me alone and kill me."

"So I might. But you are wrong about the first, shepherd. I am not, and have not been, your enemy, or the enemy of any of your kind." He cocked his head to one side. "In fact, I am the benefactor of many. And *my* kind saved your world when your kind very nearly destroyed it and made it unlivable."

I frowned. "I find that completely unbelievable. You've been massacring us since you arrived."

"Ah!" he replied, holding up one finger. "That is true. But we have not killed anything else *but* you. The creatures that are not you flourish and prosper as they have not since your kind began to take over the world. And while we were unable to reverse what you did to your world, we have been . . . mitigating the damage. You should have been thanking us; indeed, the Grand Alliance believes you should be willingly offering yourselves to us in return for what we have done for your world. Without us, your kind, along with most other life on this world, would be extinct."

I had no way to counter that. Was he telling the truth? Or had all the various disasters of the Diseray had some mitigating effect on the runaway climate and he was only claiming to have "fixed" something that would have tempered itself regardless? I had no way of knowing, so I just shrugged. "I didn't invite you here to debate you," I said instead. "I want to know why you've been helping me. And why me?"

He walked toward me slowly. Beside me, the Hounds vibrated with nervous energy, but they didn't make any moves to hinder him. He stopped when he was within touching distance—much closer than I liked, but I didn't feel as if I could move back without offending him or showing my weakness. "Because you interest me, shepherd. Of all your kind, you are the first I have encountered that was willing to speak rather than kill; negotiate rather than attack."

"Be fair," I retorted. "You're the first of *your* kind that ever tried that with me."

"Perhaps because we are more alike than you know," he countered. "I, too, am a shepherd of sorts. There are others like me who do not emulate the more . . . aggressive of our kindred. Your sheep often come to us willingly enough, and we offer them safe pasture. In the wilder places of this world, our domains are spoken of as havens of peace, and sought for. Thus, you shepherds have not often encountered us."

Well, I felt in that moment as if someone had just stunned me with a rock. He couldn't *possibly* be saying what I thought he was saying—that there were some of these Folk who protected humans and gave them—what? Places to live? Safe places?

Careful, I reminded myself. *There's no reason to think he's telling the truth....*

"As for those creatures we shared our worlds with," he continued with a shrug, "they are what they are. They cannot be reasoned with. They *can* be controlled, which is why the Grand Alliance uses them, but that control has its limits, and once they sense food, there is no stopping them."

He suddenly reached out, took my chin in his hand, and tilted my head up while he bent down. "Let me offer another small piece of information. You interest me because although I can pierce that flimsy mechanical protection you wear about your mind, I *cannot* pass the White Stone. I have not encountered this before, although I have heard of it."

His grip was firm but nothing I couldn't pull free from if I tried. His hand was just a little warmer than my face, and his skin was silken. And for some reason, his touch made me shiver. Mostly fear, but something else, an echo of what he had said back at the train, came out of my memory like a ghost: *We do not find your kind uncomely.* Was he trying some sort of glamouring magic on me? Something to get me to drop my mental protections?

Before I could object, he let me go again and stepped back a pace. "Now, I am curious as to how you knew I would be able to come when you summoned, even though we are within one of your great magic walls."

"You use Portals," I told him. "When I open the Way for my Hounds, I can make a Portal anywhere."

His eyes lit up. "Well deduced. But here is some information for you. We must know where we are going in order to pass your Walls," he said. "I told you my name in order for you to summon me, for your summons gives a place to put the Portal. Even so, though you may summon, we need not answer."

That might explain how Ace had gotten a Vamp down in the sewers, if he'd summoned one of the Folk down there. So why hadn't he gotten away from the army that way? *Probably because the Folk he was working with weren't prepared to jump straight into the heart of enemy territory.*

It was just too bad I couldn't share any of this information, because people would want to know where it had come from. The last thing I wanted to do was let anyone know I was chatting with a Folk Lord.

Yeah, that would go over well.

"That boy you have hiding under those ruins is one I know something about," Torcion said casually as all this was flitting through my head. "There are those in the city who wish to do him a cruelty that you have helped him escape from. I could offer him sanctuary. I think he would not be unhappy in my domain. Could you persuade him to accept, I would consider such an addition to my flock a favor of great price."

That just knocked me mentally sideways for a moment, because it *was* an answer to the question of what to do about Josh. It probably wasn't the best answer; it certainly wasn't the best from *my* point of view—either Torcion was lying or he wasn't, but regardless I'd never see Josh again. Still, at least it was an answer.

"I understand you would wish to know I am not offering false sanctuary," Torcion continued. "And I shall need to think upon a way to assure you that I am not. But if you will not come as a shepherd to my flock, I would gladly take him. In some ways he would be superior, for he could tell me which of my sheep is uneasy or unhappy, and why. And," he added, with a narrowing of his eyes, and a slight smile, "you are fond of him. If he is contented in my domain, in the end, that might persuade you to take service of me too."

I meant to give him an outright refusal, but my mouth betrayed my indecision by uttering the words "I'll have to think about it."

"Of course." He stepped back to the center of the street again and evoked a Portal as casually as I would have created a magelight. "But do not think upon it too long. He is ill-suited to this place and may come to grief by simple accident. There is danger here, both from those you term 'monsters' and the monsters of your own kind, and while his weapons of the mind are formidable, he can wield them against only one at a time. His masters may come looking for him, supposing he has escaped here. There are storms, and there is illness. There are small and deadly creatures that might slip into his shelter without his knowledge. And it may be summer now, but it will not always be summer." And with that, he stepped through the Portal, and it vanished.

You should sit down, Bya said, concerned. *We will watch for trouble.*

He was right; after that encounter I felt light-headed. I kept thinking about all the questions I *should* have asked. I sat down on a handy piece of rubble and put my head down. "Was I a complete idiot for doing that?" I asked the Hounds.

No, Myrrdhin said immediately but didn't elaborate.

We learned a great deal, and I do not think he was being deceptive, Bya agreed. He shook his head like a dog. *Sending your friend to him is not the worst idea in the world. Doing so would get him far away, and there would be nothing to connect you.*

It was true enough that if the Psimons got their hands on Josh, they'd ruthlessly strip everything from his mind, and Uncle and I would both be in trouble over it, even if *technically* no one was doing anything wrong.

And it was true enough that if there was any place on the face of the earth where PsiCorps couldn't get their hands on him, it would be with the Othersiders. If Ace had just had the sense to *stay* with the Othersiders who had offered him escape, he'd still be free. It was frankly only due to Ace's hubris in coming after us himself at the second Battle of the Barriers that we recaptured him. There was no surer way to go somewhere no human would find you than to go off to the Othersiders.

But I'd have to be sure that Josh would be safe with Torcion before I would even suggest it. And how in hell was Torcion going to prove that?

Well, there was only one thing I knew absolutely for sure. I was going to have to call HQ and report myself back on patrol before someone got suspicious. The storm had passed, and we should be working.

I called in. "Elite Joy to HQ. Back on patrol."

"Roger, Elite Joy. You are clear to continue. Anything to report?"

"Acute boredom," I lied. "Finally found an antenna to the surface or I'd probably be gibbering and sucking my toes by now."

The radio operator laughed. *"Roger that. HQ out."*

After that storm, things were suddenly quieter. Not *quiet,* but quieter. I wondered if maybe we'd taken more of a toll on the Othersiders than they had on us—maybe their strategy had backfired on them.

The morning after the storm, Cielle and I got a callout in the middle of breakfast. We grabbed what was portable and headed to Spillover again. We went in through a pylon access as usual and summoned our Hounds on the other side. More half-ruined buildings. This looked as if it might have been some sort of institution, like a college. There was no sign of life, other than wild birds and small animals. Since the call had come from one of the Apex PD who was running his usual patrol on the "safe" side of the Barrier, the Othersiders didn't know they'd been spotted.

"Has HQ told you anything?" Cielle asked as we marked the coordinates that the APD had given us, and I overrode the pod's Cit instructions so it would go at maximum speed to get us there.

"Goblins. Not a Goblin Fair, though," I told her. "So, if I were a flock of Goblins, where would I be?"

"I'll bet they went to bed down over there." She pointed at a roofless building that had probably been a single-story warehouse. Goblins preferred to make nests of whatever weeds and things they could find, and that building looked prime for collecting leaves and growing weeds. We hijacked the cam that was with us and sent it over to peek over the wall. Sure enough, they were there. It was the biggest swarm of Goblins I had ever seen.

If I'd been alone, this would have been more than I could handle. But I wasn't alone. I was with Cielle, and she was fresh from a nice storm day of rest.

We grinned at each other and fist-bumped.

We picked out another roofless building; this one had solid walls of brick three stories tall, but the wooden floors had all rotted away and dropped to the ground level, and the interior had filled with tall brush, even a couple of small trees. At a guess, I would say it had been some sort of factory or assembly plant, because of all the windows. This was ideal; the window glass was gone, but the framing pieces for the glass—which were steel—were still intact. The panes had only been about two inches wide and four tall. There was no way a Goblin would be able to squirm out one of those, and the four walls themselves were good and strong. To the Goblins, it would look like a perfect hiding place. Dusana helped me get onto a fire escape on the side opposite of where the Goblins would be coming from; I got myself into position at the top floor, right at one of those windows. I covered myself with a camouflage cloth. Then my pack set themselves up inside the walls in hiding, making sure the doors were covered. My *Alebrijes* actually camouflaged themselves like chameleons amid the debris; the others found hiding places under a couple of pieces of fallen roof. Cielle set off with her Hounds to chase the Goblins off their bedding ground and herd them to this building, where they would think they were safe.

It worked so well it might have been scripted.

The Goblins were in their natural form as they buzzed over the wall and flung themselves into corners, trying to get out of sight of their pursuers. Long spindly limbs, wings like a fly, snarls of hair, faces a cross between a human and a fox, with rows and rows of sharp teeth. Cielle's Hounds had them terrified; it was obvious from their frantic flying that they weren't thinking, just acting on the instinct to get away and hide.

This is the last, Bya said, as Cielle's Hound pretended to "lose" a Goblin in its natural form that went streaking into the building to huddle up with the rest.

That was when I carefully dropped the net down over the top of the whole building and securely anchored it there, because I really did not want them to come surging up out of the brush to hit the net. I was pretty sure I couldn't hold it against all of them.

They were so busy trying to get themselves even deeper into the brush, they weren't looking up at all.

"Come and get 'em!" I said into the Perscom. My Hounds heard the thought, of course, and they came up out of their hiding places and began wreaking havoc on the trapped Goblins.

Cielle strolled up to one of the doors that was guarded by Dusana, freeing him from door duty, and lined up a Goblin in her sights in a leisurely manner. She potted them with a rifle until her

Hounds could feed her magic. Her four bat-winged Hounds waited politely at the level of the vanished roof for me to loosen a corner of the net so they could slip in with my Hounds. The Goblins that managed to get into the air and got too high for my Hounds to reach found the winged ones waiting for them.

I never even had to hold the net all that tightly; no more than a couple Goblins ever bounced off. And once Cielle's Hounds went to work, she was able to mow Goblins down with deadly arcs of her powerful blasts.

I found myself elated by how much easier things like this were with a pack of eleven. I even had a moment to call HQ.

"Elite Joyeaux to HQ," I said, using the non-emergency channel.

It took a few minutes before they replied, but I was patiently picking off flying Goblins, wounding them so that they fell right in front of Hold or Strike. I kept imagining them wearing Abigail Drift's face.

Finally HQ answered. *"Go ahead, Elite Joyeaux."*

"Commendation for that APD who called in the Goblin flock here. Nice to see someone's paying attention to both sides of the Barrier," I said. "If we got more calls alerting us to problems before they got out of hand, we wouldn't have nearly as many emergencies."

I heard a chuckle of agreement. *"Roger that, Elite. Commendation noted."*

When the last of the Goblins turned into goo, I took down the net and we sent back our now-replete Hounds, and I was feeling much more cheerful. Josh was still safe. Our packs had gotten bellies full of manna, and Cielle and I were supercharged with magic. I'd even gotten in a commendation for someone who deserved it. For the first time in too long, things were "normal."

I should have known that this was too good to last.

22

THE ALARM JARRED ME out of bed, and I was on my feet and grabbing for clothing before I was properly awake. The corner of my vid-screen showed the time: five in the morning. Whatever was going on, it had to be bad. Worse, whatever fight we were getting into was going to take place in the dark.

I slammed out the door and joined Scarlet; as we ran for the armory, we were both sticking receivers in our ears and strapping on helmets. There was organized chaos in the armory itself as we all snatched up our chosen weapons, plus anything else our sleep-fogged brains recognized as useful. As soon as I got myself sorted, I raced for the airfield. Choppers were already there, rotors spinning; another bad sign. I jumped into the first open door I saw.

Hands grabbed me, hauled me in, and shoved me into a seat. I strapped down, and only then did I look around to see who was with me.

Denali was to my right, with Tober and Mei beyond him. Archer was to my left. Across from us, in the seats flanking the door, were Dazzle and Hawk. We were *all* mixed up, but since nobody had said anything yet, I queried my Perscom, saw we were in Chopper Three, and called it in as the pilot took off with a steep tilt to the side. "HQ, HQ, Chopper Three away, Dazzle, Hawk, Archer, Tober, Mei, Joy."

We call got the callback immediately. *"Roger, Chopper Three. Dazzle, Hawk, Archer, Tober, Mei, Joy. Elite Archer designated lead."*

Archer responded immediately, his voice reassuring and calm. *"Roger, HQ. Elite Archer designated lead, Team Three."* As Team Three, we'd all be on frequency three, and we tagged our Perscoms to reflect that and dialed it in.

Before any of us could ask Archer what the heck was going on, we had to wait while the other teams called in and their leaders were assigned. I was relieved to hear Cielle was with Scarlet. Only once we were organized did HQ come back on the general freq to brief us.

"We don't know a lot. This was a surprise attack. There are none of the major Othersiders, but there are swarms of the smaller ones, and they are highly organized. They attacked the town of Creedence from all sides, having apparently gotten into position during the night. The few reports we have indicate that the town is overrun, and the Othersiders are breaking into homes and shelters. The army is on the way as well, but it's going to be hand-to-hand, house-to-house,

and street-to-street fighting. No air support, no artillery support except outside of town."

Basically, the worst-case scenario, since from the report, all the Othersiders were *in* town. And they were organized, which had to mean a Folk Lord on site. My heart sank.

"*Folk Lord's been spotted,*" said Archer, confirming what I thought. "*Joy, you have the biggest number of Hounds. Keep back four and send the rest to look for him.*"

"Roger," I answered immediately.

"*We'll move as a team unless Kent says otherwise. When we hit the ground, follow me.*"

Well, that was the best we could do for planning in an unknown situation on the ground, with a Folk Lord orchestrating everything. We sat in the dark, the rattling vibration and the roar of the engine overhead, and hoped for the best.

In a remarkably short period of time, Archer got on the radio again. "*Coming in hot.*"

We hit the releases on our harnesses, and before I could even tell that the chopper had stopped moving, Archer was shouting, "*Go! Go! Go!*" We jumped out the door, hit the ground, ran a short distance out of rotor range, and summoned as the chopper lifted up and away. The area lit up with Glyphs, and the Hounds, sensing our urgency, came bursting through their Portals when we opened the Way.

Bya, take the six and look for the Folk Mage, the fancy one. There should be one bossing all the rest. Hold, Strike, Myrrdhin, and Gwalchmai with me.

Going, said Bya, and they were off, wearing their black grey-hound shape for stealth. The rest packed up around me, and as soon as I ID'd Archer we were off after him, running for the town. Parts were dark, parts were lit, and parts were on fire—not good signs. I put on my gas mask.

The first thing we hit, right at the edge of town, was a defensive perimeter of *Nagas* and Minotaurs. The Othersiders had made a poor choice for their first line of defense; neither had much in the way of Shields, and we just took them out with our assault rifles. The Hounds sucked up the manna, and within moments they were bursting with energy and we were bursting with magic.

And that was the last easy moment we had.

We got just inside the town when they hit us again. And this time they were Shielded.

There were Folk Mages there. I saw at least three—the feral kind. They stayed back, but they were Shielding their troops. And these *were* troops; they moved as a unit, they were disciplined, and they held their lines. These were nothing like the usual Othersider mobs that flung themselves at us until something got through. They used actual tactics and coordinated with each other, leaving no one too open to attack. The lights were still on in this part of town, and we could see them far too clearly for my liking.

"Joy, Tober, you have the best Shields. Drop what you're doing and cover us. Dazzle, light 'em up on my mark. Three. Two. One. Mark!"

Tober and I had already put up nested Shields over the whole group when Archer started counting down. At *"Mark!"* we *all* ducked and protected our eyes. Even so, with all the magical energy available to her, Dazzle put up a display I could see through my eyelids.

"*Lights out, Dazzle,*" Archer ordered. We looked up. The mobs of *Nagas*, Minotaurs, and Ogres were blinking blindly, unable to see. Behind them, the three feral Folk Mages stood there with tears pouring down their faces; they had lost the big Shields and only had their personal Shields, leaving their troops unprotected.

Archer took full advantage of that. "*Shields down! Hose 'em down!*" We cut loose with our assault rifles; Archer began firing off his levin bolt arrows, aiming for the nearest Folk Mage. I suddenly had a bright idea. As his first three arrows left his bow, I fired off a spell of my own, the one that made Shields brittle. My spell hit the mage's personal Shields right after the second of Archer's shots. The first two dissipated on the Shields, but the third one cracked it, and the fourth one shattered it. The Folk Mage didn't even have time to react; Archer's fifth shot took him in the head.

He went down and stayed down. As he fell, Archer nodded at me and then to the right; I targeted the second Folk Mage, and this one went down in three shots.

We turned to take out the third one, but he was gone; his vision must have cleared in time to see us killing his comrades, and he wasn't staying around to become victim number three.

Without those Shields, we made better progress. The Ogres and Minotaurs were resistant to bullets, but not bulletproof; the *Nagas* couldn't take rifle fire at all. We fought our way deeper into the town. But for every Othersider we killed, another came to take its place. Ogres were replaced by Redcaps, definitely harder to kill.

Nagas gave way to Vampires, which were smarter and stronger and had limited regeneration in the dark. Worst of all, the Minotaurs were replaced by Yeth-hounds, which could fight our Hounds one-on-one.

We were winning, but it was inch by bloody inch, and if it hadn't been for the Hounds faithfully feeding us magic ... we'd have already lost. We fought from light into darkness as we got into an area where all the power was out. We had night-vision goggles and put them on at Archer's order, but some of the Othersiders had the night vision of owls or cats. We weren't at a total disadvantage, but they were definitely better off than we were.

We battled our way around a corner, when suddenly our opposition turned and fled.

They didn't need to fight us anymore. Something more potent than Ogres and *Nagas* and Minotaurs lay around that corner.

Manticores. *Lots* of Manticores. In my NVGs it seemed like too many to count, rank upon rank of them crowding the street in front of us, stingers quivering with the eagerness to strike. And we couldn't use RPGs like we had on the first batch we encountered; we were surrounded by houses that almost certainly had innocent Cits cowering in there. Things looked grim.

A heartbeat later, Team One came around the same corner behind us, which included Hammer and Steel. I switched freqs quickly and yelled *"Manticores!"* on their freq, and suddenly those wonderful sturdy Shields sprang up to cover us just as the front rank of the Manticores charged.

We were dripping with sweat and barely holding our line as the sky lightened, and there *still* didn't seem to be an end to the Manticores. Sure, they were vulnerable to bullets, but . . .

"*Shields down on my mark!*" Archer called over our joint freq. Steel and Hammer dropped the Shields on cue, and the rest of us let loose with our ARs—but we didn't get long, twenty seconds if that. Then the Manticore tails came lashing down at us, and spearheads of three packed closely together rushed our line at the weaker points. Archer called for Shields up again, just in time to save us from those stingers.

We didn't dare have the Shields down for more than a couple volleys, because the Manticores were wicked quick. And they were *smart,* smarter than nearly every other "small" Othersider we'd ever encountered, possibly as smart as the Folk; they could tell by the way we readied our weapons when the Shields were about to come down, and they were as fast as we were to take advantage of the situation.

My Hounds were still diligently searching for the Folk Lord but hadn't found him yet. Team Four had Manticores of their own to deal with. Team Two was cut off from us by fires. Team Five was actually trapped in their street by the debris from fallen buildings, because Othersiders had deliberately toppled the buildings before and behind them. There *had* to be a Folk Lord orchestrating all this, but where was he?

Meanwhile, we—Team One and Team Three—were doing our best not to get divided up and picked off, because at this point it was pretty clear that was the Manticores' strategy. They made smoothly coordinated attacks at weak points when the Shields came down, trying to isolate someone stuck on the outside of the group. We had almost no room to maneuver. I couldn't even see past the people on either side of me.

I could certainly tell where Cielle was without seeing her. The Shield would come down, and this fat beam of energy would cut a swath through the Manticores from left to right. Unfortunately, there were so many of them, she couldn't give individuals more than a second of her attention, but her magic weapon still left them burning and howling in pain as it cut through them. The stink of burned hair and flesh was so thick that I was glad I'd resorted to my gas mask earlier to keep from choking on smoke.

Gas mask! Suddenly it dawned on me that there *was* something I could do besides fire till the barrel of my rifle was hot. I bent down and grabbed a handful of spent brass from the pile at my feet, and cast a delayed spell on it. The next time the Shield came down, I lobbed that handful of spent brass over the heads of the Manticores in front of us, into their rear ranks, and kicked off the skunk-spell that was on the casings. I could tell by the sudden agitation and bellows of outrage back there that it was working.

But while I'd been busy with that, the front ranks of the Manticores had made another push into us, and this time they succeeded in cutting someone off. I heard angry shouts, a scream—I turned my head in time to see one of those stinger tails whip down and back up again, and Archer snarled, *"They've got Denali!"*

Hammer and Steel switched tactics, and suddenly part of the front rank of Manticores got shoved back about ten feet. That gave all of us a clear view—and shot—at the Manticore with Denali in its mouth. It was midway through a turn to run off with him. There was an open Portal right behind it!

I let loose with levin bolts, Archer with his magic arrows, and Cielle gave a scream of pure rage and blasted it in the torso. In the next moment, my Hounds and Denali's swarmed the damned thing. It dropped Denali as it opened its mouth to screech in pain; two Hunters dashed in right under its nose and dragged Denali away, as Hounds nipped and tormented it, and Cielle's winged ones swooped in to harry it from above so it couldn't put its stinger into play. Hammer and Steel snapped the Shields back up again; it bellowed again in rage and pain, then pivoted on its hind legs and ran back through the Portal.

We found him! Bya shouted in triumph. *The Folk Lord.*

I looked down at Myrrdhin, who was pressed up against my legs. Without my even asking him, he said to me, *I will try to take us both to the rest of the pack. I will see to it that if we fail, we simply don't go anywhere.*

And with that, I clung on to his neck, and we *bamphed.*

We appeared right in the middle of my *Alebrijes* Hounds, between Bya and Dusana. And there, fifty yards from us, standing on a rooftop and illuminated by the first light of the sun, where he presumably had an excellent view of the chaos in the streets, was the golden Folk Lord.

I wanted to kill him. I *really* wanted to kill him. But even if I couldn't manage that, I had to get him to retreat so his flunkies would fall apart. So I levin bolted him, with the bolt carrying the embrittling spell with it. As he turned his head to look for the person who had fired on him, I let him have five bullets in the Shield.

The fifth one shattered it, and that was when he spotted me, just as the Hounds and I snapped up our Shields.

For one moment, as he locked eyes with me, the look on his face—I felt as if someone had just dumped me into an ice-covered lake at midwinter. The Folk are *not* human, and you can't read them like a human—but there was the promise of murder in his eyes, I swear it.

Then he smirked, smirked as if *he* knew something I didn't and when I found out about it I was going to hate myself. And then he opened up a Portal behind him and vanished.

In the next instant the assault fell apart. As the Hounds and I made our way back to our team on foot, Othersiders were streaming out of the town toward the open Portals on the outskirts. For the most part we pressed up close to the houses on the left side of the street, kept heavy Shields up, and avoided confrontations, although the Hounds quivered with the suppressed desire to attack.

By the time I got back to where the rest of the team ended up and reported to Kent, the last Othersiders were either dead or gone. Denali was unconscious, with a stinger-hole in his shoulder—once again, it was obvious that the Manticores had wanted him *alive*, not dead, because that strike took precision and timing.

As the residents of the town emerged from hiding, many of them screaming and crying, we discovered that there had been more to this raid than just the usual "break into the houses and eat everyone you can." And I found out just what that Folk Lord had been smirking about.

Because the Manticores had been after something else. At least half the children were gone—and according to the witnesses who could speak without weeping, they had been carried off and through Portals by the Manticores.

Kent sent everyone back on the choppers but himself, Archer, Scarlet, and Steel. As the most senior Elite, he had taken control of the area and, with the army commander, was fortifying and protecting the town while Scarlet, Archer, and Steel were taking statements.

Mark had gotten hurt—not badly, but he'd gotten blindsided by a charging Minotaur that had lost its ax and head-butted him instead, and he was bruised absolutely black all down one side, despite his body armor. I made him go to the medics even though he insisted that he was all right.

"Jessie would skin us both if you just go back to your quarters," I scolded him. "And she'll do worse than skin you if you go back on duty without being checked out."

While he continued to protest, I walked him to the medbay. I kind of hoped we could avoid his wife, Jessie, who worked there, at least as long as I was with him. We weren't the only Hunters there, either, though most of the attention was on Denali, who had been hooked up to IVs and monitors as soon as he'd been brought in.

I managed to get a medic's attention long enough for him to take scans and pronounce Mark more or less fit for duty, and pass him a bottle of mild painkillers that I knew he wasn't going to take. Just then, Jessie spotted us both there. It was too late for me to get away gracefully, so I stayed put as she turned her attention to Mark.

"What happened?" she demanded.

"Nothing," said Mark.

I snorted. "He got body-slammed by a Minotaur, and half of him is bruised, but no broken bones. Medics gave him painkillers, said he's fit for duty."

"Give 'em t'me," she demanded, holding out her hand. Sheepishly, he did so, and she examined them, then shook out two. "Hev you taken 'em?" she asked. He shook his head. "Take these here now," she ordered. He did so, dry-swallowing them, a trick I wished I could learn. "I'll track you down in six hours if'n you're not on a callout, an' make damn sure you take two more."

I pretended not to notice any of this. She peeled up the side of his tunic to have a look too, which I also pretended not to notice.

"How's Denali?" I asked, when she was done.

Her expression faded from annoyance into real concern. "He's still in a coma. No one's been able to figger out the poison those monsters used on him, an' fillin' him up with th' wrong antivenin is gonna do more harm than good. All we c'n do is support him, treat any other symptoms, an' hope it wears off in time."

I grimaced, although having gotten a good look at him before they loaded him into a chopper, this was pretty much what I had expected to hear. Short of catching a live Manticore and milking the sting for venom to make antivenin, there wasn't much anyone could do about Denali's condition.

I was about to excuse myself and get out of there, leaving Jessie to further read her husband the riot act, when Tober came striding into the medbay. "Joy, Knight, have you seen what's on the news-feed channel?"

Since neither of us had looked at *anything* since we came in, we both shook our heads. Tober aimed his Perscom at the nearest monitor, ran it back a little before we got a good look at it, and restarted it. The newsfeed channel came up right in the middle of something.

It showed a line of people in some kind of armor, standing right at the Prime Barrier on our side, spaced about a hundred yards apart. "What the—" Mark began, but Tober shushed him and turned the sound up.

"...Senior Psimon Abigail Drift's new deployment for PsiCorps," the announcer was saying brightly. "All Psimons have been pulled from regular duty to form the new Barrier Patrol."

The cam zoomed in on one of the silent, motionless figures. *Tall* figures, easily seven feet, and bulky to boot. "Each Psimon has been fitted with armor for protection, and a psionic amplifier, newly in production, that enables each Psimon to do the work of twenty." The cam panned around to the front; the Psimon was wearing really tough carbon-fiber armor, and a faceless helmet that somehow managed to look friendly. "Psimons will each take eight-hour shifts at the Barrier, not only to detect Othersiders, but deter them as well. Senior Psimon Abigail Drift had this to say earlier, at the first deployment of PsiCorps at the Barrier."

Abigail Drift's weasel face appeared; she was standing at a podium on the steps of the PsiCorps building. "Today marks a new day in the safeguarding of our city," she intoned. "Thanks to tireless work by PsiCorps scientists and engineers, we have found a way to make Psimons truly effective against the Othersiders. PsiCorps has always been a bastion of protection for the Cits of Apex, but now they are more than that; they are as effective as any army. In fact, they can do what the army cannot do—they can ensure that the Othersiders are dealt with, and there will be no collateral damage. My Psimons can turn the Othersiders against each other, quickly disrupting and subverting any attempted attack on the Barrier and forcing them to kill each other. No longer must the Cits of Apex settle for passive protection and detection of trouble, and wait for response from the army and the Hunters. PsiCorps will provide *active* protection and detection, twenty-four hours a day, seven days a week."

Mark and I exchanged an incredulous glance. "Do you suppose she figured out a way to boost her Psimons that isn't going to kill them?" he said.

"She must have—" I began, but then the screen went to a static image, the logos of PsiCorps and Apex City, side by side, flanked by two Psimons in armor, with a third in armor kneeling at the front. Their hands were conspicuously empty of weapons. "PsiCorps, day and night," the announcer said. "Guarding *your* city!" There was absolutely no doubt in my mind that this new slogan had been deliberately phrased to echo the one Apex News used with stories about Hunters: *And that's your Hunters on the job! Keeping Apex and the territories safe!*

And the screen switched to the announcer, and business news. Tober turned it off.

"What are we going to do about this?" he demanded.

"You tell me," I replied, before Mark could say anything. "Drift is not only completely within her rights to do this, she's *obligated* to, if she really has found a way to boost her Psimons without killing them. Can we stand around at the Barrier all day?"

"Well... no," Tober admitted.

"Seems to me this is a win for us," Mark observed. "You look how she's got her Psimons spaced—even if she moves them to five hundred or a thousand yards apart, that still means she's going to have to pull all the snoops in the city and armor them up to keep them at the Barriers day and night. Do you really care if they do that?"

"Well... no," Tober repeated. "But..."

"Psimons themselves are not our enemies, Tober," Mark said reasonably. "Drift, now... she's got a hatchet just waiting for Charmand, and she's dying to replace us. But the prefect knows that, and he knows never to turn his back on her. As for us—well, they can't be on callout *and* stand duty at the Barrier all day. That frees the Hunters up to patrol inside, and us to take care of trouble outside."

"Yes, but—"

"So the best way we can back him is to keep doing what we do already... excellently." Mark concluded. Jessie nodded in agreement, and so, finally, did I. "Don't forget that Psimons saved our bacon at the first Barrier Battle. If they can do now what they did then, that's going to be a big weight off our shoulders. Any amount of Othersiders they can stop at the Barrier is going to mean fewer we have to deal with in the city. And *that* means the more of us who can deal with what's going on outside."

Tober and I exchanged a glance, and I shrugged. "He's right. The one thing we *should* worry about is whether or not the Psimons really can do what she claimed without burning out and dying. They aren't going to be helping all that much if they can't. And we need to be ready for the consequences of their failure, if it happens."

Tober's face cleared. "Well, that's right. So what do we do about it?"

"The first thing we do is make sure the armorer knows all about this as soon as he gets in," I replied. "I'll go talk to Hammer and Mei. You go talk to Flashfire. Mark already knows. That's six of us. So whoever is not on callout when Kent gets in reports to him with everything we know."

Mark and Tober both nodded. Jessie got an almost-sly look on her face. "I c'n make sure Mark is here," she declared. "I wanna ice down them bruises anyway."

I looked at Mark, who shrugged. Or rather, shrugged with one shoulder. Those bruises had to be hurting, and if it meant he was going to be here to make sure Kent heard all about this, well… "Works for me," I said.

"All right," he agreed, and texted something on his Perscom. I assumed it was to Kent, asking him for contact as soon as he returned. "I'll ping you in on this if you're still in HQ, Joy," he said as he lay down so his wife could begin working on him. "I'd rather you were the one to handle this anyway."

I sighed, but agreed.

As it happened, I needn't have worried. Kent actually saw the line of armored Psimons at the Barrier as he came in, and being Kent, the first thing he did was contact someone at HQ to find out what was going on. Only when he had learned more did he answer Mark's message, and at that point he was on his way to a meeting with my uncle, along with the brigadier general who was in charge of all of the army assigned to protect Apex. The general, I learned later, was not a happy man; Drift had swooped in and absconded with all the Psimons assigned to the army without so much as an "Excuse me, I need these."

This was way past my pay grade, and I figured if there was anything they wanted me to know, they'd let me in on it soon enough. As for me, after another callout—a small one that only needed a team of four this time—I had something else in mind that needed doing.

The problem was, in order to do it, I'd have to get on the other side of the Prime Barrier. Without anyone knowing.

At night.

When my shift was over, I went to my room and summoned Bya and Myrrdhin. I patted my bed and they both jumped up and laid themselves down on it. I sat cross-legged on the comforter opposite them.

Guys, I thought at them, *I need to talk to Torcion. Which means I need to get on the other side of the Barrier.*

You could summon him here, Myrrdhin pointed out. *To this room, if you liked . . .*

No way in hell am I bringing him on this side of the Barrier to memorize a location for a Portal, I said immediately. *No, it has to be in Spillover or not at all.*

She's right, Bya agreed. *We need to think of a place in Spillover that is safe at night.*

Myrrdhin thought about this. *Or we think of a place in Spillover that we can* make *safe.*

It got very quiet. I knew better than to interrupt at this point; I couldn't think of any place that would do, and they needed to compare mental notes. Finally they both looked up at me again.

We have a place. We will need to go for a walk so you can summon Dusana. We will take you there, then you can summon the rest of the pack and we will make the place safe.

And that was what we did. I left my Perscom on the bed, made sure I was armed with my old weapons that were still in my closet, and we slipped outside. I summoned Dusana and we *bamphed* our way across the landscape, to the Barriers, through a Pylon, and to the spot the Hounds had decided on. It turned out to be the ruined building where Ace's brother had died. We lucked out. It was empty. It was also *dark.* I summoned an entire fleet of mage-lights; I figured better to chance that something might see them and come investigate than to get ambushed in the dark by something I couldn't see.

The Hounds deployed themselves around the edge, and I stood in the middle with mage-lights overhead, and called. "Torcion! Torcion! Tor—"

"Right here, shepherd," said that smooth, amused voice from behind me.

I managed to turn without looking as if he'd sent my heart right into my throat. "We need to talk," I said. Firmly, I hoped.

"I thought we were," he replied, with a slight smirk. *Somehow they manage to be alien* and *have all the most annoying characteristics of humans.*

But then I remembered what his people had just done, and I smoldered with rage. "One of your friends just staged a raid on a town today and kidnapped about a hundred children. He tried to kidnap one of us too." I had stalked toward him, and now I was right up in his face. Or at least as up in his face as I could get, seeing that I was at least a foot and a half shorter than he was. "What does he want with those children?" I snarled.

He looked down at me, as startled as if a kitten had suddenly grown the teeth and claws of a cougar. "It seems as if he has learned that one can gain more *aetheria* by keeping someone alive than by merely slaying him." His brows creased. "This does not bode well for me or for you, shepherd. What did he look like?"

Curbing my temper, I described the golden Folk Lord, and Torcion's brow creased even more. "That is Laetrenier. He is the chief architect of the Grand Alliance. I do not know if he will keep this wisdom to himself, in order to gain ascendancy, or impart it to the rest of the Alliance, in order to strengthen the whole. In either case, this is dire news for those like me, and for your kind."

"Well, what are we going to *do* about it?" I growled, clenching my jaw with equal amounts of fury and fear.

"For the moment, *we* are going to do nothing at all, for you and I are not yet a *we*," he replied maddeningly, with a slight toss of his head that made the beads in it sparkle. "You may do whatever you choose. I am going to consider my options." He made as if to move away.

"Wait!" I snarled. "I'm not done yet!"

I really, really did not expect him to stop, but he did. "The Manticores—the monsters with stings in their tails—they stung a friend of mine. He's unconscious—"

I was going to ask for the antidote, but he waved his hand. "He will awaken in time. There is no great cause for concern."

"And . . ." I stopped. Did I *want* to tell him about the Psimons and their new, supposedly boosted abilities? What if he was just stringing me along to get whatever information I'd give him? I'd been suspicious of Josh; shouldn't I be even more suspicious of a *Folk Lord*?

He peered at me quizzically, the mage-light casting flattering light on his disturbingly handsome face.

"And what are we supposed to do to get the children back?" I said instead.

"I will admit . . . this troubles me," he said, finally. "I will give it thought."

This time he did turn and walk away, far enough to cast a Portal. But before he stepped through it, he paused one more time and looked back at me.

And then at Myrrdhin.

The Hound nodded once as if the Folk Lord had spoken to him. Then Torcion said to me, "I think you and I are tentative allies, shepherd. When I have information for you, your companion there will bring you a blue rose."

Then he stepped through the Portal and was gone.

12

DUSANA GOT ME BACK into my room without incident, and my Perscom and vid-screen showed no one had tried to contact me in all that time I was gone. I felt a little weak with relief that I had managed to get out and back without incident. I was strapping the Perscom back on when my vid-screen lit up with an incoming message alert.

"Accept," I said, and sat down as the screen brightened to show my uncle.

"If you don't get any callouts tomorrow, I want you to do some research for me in Spillover," he said with a very slight lift of one eyebrow.

"Would it be acceptable if I do it after I get off shift?" I replied. "I know it'll be dark, but with all my Hounds, I should be all right."

He sucked on his lower lip a moment. "I'll tell Kent to assign you some extra protection," he replied. "But yes, that's acceptable. I see your point. If we get another callout like the one today, you should be able to respond."

"Yes, sir," I replied, and the screen went blank again.

So . . . he and Kent must have put their heads together and decided I needed to see if Josh knew anything about the new Psimon program. That was pretty reasonable—a good idea, in fact. No stone unturned and all that.

Mind you, *I* didn't think Josh knew anything we hadn't already guessed, but he was our only contact who had any real insight at all about PsiCorps. At this point we didn't have much else.

Thanks to nerves and energy expenditure, I was starving. I ate what was in my cooler unit and went straight to bed. I had a feeling it was going to be a long day.

I wasn't blasted awake by a callout alarm, at least, but I'd barely gotten dressed when the callout came. Miracle of miracles, it wasn't a full-team callout, but it was the first of four that day. I dragged back in after the last, wondering if the night shift had been hit that hard. At least the Othersiders had acted *normally*, attacking with barely controlled chaos.

I hadn't forgotten Uncle's plan, so as soon as my shift was over and I got a hot meal into me, I headed for the armory. But Kent wasn't alone.

Mark Knight was with him. Was *this* Uncle's idea of "extra protection"? I'd thought it just meant he'd issue me a special weapon or something!

"Joy, Knight, I've called a pod to take you to the Pylon at your entrance point," Kent said without any warm-up. "Joy, you can brief Mark once you're on the other side of the Barrier. Knight, you might want to pack an RPG launcher."

Well, better him than me. Those suckers were heavy.

"Report in person to me when you get back," Kent concluded, and checked his Perscom. "Your pod's here."

Nice thing about Christers. They're used to being told what to do and not questioning it. Mark kept his lip buttoned all the way to the Pylon, so to fill the silence, I told him about the Folk Lord I'd chased off back at the Manticore ambush.

He made some rumbling noises. "So I guess *he* was the one that wanted kidnapped humans?" he said at last.

"Not humans in general," I corrected. "Children, and at least one Hunter. You think that's significant?"

"Dunno. They *did* try to carry off those ag-workers. Maybe they got their hands on some adults from Spillover, and—they weren't right, somehow?" He shrugged.

"Kids are more easily intimidated," I mused aloud. "Also more easily scared. Maybe they're better sources of manna because of that? We already know Hunters are better sources of manna than Cits, so that could be why they wanted one or more of us." Of course I couldn't tell him what Torcion had told me, but maybe I could steer him in the right direction.

"You think now they want to farm humans for manna?" he hazarded. "Well, it's an idea. Which is more than we had before."

"It's a pretty ugly idea, but it's the one that makes the most sense given what little we know," I replied. Then I made a face—which, of course, he couldn't see in the dark of the pod. "I'm beginning to feel like I somehow brought a curse down on us. I show up, and suddenly bad things happen."

"I prefer to think that God knew bad things were going to happen, so He sent you," Mark countered. I blinked and looked at him hard. He sounded serious. He looked serious. Holy crud, he couldn't *be* serious, could he?

"Well, then God has terrible taste in saviors," I replied. "Because I haven't managed to accomplish much of anything."

He snorted but didn't say a word.

It wasn't dark out here after sundown; the Pylon and the Barrier both glowed with a bluish incandescence, too faint to be seen by day but quite obvious by night. We got through to the other side, put on our NVGs, and summoned. Mark turned to me once the Way was opened and our Hounds were trotting through.

"All right, what's all this cloak-and-dagger stuff?" he demanded. "I'm tired of being a mushroom here."

"And I don't blame you. Come on, I'll explain as we walk." With Bya in front, Myrrdhin behind, Mark's Angels overhead, and the rest packed up around us, I told him everything, from when Josh came to me in desperation to when Scarlet, Kent, Uncle, and Bya and I smuggled him out.

When I got to the end of that part, Mark let out a big sigh. "Darn it all, Joy, you should have come to me earlier. Josh's my buddy too, y'know."

"I didn't want you to find yourself in the crosshairs of a PsiCorps investigation," I told him truthfully. "And if anyone had asked you about him, I wanted you to be able to look surprised and worried. You're a worse actor than I am."

He rubbed the back of his head. "S'truth," he admitted. "I can't act for spit."

It was a wonderful warm night, with crickets and things making soft sounds all around us, and fireflies blinking in every direction. It was too bad there were so many things out here that would kill us if we gave them the chance. Having to keep your head on a swivel rather ruined the lovely evening. I certainly didn't dare to relax in Spillover, not for a minute.

But, oh, it was *so* good to be able to talk to Mark at length about Josh.

"... and he's been holed up in one of the old bunkers ever since," I concluded. "Now Uncle wants to know if he knows anything about what Drift's done to the Psimons. That's why we're out here, to find that out."

"Probably not," Mark replied. "If he did, I'm pretty sure he would have told you when you were out here during the storm."

I hadn't said anything about that, but now that Mark knew Josh was here, it was pretty easy for him to put that together with my absence during the storm and come up with the right answer. Mark was a great many things, but stupid wasn't one of them.

"I'm pretty sure too, but maybe he doesn't know he knows something," I pointed out. "It's worth asking." It was a relief to finally get all of this off my chest. Now if only I could tell someone about Torcion as well ...

We paused when Bya alerted me to let a flock of Willow Wisps pass in front of us. They didn't know we were there, and there was no point in starting a fight that might bring more Othersiders running when they heard the noise.

We felt our way into the ruined building, guided by what we could see in our NVGs. The stairway was pitch-black, but we managed to get down it all right, and the door lock clicked open in response to the presence of my Perscom. We all squeezed inside the antechamber—it was a tight fit—and once the outer door was closed, I tapped the code Josh and I had worked out on the inner door, then applied my Perscom to it as well.

Mark shoved the unlocked door open, allowing us to spill into the big room and turn on our headlamps. Josh was just emerging from the kitchen door. "I don't suppose you brought pizza?" Josh said.

"Not this time, buddy."

Josh stared at Mark with his mouth open. Mark took his hand, then pulled him into a back-slapping hug. "How are you holding up out here? Kent and the prefect sent us. Joy filled me in on what's going on."

"I'm doing better than I would with Drift," he replied. "But I'm glad to see you. I never thought I would miss people, until there weren't any around."

"Well, speaking of that particular devil, that's why we're here," I put in. I was giving him as much of a look-over as I could in the light from my headlamp, and truth to be told, he was looking better than he had in a while. Better rested, for one thing. In that moment I definitely envied him. It wouldn't be so bad to be out here alone with nothing to do but eat and sleep and read.

"In that case, come into my den and make yourselves comfortable," he replied.

We followed him into the storeroom, and we all sat down on

his improvised "couch" made of mattresses. He offered us water, which I was glad to take, and the Basic Ration Biscuits, which we passed on. The Hounds arranged themselves around us, making things much warmer and cozier. This was not the worst living situation in the world, but it *was* damp and cold down there.

"Well, Drift showed her hand," I said after Mark gave me a little nod, indicating that I should take the lead here. I described the Psimons in their armor, how they'd been pulled from regular duty and put on the Barrier, and how Drift was making quite the big deal out of it. Josh listened, his brows knitted, until I came to the end.

"She's not lying about pulling all the Psimons," he said immediately. "To put that many Psimons on the Barriers would take *all* the Psimons. And we're not as tough as Hunters; we couldn't do twelve-hour shifts. It would have to be shifts of no more than eight hours at a time. But I never heard of anything like this, even in the planning stage. She has to have been keeping this very quiet somehow."

"The armor didn't look all that special," Mark said after a moment. "She could have had that in the works for a while."

"But . . . if she's managed to figure out a way of multiplying a Psimon's power without killing him—that's not only new, it's a game-changer. . . ." Josh suddenly got a look on his face.

"Well?" I demanded.

"That might be more than armor. That might be life support," he said. "In fact, that might be why she put them into it in the first place. If those suits are big enough, they could hold a lot of medical equipment."

Mark and I exchanged a look. "Is seven feet tall and really broad big enough?" I asked.

Mark nodded. "Most Psimons aren't what you'd call *robust*," he replied. "There'd be more than enough room in those suits for a Psimon and his twin."

"So plenty of room for equipment." Josh nodded. "We've got a lot of life-support stuff Drift hasn't let out to the general public. Some Psimons . . . well, they're not exactly *functional*. They can do their jobs, but they have to be drugged up to do them. And some really strong Psimons kind of forget to do things, like breathe, when they are concentrating on controlling something."

We questioned Josh every way we could think of, but he still had no idea how Drift was boosting her Psimons, or what, besides the obvious, her plan might be. Finally I asked him the one thing I hadn't yet.

"Do you want to go back?" I asked. "I mean, if you know you aren't going to burn out and die . . ." I thought going back would be possibly the worst thing he could do, personally, but it was his decision after all.

"Well, that's the thing, I *don't* know that," he countered. "You can't see into those suits. You don't know what she's done to those Psimons. Why put them into faceless suits with helmets you can't see through if there's nothing to hide? They could have tentacles growing out of their heads for all I know. No, no thanks. I don't trust Drift at all. Besides, if I did go back, no matter what my excuse might be, there isn't a chance in hell that she wouldn't put me through a full Psi-assisted interrogation about where I'd been, and that would get you, Prefect Charmand, and the armorer all in trouble. I can't do that to you. I just wish you could figure out somewhere for me to go."

"Nowhere safe," Mark said after a moment of hesitation. "The attacks on the towns around Apex are getting worse, and the Othersiders have started kidnapping people now. Kids mostly, but they almost got Denali. The ones on those raids are being commanded and organized by some sort of superior Folk Mage. I don't think anything running wild out here is going to find you...." He shook his head. "I never thought I'd be thinking of the Othersiders out here in Spillover as *petty*, but compared to what we've been facing, they are. They're certainly not very bright, and even if they sensed you, I don't think they'd be able to find you."

Josh looked as if that was cold comfort. I emptied my pockets of those energy squares I liked to carry, to cheer him up. They were pretty tasty and a big improvement over Basic Ration Biscuits. "Next time I come I'll bring some kind of decent food," I promised as I stood up to leave. Mark patted him on the back sympathetically and also stood. "Oh, hey, I know—I have something with me." He rummaged around in his backpack and emerged with a hardened tablet, which was like a Perscom but way bigger. "Here," he said, handing it over to Josh. "You can at least watch vids or play games. I've got a lot of games loaded on it, vids too."

Josh lit up, and the two of them proceeded to bond over the darned thing. I did my level best not to look impatient or annoyed, although I was both. Josh was a real Cit and had probably never been more than fifty feet from a vid-screen for his entire life. He had no idea of how to keep himself entertained all by his lonesome. But then I kicked the annoyance in the head, because it was nice to see Josh being something other than worried. It was also nice to see the two of them being friends again; Mark probably hadn't even texted Josh after Josh and I had broken up. Oh, I'd explained it all to Mark so he wouldn't get the wrong idea, but Mark was a loyal guy. He'd probably think he needed to be "on my side."

Finally, Mark finished showing off every last file he'd loaded on the pad, clapped Josh on the back again, and said, "Glad I had that with me. Hopefully, this will keep you from going insane."

"I'm going to mount a holder on the front of that charging bike as soon as you leave," Josh replied gratefully. "Actually—before you leave, let me make sure the coast is clear."

He thumbed his Perscom, frowned for a moment in concentration, and thumbed it again, turning the Psi-shield off and on. "Nothing out there to worry about, and nothing at all lurking around in the building."

"Thanks, Josh," Mark said, then he gave me what he probably supposed was a subtle wink, and whistled to his Hounds to follow as he left, giving me some privacy with Josh.

Before I could second-guess myself, I sort of threw myself at him and kissed him.

At least I was pretty good at the kissing part.

"Did I give you enough time?" Mark asked anxiously as my Hounds and I joined him outside. I pulled down my NVGs and blinked hard to adjust my vision to the blurry green-and-black view around me.

"Yes. No. I don't know," I replied, flushing and glad he couldn't see it.

"I probably did, then," he said with satisfaction—a little too much, if you ask me. What is it about married people that they always want to hook up everyone around them? Couples were like that back in Safehaven too. "Let's get out of here. What's our pretense for being out here, anyway?"

"Meeting with Uncle's rebel informant," I said. "The informant told us that the rebels are suffering heavy attrition from the Othersiders, and he's looking for a way to get to another city where it might be safer."

I made it up on the spot, but it was a plausible story and one that would be impossible to disprove.

"Excellent." He nodded. "Let's get out of here fast. Any good reason why we shouldn't ride Dusana?"

"Only that we have the chance of coming up on something the Hounds can't see," I pointed out. "Just because we can all see in the dark, it doesn't mean we can see well."

Mark thought about that. "As opposed to not getting a full night's sleep . . ."

"Point." I turned to Dusana, but he had already made himself big enough for both of us to ride, and had knelt so we could mount, me in front, Mark behind. We got on, and Dusana took off at a lope, going roughly four times as fast as we could have walking.

"So, Jessie's pregnant," Mark said, too casually, in my ear. There was no mistaking the mixed emotions in his voice. Pride, of course; most men like to have their virility confirmed, especially Christers, who are invested in producing as many kids as possible. But there was worry, and given our current situation, it was justifiable.

"Sending her back to your parents?" I asked without making any of the mean remarks that I was thinking. Because to be honest, I don't care *what* his deity said, getting pregnant in the middle of a situation where Othersiders were essentially laying siege to Apex was a pretty bad idea. And Safehaven was called that for a reason.

"She's insisting on staying here." More worry in his voice now. I couldn't think of any way I could reassure him that he hadn't already used to try to reassure himself.

"There is no safer place in all of Apex than Hunter HQ," I said finally, and left it at that. I changed the subject to Denali and whether or not Mark's people had ever seen Manticores or dealt with anything that had a venomous stinger. But I was glad when Dusana got us to the Pylon and our waiting pod.

Morning began with the callout alert going off at the same time as my alarm. Thanks to Dusana, we'd made good time last night, and reciting our cover story hadn't taken all that long, so we'd gotten to bed more or less on time.

But this morning the choppers didn't take us far. In fact, the Barrier was visible from where they dropped us off.

Like many towns that had done away with their defenses because they were so close to Apex, this one was the next thing to a sitting duck—more so because the only use they seemed to have for their concrete defensible buildings was as storehouses. The good news was that we had gotten here so fast, the Manticores were only just starting to pour out of the Portals. The bad news was that those Portals were inside the town. *Right* inside the town—in the middle of it, to be exact. Minotaurs had already set up defensive lines on every street into town, with *Nagas* behind them. Once again, they were coordinated and disciplined, and this time they had something new: actual physical shields, like Romans or knights would have, along with their swords and axes. As we clashed with their lines, it quickly became apparent that the shields were the focus of individual static Shield spells.

So this Lord Laetrenier learned from his mistakes. No entrusting the Shields to Folk Mages who could be disabled by a simple dazzling spell.

Yeah, but he doesn't realize that will only make it easier to take down the Shields. Static Shield spells weren't self-renewing. Break them, and they stayed broken. "Static Shield spells on the physical shields. I'm working middle to right," I said into the radio, and proceeded to plant embrittling spells on all those shiny shields.

"Middle to left," said Scarlet, who'd learned the trick from me. Moments later, bullets started hitting the Shields, and the Shields began to fail. Spectacularly.

Just as we were starting to fight our way in . . . more choppers started arriving.

But they were *not* the army reinforcements that I had thought we would get.

No, what spilled out of the choppers were people in bulky armor in PsiCorps colors, with closed, "friendly-looking" helmets—helmets you couldn't see into.

They split up in a highly coordinated fashion, half running left, half running right. As the ones nearest us took up stationary positions, it became obvious that they were arranging themselves in a circle around the town, spaced an equal distance apart from each other.

I was too busy shooting *Nagas* and trying to get to the Manticores before they broke into houses and started abducting kids to pay much attention to the Psimons as they got themselves arranged to their liking. But I sure noticed the difference when they had.

Because suddenly, the *Nagas* near me turned their backs on me and started attacking the Manticores.

They weren't effective as attackers, since the Manticores just turned and started darting them with their tail-stingers—one after the other, killing them dead—but they *were* effective at keeping the Manticores from breaking into the buildings. Howls of rage were countered by angry hissing; the *Nagas* always lost, but they got in some good hits with those swords they carried. By the time the Manticores finished off the *Nagas*, they were all wounded and bleeding, and now they had to contend with us.

And then, suddenly, they had to contend with each other. With the *Nagas* gone, the Psimons turned the Manticores against themselves.

Slashing claws and darting stingers made wading directly into the fray a bad, bad idea ... but on the other hand, bullets and magic worked, even if we had to be more careful of where we were shooting this time because so many of the buildings were wooden-walled.

It appeared that the Manticores were immune to the venom of their own kind, but being stuck by a stinger as long as my lower arm was not doing them any good, either.

"*Break up and spread out,*" Kent ordered. "*Take advantage of what PsiCorps is doing for as long as they can keep it up!*"

The other members of my team split off to the right and left, leaving me and my pack to tackle the street alone—a task that was pathetically easy, since the Psimon about twenty yards behind me seemed to have the situation well in hand. Still . . .

Hevajra, go back and guard the Psimon. Take Hold with you, I ordered. While I might loathe Drift, that Psimon was on my side, and I wasn't going to leave him hanging out to dry.

Or her. No telling in that armor.

Alert us if something comes after him, I added as Hevajra and Hold peeled off and dashed behind us. *Or if it looks like he's having any trouble.*

Then I loaded a new clip and proceeded to stitch Manticores with lines of carefully placed bullets.

It was over as quickly as it began. The Portal at the end of the street I was on abruptly closed, leaving the few Manticores left without a way to escape. "Elite Joy. Portal closed!" I announced, but I was by far from being the only one reporting the same thing. The Portals were closing all over the town, leaving the Othersiders with nowhere to escape. In fifteen minutes, we had the last of them mopped up, and in twenty, the town was ours, without a single kidnapped or even injured Cit.

Sadly, the bodies were going to goo; I'd hoped, despite the mess it would make in cleanup, that they would have stayed solid. I had a notion of collecting stingers and poison sacs to use in making antivenin.

I walked back toward the Psimon in his armor; he was still standing there in the street, as if the armor had frozen into position. Well, if Josh was right, maybe it had. If that Psimon had completely exhausted himself, he might be on life support about now.

"You did fantastic work," I said to the helmet visor, which didn't show any sort of change. "I have to thank you, both you and everyone from PsiCorps who turned up here."

Nothing.

"Is there anything I can do for you?" I persisted. "Anything I can get for you?"

Still nothing.

I hesitated to touch that armor. It looked pretty formidable, if you looked past the pretty colors and patterns and actually paid attention to how bulky it was. There might be—in fact, there probably were—defenses built into it, defenses I might trigger with a well-intentioned touch.

"Should I call for your evac?" I suggested. I might have gone further and just done it, but at that moment the same choppers that had brought the Psimons began arriving again. As soon as they touched down, the Psimon turned and began walking back toward his ride.

But this time there was something very mechanical about the way he was moving, as if it was the suit doing the walking and he was just along for the ride. This was nothing like the clumsy but natural running he'd done to get in place. That impression was reinforced when he got to the chopper and stopped, and two men jumped down out of it and picked up the suit with the aid of a hook and pulley and hauled it inside.

So . . . maybe Drift isn't killing Psimons anymore, but they aren't in real good shape when they're finished with a fight. . . . Despite how much I disliked Drift—or actually maybe because I hated Drift—I felt a huge surge of sympathy for the exhausted person in there, too weak to move on his own.

Cielle had come up beside me and watched as the crew loaded five more Psimons into the eight-man chopper that way. "Looks like they aren't leaving under their own power," she observed with a sideways glance at me.

"That's what I was thinking," I agreed. And as the chopper took off, I added, "Let's go find out if they're all that way."

We managed to catch three more choppers loading before they were all gone. Some of the Psimons *were* getting in on their own, but most weren't. Looked as if Josh might have been right.

And that would be an interesting observation to make to Kent.

13

"DID ANY OF YOU see cams that weren't ours out there?" Kent demanded as we all stared at the newsfeed in the armory. He was looking at me as he said that, and I shook my head. The rest of the Elite and partners on the day shift crowded around, and no one looked happy about what we were watching.

"I didn't see anything like a strange cam. But I wasn't looking for cams, either," I admitted. "Because . . . well, we were busy."

Kent snorted—a *You'd better have been busy* snort—and we all turned our attention back to the newsfeed.

Which was basically a nonstop paean of praise for PsiCorps. As we stood there staring, I wondered if the Cits of Apex thought their newspeople had gone mad, because PsiCorps usually went out of their way to stay out of the newsfeeds.

This was the second time we'd all watched it; the first time it had begun on the monitors in the mess, and we hadn't much paid attention to it since it focused on the raid we'd managed to avert with the assistance of the Psimons. But then . . . things had gone sideways, and someone had shouted an indignant "Hey!" and pointed, and we'd all turned our focus on the monitors in what quickly became dead silence.

Because unless you paid close attention to the action, it looked as if PsiCorps had obliterated the Othersiders almost single-handedly. There were a few shots of Hunters, but they concentrated on us doing decidedly non-magical things, like mowing the Manticores down with AR fire. The excited commentary on the raid—focusing on how the Psimons were making the Othersiders fight each other—was followed by an interview with . . . of course . . . Abigail Drift.

The interviewer (one I didn't recognize) was practically fawning and bowing at the feet of the head of PsiCorps. For her part, Drift looked as sleek and self-satisfied as a well-fed cat. Someone had gone to great lengths to polish her up for the cams, too, since she didn't look nearly as much like a weasel as she usually did.

"Senior Psimon . . ." the interviewer began.

"You may call me Psimon Drift, Perry," she said in honeyed tones.

"Psimon Drift, then," said "Perry," and then he actually simpered. "The footage of PsiCorps in action in their new role is nothing short of amazing! Why did you keep these new developments in PsiCorps under wraps for so long?"

"Well, Perry, we at PsiCorps have a policy that we don't reveal anything to the public unless we know it's proven and battle-ready,"

Drift replied. "What's the point in promising something, making the Cits feel safe, then having those promises come to nothing?"

"She means us, of course," Steel growled. "She doesn't dare say it, because we'd be able to prove a direct lie like that, but that's what she's implying."

"She might be talking about the techs," Mei pointed out, but she sounded doubtful. "There *are* rumors that the Barriers are failing."

"If that was what she meant, that would be what she said," Kent countered, shifting his weight from foot to foot. "She knows what she's doing."

"And how long have you been working on this project?" the interviewer asked, looking as if he was hanging on her every word.

"Several years, Perry. Psi-powers aren't *magic,* after all. They are scientific, measurable, and reliable, and you always know what you are going to get and what any given rated Psimon is capable of. So we had to approach the problem of boosting psionic powers just as scientifically." She smiled into the camera. "Our biggest mistake at the Barrier Battle was not having armor, of course. Without armor, a Psimon who is concentrating with all his mind on controlling a dozen or so monsters is terribly vulnerable. Because we deployed before our armor was ready, we lost far too many valuable Psimons."

"That's probably true," Kent said thoughtfully, "but not for the reason she's implying. I have information that most of the inside of that armor is life support. They lost Psimons because the Psimons exhausted themselves into cardiac arrest. The life support of the armor is keeping that from happening."

I wondered about that. Because I distinctly remembered normal Psimons in their mid-twenties or early thirties lying dead, looking like eighty-year-olds. I was sure cardiac arrest had something to do with their deaths . . . but what had *aged* them like that?

"But, of course," Drift continued, looking sincerely into the cam, "every Psimon is absolutely dedicated to the welfare of Apex. It is an honor to be able to sacrifice ourselves for the good of the city."

"Funny, Drift, we didn't see *you* out there on the Barriers," muttered Mark.

Someone else made a gagging sound.

"Now, with the delivery of the armor, we can take up the task of providing the first line of defense for Apex. And you saw how effective we are." She smiled as the sycophant nodded eagerly. "No citizen of Apex need ever be worried about the Barriers again. Nothing can pass *us* to get to them. And, of course," she added magnanimously, "that will leave the Hunters free to deal with Othersiders far from the city where they can't do any damage."

"But—we *don't* do any—" Cielle spluttered, turning bright red with anger, which clashed terribly with her pink hair. "We never—we haven't—*oh!*"

Kent turned the monitor off, which was just as well because I think if he'd left it on with Drift's self-satisfied face on it, someone might have thrown something at it. Possibly Cielle. "That's a masterful speech," he said with no hint of irony. "She doesn't say anything that anyone can contradict—and Cielle, you can't deny that the Elite have done damage to towns out there past the Barriers. It was by accident, collateral, but we have, and I bet she has footage of it. She implies plenty of negative things about the Hunters, but since she doesn't name us, we can't confront her." He shook his head. "Perfectly scripted and perfectly delivered, and clearly a prelude to getting rid of us."

I know I'd been thinking that. I probably wasn't the only one. But when Kent brought it out into the open, the silence was so frozen you could have cracked it with a hammer.

"Well, we should talk to someone from the newsfeeds too!" Cielle blurted when nobody else spoke up.

Kent looked as if he was about to reply, but Scarlet beat him to it. "The problem is that she hasn't actually made direct accusations," Scarlet said, somehow managing to sound both worried about what Drift had said and reasoned in her own response to it. "If *we* go on record directly countering what she said, the impression that will be left in people's minds is that we are being overly defensive, even paranoid, when Drift didn't say anything about us. Which Drift will point out, then wonder aloud—'just putting it out there'—why we're being so defensive if there is nothing to defend. And that will cement her lies and implications as the truth, and nothing we'll be able to do will shake that." Scarlet shook her head, just as Kent had. "I can only think of one possible approach, which leaves us in the unfortunate position of reacting rather than acting."

"What is it?" Kent prompted.

"Wait until someone asks us the question directly, and you or the Prefect will respond with 'But Senior Psimon Drift didn't say anything of the kind.' Then she will find herself in the position of having to actually accuse us, or do some fancy verbal dancing to get out of the situation. It's far from ideal, but it's the only thing I can think of."

"I thought about pointing out that the Psimons at the Barrier Battle didn't last all that long, but reminding the newsfeeds of all those collapsed and dead Psimons will just make them into what Drift wants: martyrs in the service of Apex." Kent chewed his lip. "All right, then this is what you'll do. In case you get ambushed, your replies will all be the same: you didn't hear the feed because you were too busy patrolling the city, defending the outlying areas, and keeping the city safe, so you can't comment on something you're unaware of. If they persist, say something totally unrelated in the way of fan service and leave."

"Like 'You know, every waking moment of our time is spent in keeping the City *safe*. And thanks to all of *you* who support us!'" Tober rumbled.

"Exactly—that's excellent, Tober." Kent gave him a thumbs-up.

"I think we ought to go a step further and say good things about this," Scarlet put in. "About the Psimons, I mean."

But Kent shook his head. "Not yet. Honestly, I don't know if I could persuade anyone to—"

"I would," I said, bringing all eyes to me. I flushed. "I'd say lots of good things. The Psimon who turned up behind me did a fantastic job; with him keeping the Othersiders busy, all the Hounds and I needed to do was round them up away from the buildings and hose them down. And I don't have any quarrel with PsiCorps, just with Drift." I rubbed my temple as I thought. "Maybe we should say something about how it's good to be working together the way we all did before the Barriers were built?"

"I like that," Kent replied. "But not coming from you. I don't want you and PsiCorps to be in the same paragraph, much less the same sentence. Someone will remember about your PsiCorps boyfriend and how he's gone missing, and start asking questions you can't answer."

I felt the color draining from my cheeks. Kent was right. I did not dare remind Drift of my existence, nor give her a reason to have me questioned by her people.

"I'll do it," Scarlet replied, tossing her hair. "All I have to do is remember the Gog that was about to squash me like a bug until one of the Psimons took it over, and I can be really genuinely grateful."

"Good. This is forcing us to be on the defensive without looking like we're on the defensive, but that's all we can do right now." Kent ran his hand through his hair. He hadn't dyed it lately, and the dark roots were showing at the bottom of the red and yellow.

"Why are you so worried about this, Kent?" Archer asked. He was the only one of us who looked at all relaxed, leaning against the wall casually. "What's the worst Drift can do? Get us all assigned outside the city? Being sent out to the hinterlands and maybe ending the competition and ranking system might be a bit hard on the other Hunters, but that's *all* we Elite do, so what would be the big difference? It's not like we still wouldn't be here in HQ, and if something went horribly wrong, we're a comm call from taking care of it."

"I—don't know what she can do," Kent admitted, sitting down as if he was suddenly weary. "And that's the problem. Drift has never, ever done anything without an agenda. For all I know, she's setting us all up for something. Something big, something that would end up with the Hunters here reassigned all over the territories, leaving PsiCorps the only protection Apex has. And I don't think PsiCorps can handle it. She overreached at the Barrier Battle and lost her strongest Psimons, and she'll overreach again."

"But it's not as if she can get us all killed," Hammer told him, with a grim chuckle. "Assuming everything goes to hell and she actually gets us sent out of Apex, we'll be ready to come back with a roar when PsiCorps collapses."

"And how would you propose to do that if we end up getting split up over all the regional areas?" Kent demanded.

Hammer ran a hand over his head. "Well, I haven't figured that part out yet...."

"Let me know when you do." Kent looked around at the rest of us. "In the meantime, stay sharp, stay focused. There is way more to this than meets the eye."

I spent a restless night. On the one hand . . . if Drift *did* end up sending us all over the Allied Territories, I would be able to petition to go home to Safehaven and the Mountain, as would Mark. Drift would probably be so happy to see me going back to "Turnipland" that she'd sign the order herself. And all I would have to do would be to get ahold of some real money or barter goods—easy enough since I could probably requisition anything I wanted out of the armory—get those to Josh, and leave Dusana with him. Dusana could get him as far as the first train station on the way back home, and he could join us from there.

I had been feeling more or less at home here—but now, with this as a possibility, a jolt of homesickness hit me as soon as I went to bed, and I found myself crying into my pillow. I was so tired of all of this other crap going on when all I wanted to do was kill monsters and save people. Why did people like Abigail Drift keep making it so hard to do that? I wanted to go home, where it actually *was* that simple.

But I was torn, horribly torn, because if that happened, and if I ran or got pushed out of Apex—who would protect all the Cits here? All those children that Lord Laur-whatsis had figured out how to use? How would I save my sheep? Because the Cits of Apex were my sheep; every Hunter was the shepherd to every Cit, everywhere, but never more so than here, where no one had been taught how to protect themselves.

I could just see it in my imagination—the Psimons failing at the Barrier, the Gogs and Magogs bringing the Barrier down, Portals popping up, sending hordes of Othersiders pouring into the city...

It would be the Diseray all over again.

For the Cits of Apex, it would be the end.

So how could I possibly abandon the city and the Cits and go home?

The alarm in the morning came as a distinct relief. I reminded myself as I got dressed that this wasn't a decision I had to make right now. In fact, we might all be far too paranoid about this; perhaps it wasn't a decision I would have to make, *ever*.

I forced myself to eat breakfast. I couldn't help but notice that no one else seemed to have suffered a restless night the way I had. So surely I was fretting over something that would never happen.

Then the callout came, my nerves went all jangling again, and I realized as I threw myself into the chopper that my hands were shaking and my insides were a mass of knots. My nerves were shot. I needed to get myself under control or I'd be utterly worthless.

The choppers took us far, far past the Barriers, to a small city called Greniston, walled and fortified. So far that I was able to get my jangling nerves under control and my head more or less on straight, but I was afraid that by the time we actually arrived, we might be too late and would find a wrecked and empty settlement. We were in the air for a solid hour at least, and when we bailed out, the raid was well under way.

The good news was that this was a walled and well-defended town, and since we had been in the air for so long, we had maps and plans of the city loaded into our Perscoms, and army and air support already in place.

The bad news was that despite army opposition, the Othersiders had broken down the walls before we got there, and were already inside the city.

We came in hot and bailed, hurling ourselves out of the choppers while they hovered a couple feet above the ground. I hit the grass in a roll, came up on my feet, and summoned, quick and dirty, knowing before more than a few minutes went by I would get all that magic back and more.

"Form up a wedge on me, big Hounds in the lead, the rest flanking and trailing!" Kent ordered. We formed up into a big

wedge-shaped team and headed for the breach in the walls, with the biggest, strongest Hounds in the lead, including Dusana on the point.

No Drakken this time—maybe the Othersiders had run out of them?—but there were three sets of Gogs and Magogs between us and the city, as well as a line of Minotaurs, and although the guns on the walls had wounded the monsters, their wounds were not enough to stop them. Within a minute, Kent called over the channel, *"Heads up! There's a Folk Lord in command! Cielle, Scarlet, hunt for him."*

Of course there was a Folk Lord out there—the giants were moving with far more intelligence than they normally showed. That might well account for why they were ignoring their wounds, too.

Bya, Myrrdhin, Gwalchmai, when we get inside the city peel off and look for the Folk Lord on the ground, I instructed, as Cielle's and Scarlet's winged Hounds separated from the group protecting us overhead and streaked in opposite directions to run a perimeter search and check outside the walls.

Guys, can you feed Cielle and me with magic? I asked the rest, hopefully, because Cielle's Hounds were not going to be sucking up much manna, hunting for the Folk Lord from the air, and we could really use her big blast.

No, Shinje said with regret. But a moment later he said, *Oh! We can feed her Hounds with manna!*

That'll do! And that was all I had time for as we hit the line of Minotaurs in front of the Gog and Magog pairs.

"Joy and Dazzle, light those nearest two giants up!" Kent

ordered, as the Gog and Magog raised enormous hammers and Hammer, Steel, and Knight put up the strongest Shields they had. I waited a heartbeat to see which of the two Dazzle took, and then planted a light show on the end of the other one's nose. The bellows of outrage and confusion were music to my ears.

The other Gog and Magog pairs started lumbering toward us, but our artillery support got clear shots at all four of them. A moment after that, we were all gasping, and those of us who had gas masks were reaching for them as the stench of giant insides avalanched over us. That disrupted the light show Dazzle and I were putting on, but the Gog and Magog were pretty effectively blinded at that point. We rushed past them, and as we got inside the walls, the artillery fired the terminal clean shots at the last two, and we heard the shells whistle in and explode behind us.

And that is the last thing that went right for us.

Inside the walls, we were rushed on both sides by a mob of Manticores. The best we could manage was to huddle under Shields as they swarmed us. I ripped off my gas mask; it was taking up too much room in the scrum. We were so tightly packed together that I couldn't see where to put up the little Shield walls to trip up the Manticores, and with so many stingers lashing down at us, Hammer and Steel didn't dare drop their Shields even to give us a chance to fire into the mob. We were jammed up together, elbow to elbow, with the Hounds protected under the Shields with us. I tried to think of something I could do. The Manticores were so close I could smell their breath—metallic and hot. I couldn't see anywhere to plant the skunk-spell that wouldn't affect us too. I couldn't see any place to land a light show that wouldn't also blind us. I mentally ran through every bit of magic I had, and none of it was suited for close quarters like this.

Then, as I started running through my magical arsenal again in case I'd missed something, we were forced to move, shuffling along together in our tight-packed mob, impelled by the physical pressure of the Manticores on our left side to move in the direction they wanted us to go.

In other words, we were being herded. They had more than enough sheer mass on that side of us to overcome our resistance; it was move or be run over. *This can't be good,* I thought, just as we moved into a more open area, a kind of plaza ringed by blank-faced concrete buildings. Some more shoving, and the Manticores withdrew, leaving us in the center with a ring of nasty around us ... waiting.

Well, I wasn't going to wait. I planted a skunk-spell on the head of the one nearest me, then iced the ground at his feet for good measure. I wasn't alone; with the pressure off, we spread out, and the others did what they did best, magically speaking, until Kent ordered the Shields down and we could use firepower.

That lasted for about thirty seconds, then something white came screaming down out of the sky.

Literally screaming.

The sound this thing produced was like nothing I had ever heard before. I call it a "scream," but there was really no adequate word for this piercing, agonizing sound. The effect it produced—I went to my knees with the pain, and I wasn't the only one; three or four people next to me did the same. I clapped my hands over my ears, but it didn't help. The thing swooped once around our circle and then came to hover just above me.

It stopped screaming for a moment, and I panted with relief, looking up at it.

It looked like a woman's ghost—I mean, the way that female ghosts are generally shown in fantasy-vids. She was all filmy and white, dressed in long, floating, tattered robes with huge sleeves and a shredded veil, and you could see right through her. There were dark holes where her eyes should have been. And those dark holes were looking right at me.

Then she opened her mouth and screamed.

I collapsed, my mouth open in a scream of my own, hands wrapped around my head to no avail. My hands were wet . . . blood must have been pouring from my ears. My nose gushed blood. And the pain . . .

Like my ears had railway spikes through them.

Like my brain was on fire.

Like my bones were shattering.

I couldn't hear anything but that scream, that horrible, horrible scream, but it wasn't as if I was *hearing* it—more like it had become a part of me and I couldn't escape it. I would never escape it. It was going to kill me. And there wasn't anything I or anyone else could do about it.

Then something closed around me, softly, like a giant hand enveloping me completely. I felt the nausea-inducing jolt of a *bamph*. The pain stopped.

And that's when I passed out.

I came to in a medivac chopper—a chopper that was extremely crowded with all of my Hounds, even though my *Alebrijes* had taken their most compact forms. I was strapped to a stretcher. I panicked when I realized *I couldn't hear.*

And then the pain hit me again, pain as if every inch of me had been beaten to a pulp. I opened my mouth involuntarily. I might have screamed, I might have whimpered, I couldn't tell, because I couldn't hear what I was doing. Whatever I did, it was loud enough to get the attention of the medic, who turned around and gave me a hypospray in the side of my neck. The pain faded back to a dull ache. He had a whiteboard in his hand and he quickly scrawled something on it.

Don't move.

I mouthed the word *Okay.*

He erased what he had written and wrote something else. *Banshee. Your eardrums are broken.*

I knew that word, but only from Irish folklore. Banshees were supposed to be ghosts or spirits that warned the living that they were about to die. Looked like this one had decided to take the "death" part into her own hands.

He wrote again. *Night shift is scrambled. Army mages onsite. We're winning.*

I glared at him. If he was lying . . .

Truth, he wrote. *You were target. Archer nailed Banshee when you bamphed.*

I was the target? That meant the Banshee had been given orders *and* a description. There were only two Othersiders that would recognize me well enough to do that. One was that fancy gold one, Laur-something. And the other one of them ... was Torcion. Of the two, Torcion knew best what I looked like.

Before I could absorb the implications of that, I passed out again.

They didn't let me come to again until after everyone was back. I wasn't the only casualty, but thank the gods both great and small, there were no fatalities. I was joined in the medbay by Raynd, Mei, and Flashfire. Raynd, I learned from Jessie, had two broken arms. Mei was thoroughly concussed; they were treating her to prevent brain swelling. And Flashfire had a gash an inch deep all down his left arm and another across his back from Manticore talons.

I, of course, had busted eardrums, my brain had been rattled in my skull enough to give me the same results as a concussion, and every bone in my body had microfractures. I was pretty well contused over every square inch of skin too. That was what being the focus of a Banshee's scream did to you. Hammer and Steel were probably trying to figure out how to change their Shields to stop sound.

At least, I hoped they were.

I was all by myself in a little room with no windows and just enough space for the bed, medical equipment on all sides (most of which was, thankfully, not hooked up to me), and one chair for a visitor. I had an IV drip in the back of my hand, and something hooked up to my head.

I was in so much pain that despite being pumped full of All The Drugs, I wasn't in the least groggy. So to shut me up and prevent having to write out everything that had happened on a whiteboard by hand, Jessie arranged for a monitor over my bed and a control I could use without moving my hand much or my arm at all.

The first thing I did was queue up the vid-feeds of the fight from our cams. I fast-forwarded to when the Banshee turned up, just to make sure I really was the one she wanted, but there was no doubt. I was the complete focus of her attention, right up to the point where Shinje and Dusana bravely jumped in next to me, Shinje wrapped me and Dusana up in tentacles, and Dusana *bamphed* all three of us out of the city.

It was pretty surreal seeing all of this from outside. But there was no doubt that Shinje and Dusana saved my life. If they hadn't gone right into the cone of the Banshee's scream and gotten me out, my brain would have been liquefied.

There was only one other thing I wanted to see, but it wasn't on any of the cams: Which Folk Lord had been orchestrating this? I started going through all the cam footage in slow-mo, concentrating so hard my head began to hurt even through the drugs. But me being me, and stubborn as a hog on ice, I was going to push through the pain and find that damned Folk Lord even if my ears began to bleed again.

At this point Jessie came back, pushed the monitor out of the way, took the control out of my hand, and administered an injection, and that was all I knew for a while.

When I woke up the second time, I could actually hear, sort of. I can't really describe it properly; sound was not just dim but distorted. The little room I was in was shadow shrouded, so I guessed it was night, but which night? I moved my right arm and peered at it. The bruises had turned an unpleasant shade of mottled green, so it had to have been a couple days since I last woke up.

My stomach growled.

And I *ached*.

At least my head didn't feel as if it was going to split wide open anymore.

My stomach growled again, and as if that had been a summons, Jessie appeared in the door with a tray. "Don't move," she said in a voice that sounded a million miles away but was probably very loud.

"Yes'm," I replied. She adjusted the bed into a sitting position, arranged the tray on the bedrails so it didn't touch me anywhere, and clamped it down. "Do I need to feed you?" she asked very matter-of-factly, as if she would, without a doubt, feed me if I asked her to. I shook my head gingerly, but there was something that was very much on my mind.

"Where are my Hounds?" I asked, because I hadn't sent them back. Only their own Hunter or a Master can send Hounds back to where they came from, and there were no Masters here.

"In your rooms," Jessie said. "They've been going out to Hunt with other packs. They get a chopper all their own."

That was all right, then. They were getting fed and they had a place to go. I picked up the spoon and slowly ate whatever it was that was in the bowl. It had the consistency of cornmeal mush and tasted vaguely savory—it was probably a concentrate of some sort. There was a thick, cold drink that tasted of honey, probably the same. Whatever they were, they made my stomach shut up. Jessie came back, gave me the vid-control, and pushed the monitor over my bed again before exiting with the bowl, glass, and tray.

Once again I looked at all the vid-feeds from that raid, doing my best to analyze everything. It wasn't long before I got to the Banshee part again, and this time I stayed on the cam that showed what happened after the Hounds pulled me out. Basically, after the Hounds rescued me right from under her nose, the Banshee was startled and shocked, and acted confused. Archer took advantage of her moment of surprise and nailed her.

Then, before the Manticores could rally, the rest of the Elite unloaded everything they had on them. My Hounds remained with the team, and since all the buildings surrounding the plaza were concrete, my fire-breathers unloaded on the Manticores without restraint. "Oh, good boys," I breathed. There it was—the damn things were very vulnerable to being set on fire. It was the one thing we hadn't tried before, because every other time we'd encountered them, we had been in the middle of extremely flammable structures.

After that, the army Mages turned up in force and the town got cleared in fairly short order, my Hounds joined me at the medivac chopper, and that was the end of that.

I didn't do a search to find out how many kids had been kidnapped. I decided I didn't want to know. It would only make me feel worse than I did already.

Because, frankly, I felt horrible, and I don't mean physically.

In a way, it didn't matter if the Folk Lord that had been running this raid was Torcion or the other one. Either way, I should have said something. If it had been Torcion, I should have told someone about him weeks ago. If it was the other one, I should have guessed from the way he'd looked at me the last time that he had something planned, and told someone. But worst of all, I had solid intel on Gold from Torcion, and I'd withheld it. I knew Gold, specifically, was kidnapping people. I knew he was able to recognize me, and I could sure deduce from the way he'd glared at me that I was on his shit list.

I scanned through every bit of vid-feed and didn't see even a hint of Folk Lord anywhere. Was it possible the Folk had something like a cam? Well...anything was possible. Folklore talked about "scrying"—a way to see what was going on at a distance as if you had a cam on it—and things like crystal balls. If it was Torcion, he certainly wouldn't want to be caught double-crossing me. And if it was Goldie, well, I'd seen him twice, and I bet he wasn't going to take the chance I'd somehow put a bullet in him the third time.

I was still worrying about it when Jessie came in, took things away from me, and put an end to my unhappy thoughts with another shot.

"We're in trouble," Kent said from the chair at my bedside. He and I had been reviewing the vid again, looking for the Folk Lord in vain. I'd finally suggested that the Folk Lord could have been working remotely; he'd shrugged and said there was nothing to rule that out, which just gave us one more layer in our crap sandwich.

I could hear again, but those microfractures took special treatment, it seemed. I could break my bones—more than one of them at once—if I put stress on them, so I was still sidelined.

"How bad is it?" I asked. "The team, I mean. How many are we down now?"

"You're out. Denali is out. Mei should be out, but I can't keep her off her feet, so she might as well go active. In fact, in the old days, about a quarter of the Elite would have been benched for minor injuries, but..." He sighed and spread his hands. "The only good news is that Denali is awake again, but he is definitely not in good shape. If we're lucky, he'll be fit to go in a week. If not... the docs can't give me a number. This is all new ground for them."

"And we keep losing kids to raids," I said flatly.

He nodded. "So we're in trouble."

I hesitated, then made a reluctant suggestion. "Can we annex the army Mages? I know they're hard to work with...."

"That, and I'm putting out a plea for more Hunters from the other territories." He passed his hand over his face. "We've got to get more help from somewhere, and I'm running out of places to ask."

I'd seen Uncle, or rather, he had come to see me, and I had covertly asked him to talk to the Masters and ask them for help.

So far, obviously, there had been no response. Not yes, not no, just . . . nothing. We hadn't gotten mail from there for weeks. Were they under siege as well?

"I've tired you out," Kent said, giving me a hard look.

"Not tired," I corrected. "Scared. Depressed. Out of ideas. Scared, mostly." I didn't add "guilty," but I was that too.

I'd had time to think, and now . . . now I was wondering if *everything* I'd done to protect the Mountain had been wrong. Sure, all the people around the Monastery need the Hunters we have and the protection the Hunters and the Masters can give them—but now, Apex clearly needed all the help it could get. And yes, I was taking care of the people at home, but I was just as responsible for the people *here*. Should I have asked the Masters to send more Hunters before now? Should I have told Kent about the Monastery? If I had . . . if I had, we might not be in this position.

"I don't blame you, kid," Kent sighed. "I'll let you get some rest." And before I could say anything, he left.

When I was alone, all I could think about was if keeping my word had made things ever so much worse for everyone here.

14

THE CALLOUT ALARM WOKE me out of a drugged sleep, and I was on my feet and staggering around my little room, dazedly trying to figure out where my gear was, when an orderly came in and picked me up bodily to put me back in bed. "Stay," he ordered, as if I were a dog. I woke up enough to remember where I was, and fumbled for the vid-control. But the screen didn't show anything but archived footage, no matter how many buttons I punched, and I finally figured out it wasn't hooked up to the main vid-feeds.

I swore, and considered disobeying the orderly and getting out to where there was a live feed—because that particular alarm wouldn't have sounded in the medbay unless this was a full callout, one requiring every mobile member of the Elite and sidekicks, plus possible medical backup. I needed to know what was happening!

But they most likely had at least a cam in here, and even though I wasn't hooked up to IVs and machines anymore, they probably had passive stuff monitoring my heart and blood pressure and who knows what else. If I got out of bed again for any reason other than to use the bathroom I shared with the room next door, someone would be in here again, and this time they might strap me down.

I swore again. Dammit, I wouldn't even be able to keep an eye on my Hounds!

And then it hit me. There *was* a way I could keep track of things.

Bya! I called.

We are in our flying room, he said immediately. *We cannot return to you now.*

Flying room—that would be what Bya called the chopper. The Hounds hadn't been in one very often before I was laid up. *I don't want you to return to me,* I assured him. *They won't let me see the Hunt. Can I see through your eyes?*

Easily! he replied, and as I closed my eyes, it was suddenly like someone was playing a movie in my head. A movie with odd perspective, and even odder lighting, but vivid and immediate.

We'd done this more than once back home, when Bya and the rest were ranging out as much as half a mile from me and they wanted me to see something. But this was the first time I'd seen the inside of a chopper from a Hound's point of view.

All the *Alebrijes* had grown tentacles, not just Shinje, and they had knotted themselves into the seat harnesses or tie-down points on the floor. Hold, Strike, Gwalchmai, and Myrrdhin were each wrapped up by one of their pack-mates and tethered that way. There was no one else in this chopper, but then, with eleven Hounds, seven of them sporting masses of tentacles, there wouldn't have been much room for anyone.

Bya was near the door, and his night vision was outstanding; when he looked out, I spotted two more choppers racing alongside this one with all their lights off, in stealth mode. The ground speeding by under us wasn't anything I recognized, so I had no idea where we were going. Neither did Bya, I supposed. He wasn't sharing his thoughts with me, just his senses. The chopper motor, the pitching and vibration of the deck under him, the smell of cut hay and machine oil, night damp and hot metal.

As it turned out, I had plenty of time to sit and fret. They were in the air for a good hour and a half before the choppers came in hot. Bya's pilot must have been something special; he slid in sideways, just at grass height, exactly right for them to be able to brace themselves, keep their balance as they sucked their tentacles back into themselves, and launch themselves out the door.

They formed a wedge, with Bya, Myrrdhin, and Gwalchmai leading and big Dusana bringing up the rear in his full size, and surged through the grass, heading for the rally point. This was another walled city, and it must have had better defenses than the last one, since the walls hadn't been breached and the Othersiders were still stuck outside. Flashes of artillery fire lit up the outside, on top of the walls. Spotlights picked out some of the enemy. There were muffled *booms* as the Othersiders battered at places they perceived as weak.

Suddenly all the noise of artillery and fighting went muffled. I was alarmed until I realized that the Hounds must have grown themselves some hearing protection, in case another Banshee turned up.

I tried not to let my thoughts impinge on Bya's. He had more than enough to do with directing the pack and all. He didn't need me distracting him.

The team was not going to allow a repeat of the last time when the Othersiders had gotten inside the city; they headed straight for the spot where there were Gogs and Magogs battering at a weak point in the wall. Now I "heard" his orders along with the rest of the pack. *Myrrdhin, take Hold. Gwalchmai, take Strike. Go left and right around the walls and look for the . . .* There was no English equivalent of what Bya named, but I knew what it was. They were looking for the Folk Lord. That's exactly what I would have done.

And those four were a good choice to go hunting; they were off-black, exactly the color of shadows in the darkness, where true solid black shows up almost as well as white to someone who knows what he is looking for.

Bya and the rest were heading straight for Scarlet and Cielle, whose flying Hounds were doing the same hunt for the Folk Lord, but from the air. Without me to protect, they were free to attach themselves to anyone else who needed some coverage. As they swirled around my two friends, I felt a surge of gratitude to them. *Dusana, let us add our Shields to theirs,* Bya ordered, making me even more grateful.

Then the Hunters hit the line of defenders around the Gog

and Magog, and the real fight began. Immediately, our weaknesses showed.

They showed in the fact that so many of us were carrying RPGs and using *them* instead of magic, because the night shift was just too tired to use the magic their Hounds were shunting to them. They showed in the gaps that developed in our line. My heart sank as I understood just how big a handicap we were fighting under—tired, demoralized, with our numbers thinned.

I wanted to do something, but there was nothing I could do except watch passively through Bya's eyes.

There were two Gog and Magog pairs trying to breach the town wall; one duo went down pretty quickly, thanks to surprise and several lucky RPG shots. The second pair, however, were not cooperating. I squirmed where I was sitting, wanting desperately to tell Kent to lead them away from the walls so the missiles on the choppers could get shots in on them—

But then I realized that Kent must have thought of that and dismissed it—because these two weren't acting like the usual dumb-as-dirt giants. They were using abandoned vehicles as improvised physical shields, blocking the RPG fire. They were *looking* for the muzzle flashes and sending well-aimed chunks of debris at whoever had last fired an RPG. They were not charging blindly, roaring with pain when a hit got through. Someone was controlling them directly.

I clenched my hands hard in the sheets. I wanted to be there. I *needed* to be there!

Dazzle lit up the Gog, but instead of reacting with confusion, it hurled the vehicle it had been using as a shield at the last place an RPG had fired from. And there was nowhere for anyone in the target area to run to.

In the nick of time, Hammer and Steel redirected their Shields like an umbrella to cover the five or six people in the impact area.

But that left them open because they had to move their Shields away from themselves to cover the Hunters in danger, and was just what the Manticores had been waiting for.

Before anyone could move or react, a huge monster leapt over the combat lines and landed next to them. Its stinger came down twice, and Hammer and Steel collapsed.

The Manticore bent down to seize one of them in its mouth, just as Mark Knight, shrieking with fury and looking like one of King Arthur's medieval warriors swinging an ax, grabbed his AR by the barrel and swung the metal stock down at the monster's head.

He caught it right in the eye.

The Manticore dropped Hammer, shrieking. *Dusana!* Bya cried, but it was too late. The Manticore's lightning reflexes had already sent its stinger plunging through Mark's chest.

Dusana *bamphed* to his side and hosed the monster down with fire, as Kent and three others dragged Mark, Hammer, and Steel away.

I pulled out of Bya's head with a wrench. I heard a *crack* and felt sudden pain in my left hand as I hit the bed railing, and realized dully that—as I'd been warned—I'd just broken a bone.

But it didn't matter. The pain didn't matter. All that mattered was *I should have been there.*

I howled like a bereft dog. Orderlies and medics slammed open the door to my room, hit me with a hypospray, and the last thing I remember was someone screaming.

But it wasn't me.

It was Jessie.

When I woke up again, my throat was raw, and there was a cast on my left hand.

I also wasn't alone. Cielle was sitting in the chair next to me.

"Here," she said, handing me tissues, and I started bawling again. She kept talking. "Kent figured you were doing some kind of telepathy thing with your Hounds?" She made it a question, so I nodded, between sobs. "So . . . yeah. This makes sense, then." She made a vague gesture at my face and my hand in the cast. "We won, by the way. Well, us and the army Mages. Scarlet's Hounds found that *pissant* Folk Lord, the army Mages all unloaded on him at once, and he bugged out." But I could tell from the sound of her voice that it wasn't a "We won!" but a "We didn't lose," and that just made me bawl harder.

She could have excused herself and left, but she didn't. She stayed right there with me until Bya and Shinje nosed their way in and jumped up on my bed. She left then, but came back with a fresh stack of tissues and sat on the edge of my bed, while Bya stretched out on the other side and Shinje sat on my feet. Cielle put her arm awkwardly around my shoulders and passed me fresh tissues. I wanted to tell her to go, but I couldn't. My insides were all knotted up, my hand hurt and my head hurt, and I was *glad* they hurt because I deserved to hurt—but I was also grateful, in a cringe-worthy sense, that she was there, because I was afraid to be alone with this grief. I was afraid if I was alone, I—I didn't know what I'd do.

"That was the bravest and stupidest thing I've ever seen," she said finally. Which pretty much summed up how I felt about it. I nodded, with a wad of soggy tissue held to my face. "I—miss him too," she said, and her face crumpled like the tissues I was holding, which set me off again, and we clung to each other and cried until we were both hoarse and horrible-looking. An orderly came in and handed Cielle off to someone standing outside the door, and gave me a liter of water and a pill. "Drink all of this, and take that," he said sternly. "I'm standing right here till you do both."

To get rid of him, I swallowed the pill first, drank down the water as quickly as I could without throwing it all back up, and handed him the bottle. He took it and left, dimming the lights as he did so. I lay back in my bed with my tissues clutched in my good hand.

I should have been there. I should have. I was rested. I didn't need to do things that would have stressed my skeleton; I could have done nothing but pure magic. I could have protected Hammer and Steel while they protected the others, and they would never have been hurt, and Mark would never have needed to defend them—

And there was a bigger source of guilt. I was sitting on top of the knowledge of a reserve of some of the best Hunters and Mages I had ever seen, and I had said *nothing* about it to anyone. Oh gods, how wrong had I been? I had been protecting the people on the Mountain and the Monastery, but it was at the expense of everyone here! Would the Masters even *want* to be protected if they knew what kind of a cost we were paying down here without their help?

And now that Mark was gone . . . Jessie would surely blame me, and she'd be right to do so. But would she take her anger at me out on the Mountain? She surely knew about the extra Hunters there, Hunters that, had they been here, would have prevented this disaster. Would she betray her new home, the Mountain, and all those Hunters? Was it even betrayal when we needed them so badly?

I had to do something. I wasn't sure what. . . . I couldn't break my word to the Masters, but this couldn't go on. I couldn't keep this up without at least *trying* to get some help down here.

Bya, get me paper and a pen, please? I asked silently as my throat threatened to close up again. He looked at me with his head cocked to the side, then jumped down off the bed and trotted out. About five minutes later he returned with both in his mouth.

I took them from him and began to write.

I told the Masters how desperate things were. That we were afraid Drift's ambition would lead her to finding a way to rid herself of the Hunters, leaving the city open to invasion. That the Othersiders were thinning us down, bit by bit, to the point where Drift might not *have* to do anything. That Mark was dead. How every other source of help was drying up, and I didn't think we could hold out much longer. It was less than coherent, I was afraid, but I hoped they'd understand and figure out a way to help us. Because if they didn't, I was completely out of ideas, and from the sound of things, so was everyone else.

I rolled it up and gave it to Bya, then opened the Way for him. He looked at me as if he was going to say something. Then I got the mental equivalent of a hug from him, and he stepped through and was gone.

With my arms around Shinje, I cried for Mark until the pill knocked me out.

I felt exactly the same waking up as I had going to sleep the night before. I didn't have any appetite at all, but I guess the medics had already figured that part out, because the orderly brought me a huge glass of some thick, creamy liquid and stood there until I finished drinking it. "Thank you," I said when I gave him back the glass. He waited for me to ask for something more, but I wasn't the person who really needed support now, and we both knew it. He left after a moment, which was probably a relief for both of us.

He had also brought me a fresh stack of tissues. At this rate, I was going to deplete the stock for the entire medbay.

I wanted to talk to Jessie. The last thing I wanted to do was to talk to Jessie. I took the coward's way out and sent her a vid-message, babbling for a while about how sorry I was—and how even sorrier I was that I couldn't think of anything that seemed right to say to her. And I cried, which I thought about erasing, but they didn't look like phony tears so I left it and hit *send*.

And just as I did that, Kent came in. He looked like hell, like he hadn't slept in days, and I had no idea how many callouts he'd been on since the one where Mark was killed. All of them, likely.

"How you holding up, kid?" he asked.

I opened my mouth to say okay, but what came out was a bleat of "I don't know what to *do*!" and a gush of tears.

"None of us do, Joy," he said, sitting down heavily. "I didn't come here expecting you to hand me a miracle." He made a helpless little gesture that only made me feel worse, if that was at all possible. It was like seeing one of the Masters without an answer. "There's . . . This all just feels wrong. Like there is a big picture here that we're just not seeing . . . but damn if I have a clue."

His face was a mask of despair. And seeing him like that, I just couldn't put any more burden on him, so I mopped up, stiffened my backbone, and said, "I'd like to go back on duty, sir."

His instant reply was, "Absolutely *not*! Look at what you did to your hand—in bed!" He gestured at the cast on my left hand. "The kick of a rifle will shatter your collarbone. The kick of a handgun will shatter your other hand. If you fall down, you'll break an arm or a leg—"

"Hear me out, sir," I pleaded, because even if I couldn't go back in time and fix what had gone wrong, at least I could do something about now. "I'm all rested. I promise, I won't do anything but magic. And my Hounds will make sure that if for some reason I fall, I'll land soft. Please!"

"The docs are going to murder me for this," he muttered, then sighed and nodded. "All right. You sit here and I'll see if I can get them to release you. We're so thin now that half of us are walking wounded anyway."

So I stayed put while he went to talk to the medics. And that was when Jessie came in.

She'd been crying a lot, that much was plain, and she walked as if every step was taken in pain. But the first thing she said when she got in the door was, "You'd better not be doin' some damn fool way of killin' yourself."

That accusation took me entirely flat-footed. "What?" I said stupidly.

She waved at the medbay outside the door. "Talkin' Kent into puttin' you back on duty. This better not be so you can go get yourself killed outa guilt." She didn't let me say anything. Evidently she had a whole speech built up, and she wasn't going to stop until she had it all out. "Ayup, I tried t'blame you. I blamed you 'cause if it wasn't fer you, *he* wouldn't have gone Elite. But if he hadn't gone Elite, I'd still be with my folks, and we'd never been married. So that didn't work. So I blamed you fer not bein' there at that fight, but that was damn fool nonsense an' I knew it, 'cause I was takin' care of you myself. If you'd'a been there, somethin' woulda snapped you like a twig, an' the boys woulda still be stung, an' he'd still be . . ." Her face spasmed a moment, then she got control again. "So iffen *I* can't blame you, then *you* don't dare blame yerself. So don't you *dare* go killin' yerself."

She stalked out, having said her piece. And I was left speechless.

I was released back to my quarters on the condition that I wouldn't go on any small callouts. Nothing but the full-scale ones. And I would wear a set of arm and leg braces that were almost like casts, except they were also shock absorbent. I agreed to all of it. After the surprise of Jessie's speech, a vague idea had emerged. Maybe Kent was right—there *was* a bigger picture that we were all missing.

And maybe I knew someone who could tell me just what that picture was.

But first... I had a big confession to make, and it wasn't going to be easy. It was past time to end some of the secrecy.

So I sat down on my bed. My hand was shaking, and it was not just from weakness. *Armorer Kent, would you please meet me at the usual place at your earliest convenience?* I texted, not expecting to get an answer for a while.

But instead... I got one in five minutes. *Half an hour, usual place,* came the answer, so knowing I was going to want to steady my nerves some more, I headed for the koi garden.

A half an hour later he showed up while I was feeding the fish and trying not to remember how Mark had told me not to betray their faith, and completely failing. I just hoped that salt tears in their fresh water wouldn't do the fish any harm. I hastily wiped my eyes on my sleeve as Kent came in. "I know you better than to assume this is trivial, Joy," he said, and locked the door behind him. Then he turned to face me. "So, what is it, and—"

"Please, sir," I said, holding up my hand, the one without the cast on it. "First you have to promise me you won't interrupt me, no matter how provoked or angry or outraged you are, until I'm done."

His tired face got a strange expression on it, and he sat down. "All right. That, coming from you, tells me no matter what, this is going to be interesting."

So I started from the beginning, the first encounter with

Torcion, at the train. Then how I had been feeling as if he was stalking me for weeks after that, catching glimpses of what might have been him during my Hunts. Then the second encounter, when he tried to warn me about Ace. Kent looked as if he was going to say something right then, but he remembered his promise and stayed quiet.

But by the time I was finished, with that last encounter out there in Spillover, he looked as if he was going to explode.

I had been very careful not to speak Torcion's name, only to say that he had given it to me, and allowed me to use it to summon him. Because if all this had been some kind of elaborate ruse to get me to give him a gateway into the Hunter HQ . . . well, at least I was smarter than *that*.

"All right, that's all," I said, looking down into my lap. And waited for that explosion. Strangely . . . I wasn't tensed up. More like resigned, mixed with a little relief.

But the explosion didn't come.

"You say your Hounds claim this . . . person . . . is trustworthy," Kent said, after a long moment of silence. I looked up. His expression had changed to one of wary calculation.

"Myrrdhin and Gwalchmai particularly, yes, sir," I confirmed.

"Ace's Hounds."

"Yes, sir." I thought I could see where this was going, but I kept my mouth shut and let *him* think out loud.

"This could be a *very* long con on their part—theirs and Ace's, to get us to open up to the Othersiders," he pointed out, his voice very neutral and level.

"Except my original Hounds trust Myrrdhin and Gwalchmai,"

I pointed out. "So do Karly's Hounds. I really don't think Hounds could fool other Hounds. If we're going to start doubting our Hounds, we might just as well take down the Barriers and invite the Othersiders in right now."

He wearily ran a hand over his hair. "You have a point. And what this ... person ... has told you so far is damned interesting. In fact, it's got the preliminary shape of that big picture I said I thought we were missing." He took a very deep breath. "So. What do you think you want to do next?"

"If there *is* a big picture, and he's not part of it ... then I am pretty sure he knows all about it, the way people in Lakeland can know about politics in Apex even though they don't live here and are a lot less affected by those politics. I want to see if he'll tell us," I replied ... and winced, because that sounded pretty feeble. But it was all I had. "I'll have to meet him alone, though. I'm pretty sure he has all kinds of ways to tell if I'm not."

"I don't like this," Kent told me flatly. "But I'm desperate, and I don't see a lot of other options. And this business of him 'tending' humans ... I could be convinced of the truth of that part. It would explain a lot of things. Rumors I've heard. I thought they were just wishful thinking on the part of people who'd lost friends and family—lost kids—but maybe not." He stood up. "Get yourself a pod and get out to Spillover. I'm damn sure not going to sign off on summoning him here."

"That was never my idea, sir!" I said. "No, Spillover was my plan. With the full pack with me. And my arm and leg braces, and ... and a Taser. I can use a Taser without hurting myself, and I don't think he'll know what one is."

"Get to it, then. Leave your Perscom on so I can hear every word. Use my private channel." He unlocked the door. "Don't make me regret authorizing this. That's an order."

I sent the Hounds back, with the assurance that I was going to summon them as soon as I got across the Barrier—which I did after the pod got me to a Pylon. Bya still wasn't back, but it seemed fitting, all things considered, that Myrrdhin was in charge. After all, it was Myrrdhin who had convinced me Torcion was telling the truth. "Find me a safe and secure place," I ordered him. "I'm going to . . . well, we're going to see if Torcion is everything he says he is."

Myrrdhin's head came up. *You are going to take service of him?* he asked, with nothing in the way he asked that question suggesting that he thought this would be anything but a good thing.

"Not exactly." That was true enough. "Something a lot more complicated than that."

Myrrdhin looked me up and down and then nodded. *It would be,* he said. *You are a complicated person. We will find a safe place.*

And so they did, rather quickly: the brick shell of an old house, open to the sky—but before it had decayed away, someone had bricked up all the windows and one of the two doors. Had it happened during the Diseray? It was the sort of thing that someone might have done to make of his home a fortress and a shelter. It was surrounded by a thick wall of tall evergreen trees and bushes, so that from outside, it looked like a grove of trees too dense to force your way into. And in fact, we didn't force our way in at all. Once the Hounds found it and verified it was secure, Dusana *bamphed* me there.

There were trees inside too; their leafy cover made sure I wouldn't be spotted from the air. It was perfect—and just as perfect as a trap. Hopefully neither I nor Torcion would discover how good a trap it was.

Once again, standing in a lonely, isolated place and surrounded by all but one of my Hounds, I took my life and my safety in my hands and called his name.

A Portal formed in front of me, between the trunks of two young trees, and he stepped through. He was still dressed in lavender, although today his outfit was a lot less elaborate than it had been in the past. It was certainly more practical for being around trees and brush—the sleeves stopped at his knees, the robes stopped at his ankles, and his hair was in a single multi-stranded braid he carried looped around one arm.

"Well—" he began, then did an actual double take and frowned. "Shepherd, you are hurt."

"You can thank Lord Laetrenier for that," I said steadily. "He's decided I'm his personal enemy. He set a Banshee on me."

Torcion's frown deepened. "I like this not at all. Dark shadows gather about you, and while you remain with your kith and kin, he can reach out from those shadows at will. His memory is long, well past your lifetime. He neither forgets nor forgives those who attempt to thwart him. Surely now you will take service of me so that I can protect you."

"To do so now would be to betray my own people. I cannot, for they need me, and every shepherd." I stood straight and looked him in the eye. "It is neither right nor honorable that I desert them in their time of need."

He smiled a little. "You value honor. I like that. But . . . you asked me how I could prove that I am trustworthy, and your state gives me the way of that proof. If you will let me?" He made a little motion of his right hand, and I saw a drift of magic, like gold dust floating in the air, follow it.

Is he asking if he can cast some kind of spell on me? I asked Myrrdhin, who seemed to have the best understanding of this Folk Lord.

Yes. You should accept the offer, Myrrdhin replied. I looked at my *Alebrijes,* and none of them seemed to think this was a terrible idea. I took a shaky breath.

And right now in HQ, Kent is trying to figure out what this creature is offering to do, and having a cat.

All right, then. This would be it. My leap of faith, his demonstration he could be trusted. And if I lost, well . . . maybe I deserved to lose. I nodded.

His hands traced Glyphs in the air I didn't recognize, Glyphs that glowed with a gold-and-green energy, which drifted toward me until they surrounded me. Then, as he spread his hands wide, they enveloped me and blossomed into a gold-and-green shell that closed over me like a second skin.

I was overwhelmed with sensation. I heard something like a harp playing meandering music in the distance. My nostrils filled with the scent of roses. I tasted honey, and I was swathed completely in the sensation of warmth, exactly like sunshine on bare skin. And everywhere, I was surrounded by a glorious green-and-gold light, with Glyphs drifting through it like lazy koi.

My broken hand stopped hurting. Instantly.

It would have been easy to fall under that spell, and drift away, but I kept my eyes fastened on his and stayed alert. He smiled a little in acknowledgment of my will—or my stubbornness—and drew another Glyph in the air.

The gold-green glow faded to nothing. The harp song ended first, then the warmth. Last to go was the scent, leaving only the lingering taste of honey in my mouth. Gingerly, I removed the cast on my arm and tested my hand.

No crunchiness. No pain. "Did you just *heal* me?" I asked incredulously. The army Mages could certainly heal people, and my *Alebrijes'* spit could too . . . but not *instantly*.

"I did," he acknowledged, and then his expression clouded a little. "But I could not heal your heart. I am sorry you lost someone dear to you. That is a pain that goes deeper than flesh, and aches worse than broken bone."

His unexpected empathy almost broke me again; I choked up for a moment, but I remembered what I was there for. "I still need information before I can trust you. You seem to know a lot about me. I want to know everything about you and how you're different from Lord Laetrenier."

One long eyebrow rose. "Everything? That would take moons. Sun-turnings, even."

"Then give me the most succinct version you can," I said. He sighed a little, and cast his eyes skyward for a moment, but made another gesture. Behind us, the young trees bent and folded their trunks, and the next thing I knew, we had two seats made of interwoven trees waiting for us to use. I tried not to gawk as I sat down gingerly—it was comfortable and springy. The Hounds gathered around me as he took his seat.

"When you opened the Barrier between our worlds, we saw the earth being destroyed—and rich opportunities for those who wished to take them. Those of us who have settled here have carved out territories for ourselves and the creatures who can also cross the Veil, who are less than servants, more than mere beasts to us. There are two philosophies among my people. Those like Lord Laetrenier hold that you wantonly nearly destroyed your world, we are saving it despite you, and we are entitled to whatever we choose in order to be repaid. Those of my sort are gentle and kindly rulers, who make of our lands a paradise for your kind, and do not allow our underlings to prey upon you. We have learned that there is far more sustenance to be gleaned slowly from those of you who are happy than there is to be reft away in a single killing."

Well, gosh, that sounds just like our herds we use to harvest tissue for cloning. . . .

"I have had refugees come to me begging for sanctuary. I have taken the sick and dying and restored them to health and prosperity. And betimes, my underlings have lured parentless children, or those who had parents that yet did not care enough to keep a careful watch upon them, and brought them to my land." He seemed very proud of that, and for a moment I was angry, but then . . . those lone kids out here in Spillover occurred to me, the ones Mark and I had been feeding with game. They wouldn't last too long out here once winter came unless they found an adult to take care of them. If they were given a choice between freezing and starving, and what Torcion was offering, I knew what they'd take. . . .

"So it has been, my Folk having little to do with those who prey upon you, keeping the peace for our sheep, and slowly healing this world, while those of disparate mind war upon you, and as of old, with each other. But of late, that has changed." His expression altered to something I could not read. "Lord Laetrenier is no longer content with the bargains he made aforetime. He says that your kind are becoming a scourge upon the earth again, and that you need to be culled. He has drawn together formerly warring clans into what he terms a Grand Alliance."

I looked down at Myrrdhin.

Is he lying? I demanded.

Myrrdhin shook his head. *Not about being a kindly lord, at least. I have heard much of him.*

"Laetrenier is a deadly enemy to have, and he has singled you out for retribution," Torcion continued. He fingered the end of his braided hair. "You should take service of me. I have long suspected he covets my domain and my sheep. He may well move against me once he has attained his current goal, but with my aid to your magic, we could defend against him."

I looked back up at Torcion. "I have only your word for this, you know."

He frowned. "My word is good. . . ." He sighed. "But you do not know that." Then he brightened. "I have a plan. Laetrenier likes to boast. What if you were to go into hiding, and I were to bring him here? You could hear his plans for yourself."

My mouth dropped open. "You can do that?"

Torcion smirked. At least, it looked like a smirk. "We are old in rivalry. Cousins, in fact. I can call him with such words that he will come, and once here, he cannot fail to brag of anything that could make him ascendant over me."

"Can you put this on and hide it in your sleeve?" I fumbled at my Perscom, turned off the Psi-shield, unstrapped it, and held it out to him. He looked at it curiously, took it tentatively, and strapped it on, pushing it under his sleeve, where it was hidden completely.

"So shall I then call him?" Torcion asked. He didn't ask about the Perscom. Then again, maybe he already guessed it was some sort of recording or broadcasting device. I just hoped that nothing about him or his magic would interfere with it.

"First . . . get me into hiding," I said.

15

TORCION HAD A BETTER idea. He opened a portal that dumped us all out near the shelter where Josh was hiding. The Hounds and I bolted for the shelter while he set up what he called "precautionary defenses." I didn't see what those were. I was too busy flinging myself through the ruined building and down the stairs to the locked door—then I remembered I didn't have my Perscom to unlock it.

Bloody freaking stupid . . . shit, shit, shit . . . And then the door popped open, and standing there were Josh and Shinje.

"I figured there was something wro—" he began, but I grabbed him and hauled us both inside, followed by a flood of Hounds. I slammed the door.

"I need your Perscom," I said. Looking baffled, he took it off and handed it to me, and I sprinted for his "lair" and the antenna. Once there, after I hooked the Perscom up to the antenna, I manually tuned to Kent's personal freq, *hoping* that Kent had gotten Josh a Perscom that could actually receive it. I almost cried with relief when I got the handshake, entered the code that actually let us talk or listen on it, and got—well, what you'd expect to hear when someone was setting up magical defenses. Not much, other than some birdsong and feet shuffling through gravel. Josh came and sat down on the cement floor next to me, in the dim light from his lamp.

Making sure the thing was set to "passive reception" only, and disallowing transmission because I didn't want to startle Torcion, I turned to Josh, who looked ready to burst.

"I'll explain everything later," I said. "I promise—"

He interrupted me. "I was watching the main newsfeed. I saw about Mark. I . . ." His voice broke a little. "I didn't know him all that well, not like you, but . . . he . . ."

"Well, Cousin Torcion, for what possible reason could you have called upon me? When last we spoke, you vowed never to look upon my face again. I am curious as to why you have changed your mind, when you know I hold you in contempt."

The new voice startled us both, and we both turned to stare at the Perscom. I have to admit, short of some actor in an old pre-Diseray vid, it was the most immediately impressive voice I have ever heard. Deep and melodic, and even though it wasn't loud, it had qualities I can't properly describe. Seductive, maybe? You wanted to listen to it forever, and it really didn't matter what words it spoke. I realized neither of us had Psi-shields on.

"Can you Shield us both from psionics?" I hissed urgently, even though there was no need to whisper. He looked at me with a start, nodded, and grabbed for my hand.

"I could not but note, gentle Cuz, you and your Alliance have been spending your creatures as if they were gold and you were a new-minted, impulsive heir." That was Torcion, for sure. His voice was nothing like as impressive. I hoped Kent was recording this.

Laetrenier laughed. Whatever Josh was doing was working—while still very striking and sensual as a voice, Laetrenier's next words didn't make me want to hang on his every syllable anymore. *"How now, Cousin, are you jealous they do my bidding at my will, while yours will not?"*

"That has never been my way," Torcion replied mildly. *"And you know that."*

"If you choose to be weak, then do not weep when others take from you what you will not defend." Laetrenier chuckled. *"And do not tell me that allowing your creatures to defy you is anything other than weakness. They owe us their mere existence—"*

"This is an old quarrel," Torcion pointed out. *"We are unlikely to resolve it. But I am curious about your gathering of armies. Surely you are not attempting the siege of the stronghold yonder? After your last defeat and all that you lost there? That would be folly indeed."*

"It would be folly had I not the upper hand." Oh, the smirk in his voice.

"Cuz, we are bound by blood," Torcion said with what sounded like concern. *"Though you and I quarrel, I would not see you come to grief. I fear you are . . . underestimating the mind-warriors."*

With that, Laetrenier burst out laughing. *"You fool! You are as* blind as they. The cow that is their leader in mind-war is mine own now. She works my will, though she thinks it her own."

Josh and I exchanged startled glances. He mouthed the word *Drift,* and I nodded frantically. Abigail Drift had been working with the Othersiders! This was the "big picture" that Kent intuited we were missing.

"*Surely you do not expect me to believe that—*" Torcion began, when his cousin interrupted him.

"*They are fools, these creatures, and utterly venal,*" Laetrenier said, in a voice dripping with contempt. "*As I have maintained from the moment we arrived here, they will commit any dishonor to advance themselves. I bartered to her the means of increasing her minions' power without slaying them, and in exchange she will aid me, first against her own kind, and then against the fools in the Alliance.*"

The irony of someone who was going to sell out his own allies calling *Drift* a traitor and dishonorable was not lost on me.

"*I do not see how this favors you, Cuz,*" Torcion replied.

Laetrenier spoke as if he was explaining things to a child. "*The Alliance will destroy the shepherds until her minions are the only defense of the Citadel. Then she and I will turn upon the lords of the Alliance. After, when she is sole defender of this place, she will discover that I had intended to betray her all along, and I shall take the city. And it all comes to a head this day. The fools of the Alliance gather now to launch their attack at the barrier that keeps us out. Today, the territories of all the other lords will be mine, and tomorrow, the citadel they call Apex will be mine in all but name.*" He laughed. *"And then, when I choose, it shall be mine in all possible ways. But first, before the Alliance strikes, there is enough time to end you, sweet Cuz—"*

"Dusana!" I squeaked, and Dusana *bamphed* out. A moment later he *bamphed* in, with Torcion clinging to him.

Josh went white, scrambled to his feet, and backed into the wall. *"Joy!* That's a—"

"Folk Lord, yeah, I know," I said as Torcion let go of Dusana, dusted himself off a little, and resumed his mantle of immense dignity. "There's . . . a lot to explain."

"Then you'd better start now," Josh said shakily.

"I beg to differ, young mind-warrior," Torcion countered. "It will be only a small matter of time before my cousin finds you. I do not have such as your companions in my retinue, so he will know I have worked with the shepherd, and he will begin searching for her. I suggest that you and your companions leave here at once." He made a gesture, and a Portal appeared behind him. "Go. I shall find my own way to safety. And I shall inform the great lords of Laetrenier's treachery. Whether they will believe me or not—I cannot predict."

As he stepped through the Portal, I opened the Way and sent back Hold and Strike. Then Dusana knelt and I mounted on him, and offered Josh a hand.

He took it and mounted behind me. "How are we—" he began. And Dusana *bamphed.*

We *bamphed* all the way home; it was faster than waiting for a pod. By the time we got back to HQ, Josh was very, very sick. So sick he shut himself in the nearest bathroom to the HQ entrance and I was pretty sure he was going to be in there for some time. Meanwhile, I discovered that Kent was off doing something (I wasn't sure what) with the recordings he'd made of Torcion and Laetrenier, while leaving orders for all the Hunters to go on full standby. And he had left Archer in charge, after a brief explanation—and a sample of what he'd recorded. On Kent's orders, Archer had alerted the army that there was going to be another try at the Barrier. Kent and I knew we were all about to be in for a worse time than the previous two Barrier Battles; the only question was *where* on the Barrier were they going to appear? We couldn't count on the Psimons to alert us or stop them this time—or even help us.

Everyone left me alone, not knowing what had just happened, maybe thinking I was still too hurt to count on. But I checked in with the medics to make sure Torcion had healed me, and left them with their jaws on the floor. I was as good as new, maybe better. Then I headed to the armory. I wanted to choose my weapons carefully. Very carefully. No just grabbing things and hoping they were going to turn out to be what I needed.

I'd finished building my load-out when I realized my Perscom was still on Torcion's wrist.

I cursed and went to the techs to get another, though of course it wouldn't be nearly as good as the one Uncle had given me. I got a separate Psi-shield for my other wrist since there wasn't one on the Perscom. Then I went to the hangar and waited for the callout, thinking about what was ahead of us. The hangar was empty, open, and quiet, all things I needed right now. We were about to go into the worst fight ever, and I had to make sure all the baggage I was carrying wasn't going to keep me from doing what I had to do.

At least one of my two big secrets was out. But in the quiet of the hangar, not unlike the quiet of the meditation room back at the Monastery, I was getting my head in order.

That was where Josh found me.

"I can't believe you do that all the time," he said, looking pale but no longer queasy. "Why aren't you sick?"

"I guess you get used to it," I replied. "I promised you an explanation. . . ."

"Good. Let's hear it. Because you are clearly not the person I thought you were." It wasn't an accusation; in fact, he said it in something of a tone of wonder.

So I gave him the explanation. He listened. He didn't interrupt me. He also didn't yell at me. I sat with my elbows on my knees and my hands clasped, and kept my eyes on my hands the whole time, to avoid seeing his reactions. When it was over I glanced at him. He just shook his head. "I'm not sure if you're crazy, brave, or both."

"Both, I guess," I replied. "Where do you want to go from here? It's probably safe enough for you to go back to Uncle—"

"I'm going to PsiCorps," he replied, "and turning on my Psi-shield. That's the last place Drift will expect me to be, if she even thinks I'm still alive. But someone has to get to the Psimons and try to persuade them that Drift is the Folk Lord's tool. I'm the best one to do that." I looked up and saw that he was nodding at me slightly. He reached for my hand; I reached for his at the same time, and we looked into each other's eyes. I was pretty sure he read the fear in mine, and his eyes mirrored that fear. "I'm not going to just sit back and let her hand my city and my Cits over to the Othersiders," he continued, his voice steady. "And I can't believe every single Psimon she's got would go along with this if they knew what she was doing."

"You sound like Hunter Elite now," I replied, and my voice was shaky. "That's pretty darn brave."

"I've got a good example to follow right in front of me," he told me, and squeezed my hand. "No matter what you've been thinking about yourself, every single person that can count you as a friend is lucky to have you, Joyeaux Charmand. I've got to go. I won't ask you to keep yourself safe out there. I just ask that you remember you're more valuable to all these Cits here alive than dead. Martyrs can't help anyone."

I nodded. He kissed me hard and quick, and left, walking fast and not looking back.

Before I could have any sort of emotional reaction, Archer came in, laden with a full load-out. He nodded at me and I nodded back. "You've heard the recordings?" I asked.

He shook his head in disbelief. "Insane. If this hadn't been your doing, I wouldn't have believed it. And your Hounds all trust this . . . magician." Even now, he didn't dare say aloud what Torcion was, or his name.

"All of them," I affirmed.

"Insane. But what do I know? Nothing's been making any sense since Ace went rogue. I've got the army ready to move at a moment's notice. I'm just waiting for Kent to get back from briefing the prefect. We need a plan of attack for the first push when it comes." He sat down with me on the bench at the side of the hangar. "The plan won't survive past the first fifteen minutes, of course, but we need something to start with."

"I can tell you things you already know," I offered. "If Drift has her way, the Psimons won't help. We'll be facing just as big a force as we did at the last Barrier Battle, and we're all worn to a thread. But there won't be Thunderbirds or a storm this time, so we won't be wasting half our energy trying to keep the rain off, or trying to keep warm. So there's that."

"We'll have to do this without Mark, Steel, and Hammer." He thought about that for a moment. "Your Shields are good. Flashfire's are. Kent probably knows who in the general Hunter population has good Shields. . . ." He made a note on his Perscom. "What about finding and taking out the Folk Mages, especially the Big Bad?"

"I think that might be our only hope of getting this over with." I didn't say "quickly," because I didn't think there was any way of getting this over "quickly." I was just hoping to end it all without any more of us dying. "Is it practical to hope for gunship support?"

"Good question." He made another note.

We continued to try and think of things together, and to be honest, it was absolutely surreal. Here we were in the big, empty, echoing hangar. We knew all hell was going to rain down on us soon, but we didn't know exactly when, and right now, everything *seemed* peaceful. We knew Drift had already betrayed the entire city as well as us, personally, and yet we couldn't run around shouting this to the rooftops, even though we wanted to. Or I did, anyway.

"Do you think your friend is really going to do what he said he'd do?" Archer asked at last. "Because that could make a big difference." I knew he didn't mean Josh; if he'd meant Josh, he'd have said boyfriend, or Psimon. So that meant Torcion.

"Only if the lords of the Alliance believe him." I made a face. "And we're talking about creatures whose motives we probably don't really understand."

"I dunno . . . I've known cats that understood revenge. And the gods know that crows do. Your friend probably wants revenge on his cousin right now for trying to kill him." He took out a knife and began putting an edge on it.

And that was when my Perscom alerted me to a text. As Archer looked over my shoulder, I pulled it up so we could both see it.

It was from Josh.

Three-fourths of those suits are empty.

"What the—" Archer didn't quite gasp, but it was pretty clear he was as shocked by this as I was.

"But it makes sense," I said after a moment. "How many Psimons did she lose? I watched techs walk those suits into the transport, rather than the Psimon who was inside doing it. That means the suits are autonomous. She could just walk the empty ones out and leave them there; it's not as if anyone was going to know they were seeing an empty suit. And there are a *lot* of suits at the Barrier. She knows where the attack is going to be. She can put the manned suits there and nowhere else, if she intends to help the Othersiders."

I texted back, *Where are the manned suits?*

I got back what had to be the feed from whatever control room was monitoring those suits—a screen with a map of the Barrier, with red dots in a line along it everywhere except a small section in the south, where the dots were green. A new place, one the Othersiders hadn't attacked from before, probably because the army base was there—

"*Shit!*" Archer swore. "They're planning on hitting the base first!"

He got on his Perscom and began muttering into it—presumably telling his army contact what was about to fall on their heads. Meanwhile Josh had texted me again.

I'm going to do something about filling those empty suits.

Okay. That made no sense. With *what*?

But then suddenly I remembered something he'd told me when we had first met. About all the low-level psychics that Drift deemed "insufficiently talented" to join PsiCorps. How they got enough training so they could use the little they had, then went out to a separate school (more like normal people, I'd bet) and went on to get jobs that needed just a little bit of psi. Like . . . with the vid-channels.

And those suits amplified psionics. A suit turned a regular Psimon into something amazingly powerful. Would it turn a marginally talented psionic into a Psimon?

. . . the Marginals? I texted back.

I could almost see him grin. *Got it in one. Gonna be busy now. You kick some butt.*

Archer ended his conversation. "All right, they're alerted. I don't know what else I can do."

"Maybe tell everyone to get their load-outs and wait?" I said, floundering a little. I'd never been in a position like this before.

"Already done. I only skipped you because I thought—" He finally took a look at me. "Why *are* you loaded up? Where's your cast?"

"My 'friend' healed me to prove we could trust him." Archer's eyebrows practically hit his hairline. "And I mean healed everything. Healed things instantly, like, faster and better than I've ever heard of."

"And how do you know he didn't just—I don't know, make you *think* you were healed?" he retorted.

"Because I'm not stupid. First thing I did was check with the medics. It didn't take long. One bone scan, in fact. He might be able to mess with my head to make me not notice pain, but I don't think he can jinx the bone-scan machines."

He was going to reply, when the alarm went off. In the next moment, Kent came charging into the room with his full kit. "You two with me, Chopper One!" he yelled as he went by, the hangar door opening for him automatically. We followed right on his heels.

We picked up Cielle, Scarlet, and Tober in short order, and Kent directed the chopper away. We were no sooner in the air when we saw explosions in the distance—right where the army base was. "*What the—*" Tober swore over the comm. "*How can they—*"

"*I'm finding that out! Stay off the freq for a second,*" Kent ordered, one hand to his ear as the chopper powered its way toward the base. Then Kent's face went cold. *"They sent suicide squads of Ketzels over the Barrier to attack the choppers. Fully fueled choppers."*

I felt all the blood drain from my face. Fully fueled bombs was more like it. . . . Whatever protection against static, sparks, or lightning those choppers had, it wouldn't be enough against a whole flock of Ketzels. Especially not if the Ketzels had been controlled to attack without regard to their own safety.

We were already off to a bad start.

We flew over the airfield on our way to the Barrier; there *were* some choppers in the air, and a lot of soldiers out there doing their best to gun down the Ketzels, or at least keep them away from the choppers and the fuel tanks. But we flew past them too fast, and I couldn't see how that was going. All I could tell for sure was that there were far too many burning choppers on the field, huge billows of black smoke and flames coming up from the ones that the fire crews hadn't gotten to yet.

"There goes our air support," Archer muttered, saying aloud what we were all thinking.

The chopper we were in engaged the field that let it pass through the Barrier; there was a feeling of resistance, and tingling all over, then we were setting down right next to the Barrier. There were a few troops here already, and some artillery pieces.

And the Psimons in their armor . . . were gone.

No one commented on that. At least it meant we wouldn't be attacked from behind by people who were supposed to be on our side. The best I could think to hope for was that Josh had gotten through to some of them. They couldn't *all* be toadies to Drift, could they?

The chopper set down and we bailed. The other choppers were not far behind ours, kicking up dust as they touched down just long enough to let the rest of us off. There were Portals blossoming all over the bean fields in front of us, so we lost no time in summoning our Hounds.

Some of the others were summoning fast and dirty, but I was thinking of the long slog we were going to have in front of us. To conserve energy I used the Glyphs—and the first Hound to burst through the Portal once I opened the Way was Bya.

I wanted to fall to my knees and hug him, I was so happy to see him, but the rest were coming through right on his heels—and within sight of us, Othersider Portals were spewing nasty things.

I am happy to see you too, he said in answer to my unvoiced thoughts, as he took his proper place at my side. *Are we to Shield?*

Yes, we have to make up for Hammer and Steel still being unconscious. I didn't mention Mark, but Bya got up on his hind legs and gave my cheek a sympathetic lick.

Then we will was all he said, but he said it with feeling.

The Hounds and I put up our Shields, twelve layers interwoven. We tested them for strength and expanded them as far as we could, before toughening them against everything that the Othersiders could throw at us. Then we made sure they were transparent to magic on the inside, so we could throw spells when they were up. We were able to cover roughly the same area as if Hammer and

Steel were there, although people had to crowd in a little closer than usual to fit inside. I listened with half an ear to Kent as he explained to the rest what was going on. He played an edited version of the recording for them; their reaction was pretty much as might be expected. There was a lot of rage. There was also a lot of fear. I think a lot of us had counted on the Psimons having our back, and maybe doing even better than that, what with the new suits and their boosted abilities.

"Now listen up, Hunters," Kent said over the comm when he'd finished giving them the situation. *"The important part of all of this is that the Othersider leader is counting on taking us out in this fight. If he doesn't, he loses. He'll be concentrating on us and not on the Barrier this time. All we have to do is outlast him until one or more of his allies starts to get doubts."*

That seemed a much too optimistic reading of the situation to me, but I kept my mouth shut.

"So don't waste anything. Not a bullet. Not a levin bolt. And most especially, not yourselves. Make everything you do count. Save your strength. We can *outlast them. We've done it before, and we'll do it again."*

Meanwhile, on the other side of the bean fields, the Othersiders were pouring out of yet more Portals and forming up into ranks, just like the army that they were. Then *finally,* whoever was in charge of the army base woke up from his shock and realized that while living things couldn't go through the Barrier, inanimate objects did just fine. All the artillery and tanks suddenly swiveled their barrels. We all heard the whine and grinding of gears and turned—to see every barrel that had been pointing somewhere else now pointing at those Portals. Then came the *booms* as they began pounding the Othersiders.

Shells screamed overhead, more than low enough for us to see them clearly, and hit on the Othersider lines. It looked as if they were letting loose with whatever they could load. I saw explosive shells, incendiary, frags. . . . There wasn't much consistency, but then given what we were up against, a mix was probably better anyway.

A vicious roar came up from the Othersider ranks as the first shells landed among them. Evidently getting pounded like that broke whatever power kept them disciplined and holding rank, and they charged straight for us.

At that point I found out just how hard it was for Hammer and Steel to do what they did. Whenever anything solid hit the Shield, it resonated unpleasantly with me, and magic energy drained away. I was constantly replenishing the thing—and so were the Hounds. They all hunkered down, even Hold and Strike, almost as if they were being beaten, and closed their eyes, concentrating on helping me.

Elbow to elbow, back to back . . . I was in the middle, somewhat protected, but having to keep track of everything.

I had to listen hard through the cacaphony for Kent's instructions to bring the Shields down and put them back up. I had to keep an eye on all the people I was supposed to be Shielding to make sure none of them got separated from us while the Shields were down, and if they started getting pushed or dragged away, I sent a Hound to drag them back. Dusana, preferably; he was big enough to haul anyone back by the belt.

We were surrounded by the enemy now, at least six deep, maybe more, but I couldn't see past the row of Minotaurs. I also didn't see any sign whatsoever that Torcion had gotten to the Folk Lords of this "Grand Alliance." The Othersiders didn't seem at all inclined to fight one another.

So things are going according to Laetrenier's plan. Well... crap.

This was insane. The noise was incredible. Shells screaming by overhead; Othersiders howling, screeching, bellowing, in a dozen different voices. Gunfire and grenades when the Shields came down; magic explosions and the sounds of levin bolts and fire bolts hitting when they were up.

Although I was in the center of the group, I was getting my hits in too. Specifically, I made liberal use of the skunk-spell. I'd picked up an old-fashioned slingshot and some bullets for it; I cast the spell on a bullet and let it fly over the heads of the Minotaurs, then triggered it. I didn't care where it landed—anyplace would do. The point was to get the skunk-spell as far as possible from *us*. Anywhere it landed after that would do damage.

I alternated that with perfectly physical firepower and steel-jacketed bullets when the Shields were down, taking care to make every shot count. And when the Shields were down, my Hounds took the opportunity to dive into the packed lines of the Othersiders, grab a few, and drag them into our lines, where they got hacked to bits. The Hounds were too agile for the Othersiders to return the favor.

No sign of Drift. No sign of her Psimons. Could Josh have gotten through to them? If he had ...

"Shields down!" Kent shouted. The Hounds and I dropped the

Shields. I fired stink-bullets. The Hounds dashed into the mob in groups and dragged a trio of unfortunate Othersiders into the range of our edged and pointed weapons. One thing always seemed to work on the Othersiders—iron and steel. Knowing I'd be in the center of the group, I'd equipped myself with a spear with a crossbar just behind the point. Where I came from, it was called a "boar-sticker," and it was used for hunting wild pigs. The crossbar kept an enraged boar or sow from coming right up the spear to gore you. It did the same for the *Naga* I impaled when Dusana dragged the damned thing within reach.

"Incoming by air!" Kent reported as the thing squirmed and died. *"Winged Hounds up!"*

There was a thunder of wings as the flying Hounds went up. As tightly packed together as we were, the most expedient way for them to get airborne was to use us as launching platforms, running up our backs and jumping as high as they could before opening their wings at the peak of their jumps. Dusana patiently let himself be used that way four times, even sitting down to make a ramp out of his back.

When the winged Hounds were safely clear, Kent shouted, *"Shields up!"* and my Hounds and I went back to holding against the battering of the mob.

Those who had offensive magic joined their Hounds in picking off our airborne attackers: a mix of Harpies, Ketzels, and black feathered things that looked vaguely like oversize ravens. Fluids and body parts began to rain down on the Shields, sliding down the curve and gradually vanishing as they reached the earth.

Our winged attackers weren't as disciplined—or maybe as

controlled—as the ones on the ground. After fruitless attempts to get past the Hounds, one of the Harpies screamed something unintelligible, and they all scattered.

"*Shields down!*" Kent ordered so the winged Hounds could rejoin us and get their breath back. As soon as they were all tucked in among us, he ordered the Shields back up again.

Everything started to blur together.

How long had we been fighting? It seemed like forever. I was pacing myself, and I was fresh off several days of bed rest (not to mention that healing trick Torcion had done), yet *I* was tired and wearing out; a glance at the faces nearest me showed me nothing but the set expressions of people fighting through pure exhaustion.

And yet . . . we were holding our own. Enough that squads of Army skirmishers had now managed to get across the Barrier to join us. Rather than depending on Shields, they were all wearing combat armor, and I was pretty darn sure they were also sporting Psi-shields. They fought their way to us and spread out on either side, giving us flanking wings of firepower.

And finally, the remaining choppers got into the air, thundering overhead to unload a furious barrage of chain-gun fire into the ranks behind the Othersiders we could see. The pressure on us eased a trifle.

Where were the Psimons? That was my big nagging worry. Because if Drift unleashed those on us . . .

"*Joy, I've got word from your boy Josh.*" That was HQ on my private freq.

"Roger, go for message," I said breathlessly—because this could be very good, or very bad.

"He says his troops have Drift's locked down for the duration, and you'll know what that means. Out."

A thrill of elation struck me like a Ketzel's lightning. He'd done it! He'd actually done it! "Kent, update," I said on the general freq, knowing this would be something everyone would want—no, *need*—to hear.

"Go for update."

"PsiCorps is locked down. Repeat, the Psimons are locked down."

I heard several whoops of glee over the freq, and smiled grimly. This was the first good news we'd gotten since we started this fight. With the Psimons out of the picture, we might actually be able to not just hold our own, but to win this thing.

"Good news. Don't get cocky."

I don't know about anyone else, but "cocky" was the last thing that described my state of mind. Scared bloodless . . . that was more like it. Grimly determined not to let another friend die? Definitely.

And that was when Drift made her move.

SUDDENLY, NONE OF US could move. I was literally paralyzed; I couldn't even twitch, I could barely breathe, and I was so overcome with confusion it was hard to think. Through blurring vision, it looked like everyone else was struck at the same time.

Thanks be to all the gods big and small, whoever was in command of the army units noticed this immediately. And just as my Shields went down, the Othersiders were moving from flanking us to surrounding us. The Hounds were not affected; they kept up their Shields, and the few who had magic-based weapons, like my *Alebrijes* fire, went on the offense. The choppers came in with close air support, chain guns pouring bullets into the mob, using incendiaries as the ammo most likely to do damage.

We were aided by the fact that some of the Othersiders had gotten locked down too. That put a wall of immobile meat between us and the rest. Confused by this, some of them turned on their frozen fellows and ripped them apart.

But it was horrible. All I could do was breathe and watch those soldiers try to protect us . . . and watch some of them die. And there wasn't a damn thing I could do about it. I couldn't even scream! Despair and fury filled me until I thought I was going to explode.

We were going to die. We were all going to die. Because one of our own kind was so ambitious she was willing to kill us, willing to kill *anyone*, so long as she could be top dog.

Still, I struggled, and I know the others were fighting her too.

That was when the Drakken and Gogs and Magogs arrived, each one protected from the artillery barrage by a Shield cast by a Folk Mage striding along next to it. One Folk Mage for every single one of the Drakken and Gogs and Magogs. Two dozen at least.

The ranks of Othersiders surrounding us pulled back, so we could get a good view of our doom.

Because there was no doubt: we could not take that many giants and Drakken on. Even if the army could launch Hellfires, they'd just dissipate fruitlessly on the heavy Shields that shimmered around them. And our Shields were not going to be able to hold for long against the purely physical pounding that Gogs and Magogs and Drakken could dish out. Behind them was a single figure in a suit of Psimon armor, also with a Folk Mage at her side.

Drift. Come to watch the fun. And on her other side, a glistening golden creature standing in midair with his arms crossed over his chest in a posture of relaxed satisfaction.

We were about to be squashed like bugs.

Then Drift, the sadistic bitch, let us go. So she could get a good look at us fighting and dying, I guess.

My heart stopped. I went cold all over, and . . . "the blackness of despair" does not even begin to describe how I felt at that moment. Even Hold and Strike whimpered.

Things went very, very quiet.

The monsters stared at us. They were gloating; you could see it in their faces. They knew they'd won. The Folk Mages all wore the same identical expression of smug superiority. You couldn't see Drift's face because of the helmet, but the Folk Lord had a nasty smirk, like a spoiled child that has gotten its way.

Somberly, we all looked at each other, nodded, turned back to the enemy, and braced for the attack. No one looked anything but determined. No one ran, or even looked as if they wanted to. I know I was petrified, and probably so was everyone else. But we were Hunters. This was what we did, and this was how we would die. Defending the Cits. Saving people. We weren't going to give up now, not even in the face of certain defeat.

Silence. The Othersiders didn't move. I sensed they were hoping for us to break—or maybe they were just enjoying their moment of triumph.

I kind of expected something, some short speech from Kent. That was the sort of thing he did, after all—that was what made him such a brilliant leader, knowing the right thing to say at a time like this. But that wasn't who spoke.

Open the Way, Bya said urgently into my head. *Open the Way!*

I looked at him in confusion at first, and then with a sudden feeling of complete betrayal. *You want to escape?* I asked him dispiritedly.

NO! he shouted. I winced. *Open the Way!*

So I did. Swiftly, I cast the Glyphs, threw them to the ground, and opened the Way. The Portal appeared just outside our Shields, and the Othersiders nearest it looked suddenly bewildered by a Portal appearing in their midst.

Now! Tell us, Pack Friend, Sister to the Alebrijes. *Tell us you need help. This is your right, to call the Great Hunt. Tell us all!*

This didn't make any sense but . . . I opened my mind and tried to speak to every Hound that could hear me, not just mine.

I am the Pack Friend, Sister to the Alebrijes, *and I beg you, if you can bring us help, then call it now! Please, I entreat you, call the Great Hunt.*

Then Bya raised his nose to the sky and . . . sang. I call it singing because it wasn't a howl—it was like a horn call. Then Dusana joined him, and Shinje, and then all of my *Alebrijes,* in a beautiful, many-voiced, silver-throated chorus. Then Hold and Strike, with real howls, and Myrrdhin and Gwalchmai, and then all the *other* Hunters' Hounds, in dozens and dozens of harmonic notes and voices, as the Othersiders stared at us, confused and baffled. The chorus swelled and grew until the air itself vibrated with all the notes contained in it. I lost my fear. It melted away in that amazing sound. For no damn good reason at all, my heart lifted and my spirits rose into the sky with that music. I would not have been the least bit surprised to see—well, even a Christer angel, at that point.

Then the Portal began to grow.

I wasn't doing anything, but as the Hounds called, the Portal expanded and widened—scaring the heck out of the Othersiders, who began backing away from it—until you could have fit a Drakken through there.

And then they came, charging through the Portal. Our salvation.

Alebrijes, first. Two, ten, dozens . . . including one that was easily the size of a Drakken and was such a crazy quilt of patterns and spikes and knobs and horns in eye-blinding colors that it was painful to look at. It was as if the toy boxes of an entire village of children had spilled out their contents through the Portal; there were more shapes and colors and sizes of creatures flinging themselves across the threshold than I could ever have envisioned in dream or nightmare. Then a pause, and I thought that was all—but more, more Hounds of every possible shape and size and type, by tens and twenties, a river, a *flood* of Hounds followed them, spreading themselves out between us and the Othersiders.

We had an army. An army of Hounds. Thousands of them. And now the Othersiders, even the Gogs and Magogs, looked paralyzed and afraid.

The Drakken-size *Alebrije* bent its long, long neck down until he was face-to-face with me. He had a head like a deer, complete with antlers and big flexible ears. The bright blue head, at least, was free of pattern; his antlers were pink, matching the insides of his ears. His eyes were the size of Bya and were like opals, with black, black pupils. I saw myself reflected in them—disheveled, bloody, and bruised like everyone else.

You have summoned the Great Hunt, little Sister, he said into my head, a voice that boomed and echoed inside my skull. *What is it that we Hunt for you?*

There was absolute silence. I couldn't even hear my fellow Hunters breathing—I think they were afraid to. It flashed into my head that this was one of those times my Masters had warned me about—when words were critically important, and the wrong ones would unleash dreadful, unintended consequences.

Like, if I said "Hunt the Folk," what if Torcion was out there? I had gotten nothing but help from him, and if what he'd told me was true, if he died, there would be yet another population of humans that would now be helpless against the Folk who only wanted to kill them.

And that would leave so many Othersiders still perfectly prepared to pound us into paste. Drift was still out there too.

So I considered my words, took a careful breath, and said aloud, "Please, of a courtesy, Hunt those on this field who would harm me, my fellow Hunters and Hounds, my fellow warriors, and all those in the city behind us who I am sworn to protect."

The thing grinned. I have never seen so many big, sharp teeth in my life, not even in the mouth of an Othersider. *Wise choice, little Sister. So let it be done.*

Then the creature flung its head into the air and bellowed, and all the Hounds on the field charged. The huge one went straight for the nearest Gog and tore through the Shield like it was made of paper. A second later it had sunk all those long, sharp teeth into the Gog's throat and was shaking it like a terrier with a rat. But because of the mass of both of them, the movements were nightmarishly slow, and every detail as it ripped the Gog's throat out clearly visible....

And then it turned on the nearest Drakken.

Meanwhile, the rest of the Hounds engaged the Othersiders like...well, I had never seen anything to compare with it. There were so many of them, they could actually swarm individual monsters, immobilize them by sheer numbers, and tear them to pieces.

Our Hounds joined in the fray with sheer homicidal joy. I felt that bloodthirsty elation from mine, and I am sure the others felt it as well.

"Hold your fire! All stations, all units, hold your fire!" Kent screamed over the general freq. *"Friendlies on the field, friendlies on the field! Hold your fire!"*

The Folk Mages with the giant monsters were the first to react ...and they fled, opening Portals and vanishing, leaving their underlings to fend for themselves. Without any direction, the monsters panicked, as well they should have, trying to escape in every possible direction, some of them actually running into the Barrier and committing suicide on it rather than face the Hounds. The enormous *Alebrije,* deprived of equal-size prey when the remaining giants and Drakken fled, loped off into the distance. Meanwhile the smaller ones—and believe me, "smaller" often still meant things the size of a cottage—tore through everything in sight.

And what did we do?

You might have thought that after all we'd been through, we'd have been falling down on the spot. A couple of us, badly hurt, did. But the rest of us went charging out after our Hounds—except for me. Poor Kent was flat on his back in the dirt with his eyes closed, and didn't look in any shape to take charge.

"Is anyone hurt?" I asked over the general freq.

"We could use a half dozen medics," the reply came. *"You?"*

I was startled to find a slash down one arm I hadn't felt, and looking over the soldiers I could actually see, there were a lot of injuries. "Yeah, I think it's safe for the medics—and evac choppers," I replied. And then I went out into the chaos on the field, looking for Drift and Lord Laetrenier.

It was sheer chaos out there; Bya, Dusana, and Shinje loped up to join me, but the rest were somewhere deep in the free-for-all. Initially, we Shielded to protect ourselves, but it became apparent that we needn't bother. Occasionally, when I saw one of the Hounds had taken on something too big for it, I sent a few bullets into the fray, but mostly we four concentrated on getting to where we had last seen Drift and Lord Laetrenier, and not getting caught up in the snarls of combat.

I didn't realize how much I had let my guard down as we hunted for those two enemies, until a flash of gold materialized next to me, grabbed me, and we *bamphed* away.

I fought myself free of him as we landed, stumbling over the harrowed rows of another field, and realized I was surrounded by Manticores. And facing me: my kidnapper, Lord Laetrenier.

I Shielded immediately, so pumped full of magic by my Hounds that the thing popped up as strong and sturdy as anything Hammer could have made. The Folk Lord and I stared at each other—he glaring death at me, and me . . . well, I hoped I managed to keep my expression from giving anything away.

"You did this!" he spat. "*You*, you puling, weak little worm, you did this!" I said nothing, but I did trigger the Psi-shield. If Drift was here too, I wasn't going to get taken by her again. He had caught me unguarded and brought me here—which could not be far from the combat since *bamphs* couldn't take you that far. It wouldn't be long until my Hounds found me, and I knew they would bring the others with them.

"Is there something you want, Lord Laetrenier?" I said politely as I examined every detail about him. He started as I spoke his name.

He was slightly the worse for wear; something must have gotten through to him before he retreated and summoned this body-guard of Manticores. His hair was mussed, there was a smudge along one perfect cheek, one of his fancy sleeves had been ripped off, and he wasn't floating.

"I want my *victory*, you mud-born ape!" he snarled.

I needed to stall. Right now, it was just me. But there was one sure way to make certain he did not sic those Manticores on me . . . or sic Drift on me, for that matter.

"If you want a victory, you must take it, Lord Laetrenier," I replied, and bowed. "I see you, Magician. I call right of challenge on you."

His pupils dilated. He had not seen *that* coming.

"Who has told you these things, ape?" he snarled as his face twisted into an expression of pure, unadulterated rage.

"No one told me these things, Magician," I replied, bracing myself. "Your ways are not so secret as you think. Now," I continued, making sure my voice was very calm, "I have called challenge on you. Will you accept? Or will you take the name of coward and flee? You have only those two choices."

"By what right do you challenge me, insect?" he countered. But I was ready for that one too, and keyed my Perscom.

"By the right that you allied yourself with a traitor to me and mine," I said sweetly. "By the fact that you did bargain with her to fulfill your wishes. By your own words, this was your doing." By the time I had finished that sentence, I had the broadcast from Apex that was airing the recording Torcion and I had made of Laetrenier; I punched up the volume and let it play, and watched as his face went from blank recognition to incredulity and finally back to rage.

"Those are your words, in your voice. Twist how you will," I continued. "Now, do you accept challenge of me?"

His answer was to fling a double-handed fireball at me, which splashed off my Shield. "I'll take that as a yes," I said, and let him have it with a skunk-spell.

It was the very last thing he was expecting. He coughed and gasped, his eyes watering, as he staggered away from the patch of earth I'd made so pungent. Finally he iced the area, which sealed the smell in.

I had a particular intention in this fight, because as I said, I was stalling for time. I wanted to make him look ridiculous. Granted, there were no others of his kind here to grandstand in front of, but nevertheless, he'd feel ridicule more keenly than if I played this seriously. He'd be angry, and his control would be off.

Most importantly, now that he'd accepted the challenge, for a while at least, he'd have to play by the rules. Mind, I expected him to cheat eventually, but by that time, my help would be there.

I hoped—I really, really hoped—I was right about all this. My life literally depended on it all.

Outside I was cool.

Inside I was racing around in a panic.

But the last time I'd faced off with Ace, I'd put a spin on my Shields to deflect his attacks rather than block them. I did that again. It wouldn't matter if this Folk Lord figured out what I was doing; there was no way he could alter his offensive spells to deal with the spin. Spinning the Shields made them work very much like Aki-Do deflections; instead of the energy going *into* the Shields and damaging them, most of the energy would remain with the attack and be flung off in the direction of the deflection.

As I suspected, the Folk Lord didn't even notice what I had done. He hit me with a barrage of levin bolts, and they careened off in twenty different directions as they struck, pinging off into the Manticores around us with a little added velocity from the Shield-spin. It took everything I had to keep from reacting as those bolts of pure magic energy raced toward my face.

The Manticores didn't move. Not even when their own master's magic hit had injured them. They formed a near-perfect circle around us, all of them facing inward, all of them motionless.

Drift. Drift is controlling them. She has to be—he *is in no mental state to do it.*

"Oh dear," I taunted. "What's the matter, oh mighty one? Have you been indulging in a victory binge too early? Your aim appears to be off."

The angrier I got him, the wilder his attacks would be and the more force he'd put into them. I might be able to bleed him of so much magical energy he'd lose his Shields.

My heart raced, my hands were cold with fear, and I was glad that the noise of fighting covered up the fact that my voice was shaking. But I realized that although I should have been bleeding magic, I still had all I could hold. Somehow, even though they were nowhere near me, my Hounds were keeping me supplied. I had a nearly infinite source of magic power.

He didn't. And that just might be what allowed me to survive this. *Please let me survive this....*

I stayed on the defensive, hitting him with tiny attacks meant to sting, to annoy, to make it look as if I was playing with him. I set the field upwind of him on fire so he choked on the smoke until he moved, only to find that I had created a miniature skating rink under his feet. "Where are your allies, great lord?" I mocked, as he slipped and slid until he got the ice thawed again, then discovered he was ankle-deep in mud. "Oh, that's right. They've deserted you. They've discovered you intended to use the human traitor to help you take their domains. You're all alone now." *Alone, like me.* "In fact, you'll be lucky to discover they haven't decided to take *your* domain and divide it up among themselves. What happens to a landless little creature of your kind, anyway? Do you have to take service? Do they make you clean their floors with your tongue?"

I thought all of that was pretty mild, but evidently *something* I said struck a nerve, because he let loose with all the brute force he had in his arsenal of spells.

It wasn't far off from being at ground zero of a Hellfire strike,

• 274 •

with a few artillery shells and maybe an RPG thrown in for good measure.

I cowered down and made my Shields as tight and dense as they could be. All I could do was keep my head down and up the spin on the Shields in an effort to fling off as much force as possible. The area around me was churned up with concussive blasts, deflected levin bolts flew in every possible direction, and finally a plume of bale-fire washed over me.

This was it. I was about to die.

I expected at any moment that the Shields would fail. "Terror" doesn't quite cover the feeling I had with all that destructive force pinning me in place.

But I didn't break. Someone else did.

The Manticores suddenly came to life, bellowing with the pain of their wounds—and it was obvious where the attacks were coming from, even to them. They roared their anger at their erstwhile master—their hurt and their sense of betrayal—and scattered.

Drift had abandoned her ally to save her own skin. His monsters had abandoned him. And now he was alone—no Psimon, no army, just him. He had probably intended to turn those Manticores on me, but Drift had twisted that plan right on its head—whether because she had intended to betray him all along, or out of panic, it didn't matter.

I'd won. Somehow ... I had won.

His barrage suddenly ceased, and I stood up inside my Shields, unhurt. We stared at each other across the stretch of churned-up, charred earth. I saw his eyes widen with disbelief and then fear. And that was when I went on the offensive.

I looked at this creature, and all I could see were the faces of my friends that were dead because of him. What I felt was not so much rage as a grief that was as powerful as anger, a great tsunami of feeling that rose up inside me and *demanded* an outlet, a grief too strong, too profound for mere tears.

While he stood there staring at me, I gathered my wits, my strength, and my magic. I whispered, "This is for you, my friends," and hit him with a Shield Bash, exactly the way Mark would have, if he'd been here.

His Shield wasn't anchored, of course. I expected to knock him off his feet with his own Shield, the way I had with Ace.

Instead . . . the concussive force shattered his protection, leaving him standing there with nothing between us but air. He stared at me in horror.

And then—he *bamphed*.

Until that moment, I had not realized that I knew as many curse words as I did. As the huge mob of Hounds surged toward and past me from behind, led by the giant *Alebrije*, chasing a wildly assorted herd of Othersiders before them, I filled the air with invective. Monsters in a complete state of panic ran around me, even bounced off my Shield, and I still didn't stop cursing until I found myself surrounded by my own beloved pack, all of them looking expectantly at me.

All my emotions suddenly ran out of me, and as the adrenaline I'd been flying on dropped, so did all my energy. I banished my Shield, and my Hounds—my faithful friends, my best companions—came crowding around me. I hugged them and praised them until I was hoarse.

Then we began what turned out to be about a half-mile walk back to the Barrier. And not a hair nor a tooth nor a horn did we see of a single Othersider.

When we got there, everyone else was gone—except for that enormous army of Hounds, waiting. They all looked at me expectantly, and finally my fatigue-dulled brain put two and two together, and I realized they were waiting for me to open the Way for them so they could go home.

Not yet, Bya said. *Ah—look! There he is!*

I saw the giant *Alebrije* coming toward us, and every line of him said to me that he was extraordinarily pleased with himself. He was moving very slowly, and as he approached, I saw that he had something in his mouth.

No, not something. Some*one*.

Lord Laetrenier.

The Folk Lord did not appear to be conscious, although he could have been under some sort of spell, stunned, poisoned, or just feigning it. But the huge *Alebrije* bent down and came eye to eye with me, the limp form held carefully in his mouth. I stared into that one huge eye, and I should have been afraid, but I wasn't. Instead, I dared to put one hand on his soft cheek (surprisingly, astonishingly soft, like deerskin) and whisper, "Thank you. You saved us. There is not enough gratitude in the world to repay you."

And that, little Sister, is why you are worthy to call the Great Hunt, he said with affection and amusement warming his mental voice. Then I sensed affection changing to warning. *But do not think—*

"I would never, ever, ever dare to do this again," I replied, my voice shaking with emotion . . . and yes, some respectful fear. "Not unless Bya said I could."

The warmth and affection came back. *And that, too, is why you are worthy to call the Great Hunt. But I have a thing I must ask you.*

"You can ask me anything, and ask anything *of* me, and it won't be enough to repay you," I told him fervently.

This . . . He shook his head slightly, and Lord Laetrenier's limbs flailed loosely. *Rightfully this is your prey. But he has much to answer for to my kind.*

I thought about justice. I thought about revenge. I thought, for a long, long time, about Mark.

And then I thought, *Maybe they have a better claim on justice or revenge than I do. . . .*

Besides, who was *I* to render justice? And revenge generally turns out to be a lot less satisfying than you think it will be.

"Take him. He's yours," I replied. "If that goes a tenth of the way to repaying you . . ."

It pays the debt, he said with immense satisfaction. I wondered, then, just what kind of atrocities this Folk Lord had perpetrated on the Hounds that *this* was the response. But I wasn't going to ask. The Hounds told us what they wanted, when they wanted, and that was that. *Of a courtesy, would you open the Way that we might go home?*

"With pleasure," I replied, and cast the Glyphs, opening the Way. The Portal appeared—somehow, though I have no idea how, managing to be big enough for the giant one to go through.

Step through he did, followed by a slow-moving river of satis-fied, manna-fat Hounds of every shape and size, so many of them that I quickly lost count, until at last, bringing up the rear, came my beloved pack.

They paused beside the Portal and looked at me as one.

"You guys ready to go home for a while?" I asked. Myrrdhin and Gwalchmai grinned. Hold and Strike dog-laughed. The rest nodded. I bowed, and gestured toward the open Portal. They all went through but one.

Bya lingered. I looked down at him, then knelt and hugged him until my arms ached and that slash burned. "I love you," I said with every fiber of my being. "I don't know how I deserved what you did for me, but—"

Oh, hush. I love you too, he said fondly. *Unfortunately, I have some bad news. That evil she-beast got away, and she took some of her minions and your old enemy with her. I tried to track her, but one of the big Lords opened a Portal for her and it closed before I could see where the Portal led.*

So Drift got away and took some of her Psimons and Ace with her? Well . . . crap. But for now, it didn't matter. "Not your fault, and we'll deal with her another day," I said. I heard footsteps, and I looked up to see someone in army gear approaching.

But . . . I thought the soldiers had all gone. Had someone gotten so far separated from the rest that—

Oh, that's not who or what you think, Bya said, and wagged his tail.

"Your companion is correct," said the newcomer in a *very* familiar and mellifluous voice. "I had rather not be attacked just now, and we are somewhat too near your great magic-wall for the safety of my true form."

True form? I tried not to show my surprise, but this was the first time anyone had ever had any confirmation, both that the Folk could make themselves look like one of us, and that those ridiculously gorgeous visions were their true forms.

"You asked me how I could prove that I was worthy of your fullest trust," Torcion said. "Whilst you were engaged with our mutual foe, I realized he would not have his eyes on his own holdings, and that there was something I could do that would prove this to you once and for all." He paused. "As I suspected, the whole of his guardian forces were *here*, allowing me to slip into his fiefdom and do as I would. And, besides . . . it was just the ethical thing to do."

"Um, you're going to have to be a little clearer than that," I said. I was beginning to wonder if the most difficult part of dealing with the Folk was their habit of beating around the bush so much that they knocked all the leaves off.

"Better still, I shall show you." He made a little gesture, screening it from the other side of the Barrier with his body, and a second Portal opened in front of mine. From the army base, it would look like there was still only one Portal there. "You may come through now," he called out loud. "You are almost home."

What . . . ?

Human children—and a few adults—began stumbling out of the Portal. Shabby, filthy, some still in tattered nightclothes, starved and frightened-looking, they took one look at me and lit up.

"*Hunter Joy!*" screamed one little girl, and flung herself at me. Suddenly, I was surrounded by kids and those few adults, all babbling at once, most of them crying, most of them pretty incoherent.

I stared, my mouth dropping open.

While I'd been fighting Laetrenier, Torcion had gone to his domain, and rescued the people who had been kidnapped by the Manticores. To prove I could trust him.

And because it was the "ethical thing to do."

A Folk Lord.

I was going to have a lot of thinking to do.

Torcion somehow slipped away while I got some help from the base. Then it was just a matter of getting the rescued people across the Barrier and into quarantine. I didn't think they'd much mind— those kids would probably be spoiled within an inch of their lives, and the adults looked as if all they wanted right now was sleep, food, and a lot of quality time with a psych-counselor.

When I was alone again except for Bya, I was unsurprised to hear Torcion's voice behind me. I turned. He was still wearing his disguise of a soldier, but his eyes were his own again.

"How did you get them to come with you in the first place?" I asked.

He laughed. "I wore this guise and told them I was a magician who had been sent to rescue them. I took them first to my domain."

"Because you didn't know at the time we'd win?" I asked.

He shrugged. "It was possible. And better with me than the alternative."

I nodded. It was the same thing a human probably would have done. After all, why send them home if home was about to be overrun?

"I come to ask you, once again, will you take service of me?" he asked. "Your people are safer for now. I returned the ones that were stolen away. The Grand Alliance is no more. Laetrenier has vanished, and I cannot find him in any of the realms. Although," he added thoughtfully, "the queen of the mind-warriors is at large, and with her some of her minions and your old enemy."

He can't have known Bya just told me that . . . so . . . holy crow. He's just given me free information again.

"I cannot," I said. "Regretfully. My vow is to my Hunter clan."

"I would not esteem you half so much were honor not paramount with you," he replied, with a little bow. "Nevertheless, I shall not cease to ask."

"And I . . . won't ask you to stop asking," was the only thing I could think of to say.

He smiled a little, gave me that half bow again, then opened a Portal behind him and was gone.

Kneel down and give me your arm, said Bya, and licked the slash thoroughly. Then he yawned hugely. *I have a big meal to sleep off.*

"Go do it, then," I replied, and he walked with tail high through the Portal, which closed behind him.

And I walked to the Pylon to join the rest of the Hunters, waiting for a truck or a pod home.

I'd barely gotten out of the truck when a Psimon-suit came galumphing clumsily toward me. *"Joy! You're all right!"* cried a metallic and highly amplified voice. I winced. The suit came to a halt, and the helmet visor came up; it was Josh. "They said you were all right, but I never know with you Hunters if that means *'She's fine,'* or *'Well, at least she survived.'* I—"

I silenced him by jumping up and more or less climbing the suit—it was about the size of Hammer, for heaven's sake!—and planting a huge kiss on him. I was so grateful to him and so relieved to see him that I didn't care that we had an audience of interested and wearily chuckling Hunters. But when I couldn't hang off his shoulders anymore, I let go and dropped to the ground again. "How did you manage to lock the Psimons down?"

"I didn't lock all of them down. Drift got away with some," he said. "But I managed to round up all the Marginals in the city and scrambled them into suits, with techs to help them. And maybe one-on-one we'd never have been a match for the PsiCorps Psimons, but I had enough folks that we could dog-pile four or five or even half a dozen on every one of Drift's flunkies." He grinned and flushed a little. "Then we got the techs to hit the shutdown on each suit, and that was that." He looked around, and after a moment, I saw what he was looking for—another five of the suits, with the helmet visors open, were heading in our direction from a transport. He waved to them; they put on more—if clumsy—speed. "Joy, these are the real stars. If it hadn't been for them, I'd never have found all the Marginals in time. This is Larry Smith, who's a celeb-chaser for the clubbing channel, and this is Sally Kobee, who's a stringer for the top-ten Hunter channel; these are

Sue Acord and Trey Chipman, who—" I was so tired by now that they all sort of blurred together, but I gathered that these were all marginal psychics who worked for the vid-channels. Apparently they'd been able to use their authority to break into all the broadcasts, air the story of Drift's betrayal, and put out a plea for other marginal psychics to come help. Which was how Josh had managed to get so many so fast.

"And that's basically what happened," he finished.

To his open astonishment, he was saluted by weary but genuine applause from some of the Hunters who had climbed out of the trucks to hear it all. Then Josh and his coconspirators found themselves pried out of their suits and carried off to retell their story, leaving me standing there with the empty suits.

I started to laugh. And once I started, I couldn't stop. I laughed until tears poured out of my eyes. And oh ye gods, it felt so *good* to laugh, even if it was entirely hysterical laughter.

I got myself back under control and followed everyone else back into HQ. I had a lot of debriefing to do.

OUR LUCK HAD COMPLETELY turned, for the next day, a ridiculously huge storm blew up, practically out of nowhere, big enough that we had three solid days of rest and recovery time. I'm pretty sure everyone spent the first day of it doing nothing but eating and sleeping; I know I did. The only thing I did that day was visit Hammer and Steel in the medbay; they'd woken up, and I wanted to make sure they were all right. By the second day, I felt up to talking to Josh and put in a call to him, only to find him practically babbling with all the news he had to tell me.

"PsiCorps is now under Prefect Charmand," he said. "And *I* just got a promotion to his chief psionics advisor! Can you believe it?"

"That's fantastic!" I replied. He was grinning like a cat in the cream. "Are there any other Psimons you guys can trust?"

He lost a little of that grin. "Well . . . yeah, that's a problem. There's some I know were in on this with her, and we have them locked up for now. But the rest . . . I dunno, Joy. I'm not sure what to tell him to do about them."

"Find a way to get into their heads. And keep them away from the suits," I suggested.

"Yeah, we're going to give the suits to the Marginals. In fact, there aren't going to *be* any Marginals anymore. Just PsiCorps Psimons who either use amplification or don't." He sounded adamant about that, and honestly, I was glad to hear it. In fact, he was cheerful and confident. "The vid-channels and anyone else who used to hire them will just have to do without them. Oh, and there's going to be some changes in how the youngsters are brought up. In fact, there's going to be a lot of changes in PsiCorps."

I felt a pang. After a moment, I identified it as something like jealousy, if you can be jealous of someone's job. "Sounds like you're going to be busy," I replied, cautiously.

"No busier than you," he pointed out rightfully. "But we'll be all right. You and me, I mean."

I relaxed a little. "So what's it feel like to have everyone calling you a hero?" I'd flipped through the news channels from yesterday and the day before, and Josh and his new friends had been all over them. Next to Abigail Drift's defection, Josh's last-minute save at the Barrier had been the biggest news. We Hunters came in third.

No one mentioned the miraculous return of all those kidnapped people. But then, no one had mentioned them being kidnapped in the first place. Their return, like their abduction, was being kept a secret. After all, no one was supposed to know about the Folk, much less that they had taken to stealing children. I didn't much care, because I didn't want to have to explain how they'd materialized in front of me. I'd told Kent all about it, of course; Kent still didn't know what to make of Torcion, and truthfully, neither did I. If he was an enemy trying to trick us, he'd done an awful lot to undermine his own cause.

I hoped he was an ally. Even a friend.

"Hey!" Josh said, interrupting my thoughts. "Got something to show you. My first project as the prefect's advisor. He gave it the okay today!" And before I could say anything, the screen blanked out for a moment, then returned with a vid-cut.

An image on a bright blue background fading out to black on the edges appeared. On the left stood a suit of Psimon armor, with its hand resting protectively on the shoulder of a little boy. On the right . . . was *me*. With Bya on one side of me, a whacking big AR slung over my shoulder, and my hand resting similarly on the shoulder of a little girl.

Between us, the joined logos of the Hunters and PsiCorps, superimposed over the skyline of Apex, with sunrays behind it. *"That's* your *Hunters and PsiCorps!"* trumpeted an announcer. *"Keeping Apex and the Allied Territories safe!"*

The screen blanked out and Josh returned. "What do you think?" he asked, beaming at me.

"I—" My immediate reaction was great discomfort at being made the "face of the Hunters." But I stopped. "It's a great splash," I said finally. "And you guys are right to put it out now, while people are still thinking about the save you and the others did."

"I thought it made sense to ally us with the Hunters, and

specifically the Elite, and get some of that positivism smeared over onto us," he replied, still beaming. "We'll rotate in each of the Elite on that splash, probably on a weekly basis, but I thought we should start with you. I mean, you're a hero too, Joy."

"Well, crap," I said, making a face. "This is unfortunate."

"What?" His face fell.

"This means we'll have to start letting you PsiCorps creeps in through the *front* door." I sighed. "At least learn to wipe your feet, will you?"

"It's a good thing there's a mile of rain between us, woman," he replied with a mock snarl. "Let's play a game."

"Have you got time for that?"

"I'll make time," he said firmly.

I smiled with relief. "Then game on!"

I had never seen the main train station here at Apex before. When I'd come here, I'd been let off at the premier's private platform, which was right at the army base. There hadn't been much there but the cement slab—anything the premier needed was brought in especially for his arrivals and departures.

But this was impressive. *Very* protected; it would look like a giant 'crete cave except for the lighting and the faintly warm beige color that had been infused into the 'crete. There were six tracks, all ending here, surrounded by 'crete platforms. All the walkways funneled into a single entrance and exit in the back wall, but the fact that there wasn't a sharp edge or a straight line in here softened the interior and made it seem welcoming rather than oppressive.

We'd come in through that single entrance, but Jessie Knight's ticket had given her special treatment and she had been whisked past the lines and straight out to the platform—despite the fact that the two of us were wearing some of our old clothing from home, and the only way anyone would recognize one of us was by scanning our Perscoms.

Only one train was currently in the station; we were next to it, waiting for the armed car and the engine to be put on it.

Jessie kept her eyes on the transport that would take her back to her parents and her people. Did she think of the area around the Mountain as home yet? I didn't know.

"Ah'm glad you came to see me off, Joy," she said finally.

That was just about the last thing I would have expected to hear out of Jessie Knight—but the third day of the storm I'd bitten the bullet and gone to see her, and we'd had a long talk. We'd never be real friends, I thought, in no small part because I think she would probably never give up trying to convert me to being a Christer if we were. But she'd managed to talk out a lot of her resentment and anger, and we'd cried on each other's shoulders for a couple hours. In the end, she was the one who said that more good things had come from me and Mark being friends than bad.

And if nothing else, we shared the fact that we both cared about Mark Knight a lot, and we both mourned him deeply.

"I couldn't let you wait here by yourself," I replied. "I'm glad Uncle got you a private compartment." That had been my doing, actually. When Jessie said there was nothing in Apex for her anymore, and wanted to go home, I pointed out that getting her a private compartment where she wouldn't be pestered was the least that they could do for the pregnant widow of an Elite hero. Didn't take much to sell *that*.

"That's a pure kindness; Ah didn't much care fer all them people starin' down their noses at me comin' out here," she said.

"Yeah, they don't know what to make of us turnips," I agreed. "That's all right. Three days and you'll be with your own people again. Never have to leave unless you want to."

"Ah ain't gonna want to," she replied, and managed a ghost of a smile. "It's like paradise out there compared to what we come from. An' our baby ain't gonna haveta worry 'bout where he plays, or what he eats, or if'n his water's safe t'play in or drink."

"Not ever," I agreed, and dared to pat the hand that rested on her bags. She was going back with a lot more stuff than she had arrived with; with the private compartment came the privilege of unlimited cargo. I was pretty sure that every single one of us in the Elite had gotten her a gift for the baby. She shouldn't need anything at all. One of those bags alone had enough diapers for *two* babies; I know, because that was Scarlet's gift. And I think the fabricators in the Style Center had gotten a lot of fun out of creating baby things for a change.

She'd probably make baby clothes anyway, which was why another bag held a lot of appropriate fabric and matching thread. That had been my present. It'd be good for her to do that, concentrating on what was coming instead of what was lost.

The engine and armed car arrived, hooking up to the passenger cars with a lot more noise than I had expected. The entire train shuddered and moved back a little, then settled. As it did, a second train pulled slowly into the station.

Only the few passengers that were taking the private compartments were on the platform at the moment, and the attendant in charge of that car came down the platform, checking tickets and escorting them one by one to their compartments, while a porter directed the trolleys to the baggage car. We were the last ones on the platform. Jessie turned to me and gave me an impulsive hug. Very surprised, I hugged her back.

"Remember, I wrote my best friend, Kei, about you," I told her. "If you need a real friend, get ahold of her in Anston's Well."

Jessie nodded, but I never did figure out whether she was actually going to contact Kei or not before the porter and the attendant finally got to her. As the passengers on the other train began to disembark, I watched the attendant gravely escort her into the car. She didn't turn back to wave.

When she was safely on board, I turned and started to join the trickle of passengers from the second train, heading for the exit.

And that was when I heard a familiar voice behind me.

"Excuse me, could you direct us to Hunter Headquarters?"

I whirled and stared at him in absolute disbelief.

Master Kedo Patli waited patiently for me to get over my shock, eyes twinkling. He was a little grayer, a little more weathered, but otherwise unchanged, right down to the weathered poncho-thing he always wore. With him were seven people I didn't recognize.

But in the instant before I would have flung my arms around him with a squeal of glee, he made a tiny motion with his hand, signing to me that I was to pretend he was a stranger.

I got control of myself and schooled my expression. "Of course, sir. I am on the way there. I will be happy to escort you. Will you come with me?"

I led them to the exit. Since Master Kedo and his entourage were only ordinary passengers, not having registered themselves as Hunters when they got their tickets, we all had to go through the tedious business of waiting for baggage, getting baggage, proving they were the proper people to *have* that baggage, before we all ended up on the street. By that time I'd summoned a pod big enough for all of us. Once we were safely inside it, I flung myself at Master Kedo, who laughed, called me *chica*, and hugged me back.

"I am very sorry it took us so long to get here. As soon as Bya brought us your message, I volunteered to take a group to join you here in Apex, and we began recruiting those who could be spared," he explained. All the unhappiness I had felt that the Monastery hadn't answered me melted away. "These are all first-year Hunters, Joy, but as they are now *my* apprentices, they are, of course, the best." He grinned, and they blushed. Unlike the Masters who followed the paths of the Monastery's founders, Master Kedo did not believe modesty to be a virtue. "This is Lee Strong, from Anston's Well—you know his brother, Steve."

I recognized the Strong family chin; so square and jutting it was the most prominent feature of Lee's face. I did know his brother, but I didn't recognize Lee. He grinned at me.

"These are Terry and Tanya Deschene, brother and sister, from Becenti," continued Master Kedo. They were twins, and had the Dineh look; Becenti was about half Dineh and half Hopi, with a scattering of us Mountain mutts. They looked very somber and very determined, about two years older than me.

"This is Sigurd Olafsson, from Midgard." I knew Sigurd by reputation as a game and vermin hunter; he must have popped Powers after I left. He was a tough middle-aged blond, from a settlement quite a bit north of the Monastery, a settlement that had allegedly started out as . . . well, not nice people, but in the Diseray they quickly learned that how blond your hair was didn't matter nearly as much as how willing you were to help out a stranger.

"This is Lila Thorn from Safehaven—the Thorns arrived after you left." Lila was a pretty, petite woman with a ready smile. I had the feeling that she'd be very popular on the feeds.

"This is Cody Pierce, who I sent for from—well, never mind that, you won't have heard of it." Cody nodded at me. He was tall, black-haired, dark-skinned, and moved in a way that told me he was used to being in the wilderness.

"And this is Wolf Tavy, who strolled into the Monastery with his pack about six months ago," Master Kedo concluded. Wolf was a redhead with an engaging grin that made you grin back. "We'd have been here sooner, but . . . there were storms and some interference with the trains." He shrugged. "We watched the newsfeeds. It looks like you handled everything well enough without us."

"But if you mean to stay, we'll handle them much better *with* you," I replied fervently. "Nothing's changed insofar as needing more Hunters here badly. And . . . I have a lot to tell you. All of you. Most of it wasn't on the feeds. For that matter, a lot of the Hunters here don't even know about half of it."

Master Kedo raised his eyebrows and settled back in his seat. "Well, then! It sounds as if you have had some interesting times, in the sense of the ancient saying. But this can all wait until we present ourselves and our skills to your chief. I hope he will be as happy to see us as you were."

"Happier," I replied firmly, and texted Kent.

Kent met our pod himself, and if Master Kedo had any doubt about his welcome, Kent certainly made it very clear how badly we needed all of them. Then he ushered them all off to be processed, thanking me for bringing them, and leaving me at the curb.

Well, it wasn't as if he needed me to process them. And none of them were the turnip kid I'd been when I arrived here. . . . They might be from the hinterlands, but it was obvious from everything about them that they were all tough, experienced, and ready for just about anything.

Including Apex.

And, of course, none of them had arrived burdened with the baggage of being the prefect's niece, or the reputation of someone who had faced down a Folk Mage. The Hunters of Apex, and the Elite, were also a different organization than they had been when I arrived. They'd fit right in.

And just as I thought that, my Perscom went off. There was a flock of Gazers in Spillover, and Cielle and I were being scrambled to deal with it.

"Same song, different verse," I muttered to myself, and ran for the choppers. Master Kedo and all the things I could tell him would have to wait.

I am a Hunter, and this is what I do.